The Wedding Crush

The Wedding Crush

A Fortemani Family Novel

Mia Heintzelman

TULE
PUBLISHING

Dedication

To my gorgeous, loving, growing Sister Circle.

Author's Note

Please note that this book contains sensitive topics such as grief due to loss of a spouse, parent, and grandparent. Includes profanity, sex, and mentions of infertility, divorce, and aging.

CHAPTER ONE

Stefano

N O ONE EVER told me getting married meant getting used to gray hair.

One day, I was saying "I do," and we were in love and ridiculously happy. Then suddenly everything that used to be funny and adorable set her off, and another gray strand appeared. But I wasn't worried because I had my person, and we were growing old together.

Now, twelve years later, the ink isn't even dry on my divorce decree, I've got the same face—plus or minus a few laugh lines—and a full head of salt-and-pepper curls that I can't tell whether they make me look distinguished or just older.

I adjust the rearview mirror, leaning in to examine my hairline before I turn up the volume on the "Confidence and Cologne" podcast I'd been listening to on the drive here to the vineyard. This episode aptly is titled, "Grieving, Graying, and Getting Back Out There."

At least it's not thinning.

Johnny Timmons's laugh filters through my speakers like he knows my secret.

"The thing is, after my divorce, I used to be hopeless with women. Like, *so* bad." He chuckles. "If there was a *Don't Do XYZ or Risk Turning Off Every Woman in a 100-Mile Radius* list, I would've been the poster child. Women didn't want me because I was forthright about my faults to a fault…"

I deflate back against my headrest.

Good God.

I should probably table this episode for now.

Currently, I'm parked in the brush, off the steps of my family's vineyard, not even five hundred feet away from the massive silk-lined tent on the main lawn. It's teeming with my three siblings, friends, and most of Napa's nobility.

They're all here to celebrate the matriarch of our family.

Not that Mother does any event on a small scale. Today, though, we're marking the occasion of Victoria Fortemani's sixty-fifth spin around the sun, appropriately with an outrageously lavish high tea.

It's more than chamomile and crustless cucumber sand-wiches. There'll be a full catering army ready to serve and tend to Mother's every whim. A long, single fifty-seater table will be dressed in white linen with fine china, bustling purple peony centerpieces, and collectible teapots. There'll be dessert and sandwich towers for guests to nibble on as they chat about every salacious piece of gossip they can get their hands on.

That's what I'm worried about.

The Gossip Set loves nothing more than spilling tea about business, real estate, weddings, divorces, who's dating who.

After my ex-wife Carina's post this morning, they won't want to talk about—or celebrate—anyone else.

Why waste time chatting up the belle of the ball over scones and jam? Why not speculate about her eldest son making his debut back into society as an unmarried man on the day that his ex posts a picture holding hands with a younger, more athletic, virile man without a gray strand in sight?

"Jesus, why do I even care?"

Because I failed our marriage, maybe? Because I failed her? Because she deserves happiness, even if I couldn't give it to her?

"Goddammit. You had to post this today, Carina?"

Glancing at the time on my dashboard, a full-chested sigh works its way through me.

Just a few more minutes.

I scrape my hand through my graying curls then tune back in to Johnny.

"What I'm saying is, confidence isn't just attractive to women," Johnny says before he clarifies. "It's the MOST attractive thing to women."

Whether I want to listen to this guy's "instant results with women" spiel or not, my ears perk up.

I'm hiding in my car to spare Mother my drama and avoid answering questions about the state of my love life (spoiler: it's in shambles), and Carina is moving on. She's dating and holding hands with an oil-slicked Instagram fitness model, and I'm getting self-help advice from a motivational speaker wearing an inordinate amount of hair gel.

So, yeah, I'm a little insecure.

"Conversation skills are important." Johnny's voice weaves into my headspace. It's like he's talking directly to me, as if he all but whispers, *Stefano Fortemani you've got to learn how to talk to women again.*

Which just feels rude.

A voiceover sound effect punctuates his point with, *I'm listening, honey,* and Johnny's groan bleeds into a laugh.

"All women want to do is talk. It's how they show they care, which means you need to learn how to actively listen and hold an engaging conversation. Period," he advises.

A pang of nostalgia settles in the pit of my stomach, remembering how Carina wanted to download about everything from the meals she ate to the man who cut her off on the freeway.

She's probably telling everything to Mr. Instagram now.

"Yes, looks matter, too. No woman wants a guy who needs a relationship with a barber more than he needs one with her. Get some new threads and some cologne, too. This is permission to spend money on yourself." I let my gaze drift over my pale gray, starched suit and burgundy tie, feeling vindicated about my tailored suit wardrobe before he clears his throat edging toward seriousness. "At the end of the day, though, it comes down to mental and emotional strength. It's nonnegotiable. Your confidence has been knocked, but you've got a decision. Do you want to win her back or do you want to explore sexual and romantic relationships with—"

"Jesus Christ—"

The Lord's name dies on my tongue as I swivel around to my window, blinking slowly.

It's not my brothers, Dante or Marcello, rapping on the glass. Nor is it Mother or my sister, Chiara. Instead, they've sent Dante's live-in girlfriend Morgan's overprotective best friend, Avery Ellis, to summon me.

You can't be serious.

"Hi there!" She beams, tossing me a small wave as the inflection in her voice rises cheerily, expectantly.

She's waiting for me to return the greeting or at the least, acknowledge her. Which, now, I'm incapable of doing. I'm frozen, still clutching my chest, and futilely trying to make sense of a woman who is the human equivalent of a Rubik's cube—colorful, marketed for youthful fun, but mind-boggling.

Why is she here?

I'm just about to ask why she's snooping around the circular drive when the party is on the main lawn, right as Johnny doubles down.

"Don't wait to get back out there. Date, have sex… Lots of sex."

Panic streaks through me as I watch Avery's sparkly brown eyes widen with amusement.

Heat swarms my skin as I jolt around, reaching for my phone to stop the podcast.

Except, when I tap the button to pause it, I hit it too many times and it repeats, impossibly loud like a commandment.

"Date, have sex… *Loooottttttsss of sexxxx!*"

Embarrassment coils around. I feel like my ribs are closing in on my heart when I turn back in time to see her lips twitching.

"Uh...that was just, um..." I stammer, but Avery, the saint that she is, finishes my sentence.

"Some grade-A messaging you've got there." She giggles, and the infectious sound... Dear sweet Lord, it's like gasoline on fire, burning me up from the inside.

My skin tightens and flames singe my eyes and cheeks.

The thing about this woman is that she's insufferable.

Oh, Avery "sunshine all the time" Ellis is nice. Too nice, as in Pollyanna, traipsing through the meadow to solve all the world's problems. For her, life is literally a party. She's an event planner. Weddings, anniversaries, *quinceañeras*, any excuse for a celebration. In fact, high tea is her brainchild, which she pulled off in less than three weeks after Mother canned her Bermuda trip.

Avery to the rescue!

Deep down, I know she's one of those perky people who, at the end of an interview when asked about what she thinks her weaknesses are, gives a glaringly false negative. *I'm too detail-oriented. I've got checklists for everything. I always forget when the workday is over.*

Give me a break.

Miss punctual, professional, beautiful, gets along with everyone, and she's fiercely loyal.

Which...that's where we butted heads from the start.

When it comes to her Sister Circle—Seneca, Monica, Valerie, and Morgan, Dante's girlfriend—Avery Ellis is a ruthless warrior. Much the way I am for my siblings, what she'll do for them is limitless. Loyalty is the only thing we've got in common, which Avery learned firsthand over the last six months.

She's completely blown it out of proportion now, but in January, after my family realized we were losing Dante to grief, I helped Mother orchestrate a diabolical family hoax, threatening to sell the vineyard.

Now, I know that sounds horrible.

Who goes to those extreme lengths to prank their brother who's already struggling with the loss of his father and grandfather?

Only loved ones who know they've got to do something drastic to light a fire under him to pull him out of said grief, that's who.

It was out of love, and there was nothing he wouldn't do to save our two-hundred-plus-year-old vineyard and winery, so we took our shot, and it paid off.

Big time.

At Dante's first event meant to draw crowds, he met and ended up contracting Morgan's business consultant firm. They fell deeply in love in the process and the rest is history.

Except, Avery still harbors resentment toward me since her best friend's relationship *could've* been the collateral damage of our risky gamble.

It wasn't, but it could have been, she reminds me every time we see each other.

Now, this woman who I've clashed with from the second we met, is snooping outside my window in the sweltering midday heat, right when the word "sex" is broadcast to the hilltops?

I'm mortified.

But also, cautiously curious why she's here.

I flit a quick glance at my phone to ensure the podcast

app is closed before I straighten and clear my throat.

"How can I help you, Avery?"

Who better to practice that nonnegotiable confidence on than a woman intent on questioning me?

She steps closer and I get my first good look at our sparkly-eyed sunshine warrior, fittingly wearing a bold yellow-and-white polka dot sundress with her sleek blonde lace-front swept over her sun-kissed shoulders. It's perfect for high tea on a bright, summer afternoon.

No surprise there.

Avery Ellis is perfect in every way, right?

Call me cynical, but I've found most people aren't trustworthy. Generally, they're not bad but no one is nice or selfless all the time. Not without ulterior motives. And there's always, *always* a catch.

"Hi, Stefano." Avery's tone is upbeat and clear as she bounces on her heels. "I didn't mean to interrupt your self-help podcast, or anything..." *You're thoroughly enjoying this, aren't you?* "But everyone was looking for you inside the tent, so I volunteered to look around, and bring you back if I found you."

I cut the engine and step out onto the gravel.

"Looks like you did. Great job."

That was a bit harsh.

I stand to my full height, and shut the door behind me, taking my time to press my hands over the wrinkles in my pants.

As Avery glances over her shoulder toward the path that leads to the main lawn, though, my focus zeros in on the thin laugh lines, crinkling around her full, sweeping eyelashes. I watch as they slowly smooth, and she lowers her gaze. I catalogue how her delicate bronze shoulders curl over her chest, and I immediately hate that my default response with Avery is always on the defensive side.

"So, how's the party going?" I ask, hoping to put her love of talking to use while we walk toward the main lawn since my conversation skills clearly need work.

I'm fishing.

Are they drinking tea or spilling it? Both? Is it about me and Carina? Am I blowing this whole Instagram post out of proportion? How's my confidence? Do women even notice me anymore?

Wait, what?

"Oh, my goodness, it's like a dream in there. It's elegant and charming, and the food and the English tea sandwiches…" Avery moans, clearly unaffected by me or my fishing bait. "And Victoria is having a ball."

So, maybe no one has seen the post yet.

Cool relief rushes through me and my stride quickens. Suddenly, the tension in my shoulders loosens and I feel lighter, giddy. I'm impressed. The corners of my mouth tug downward, lower lip protruding. I'm nodding to myself as the larger-than-life white tent beams into the path before us.

Yes, this is good.

"Now, English tea sandwiches, you say? Are those the ones with the smoked salmon—"

I toss her a sidelong glance just as she stumbles over a clump of grass. She tips forward, and I grab her elbow, steadying her on her feet.

We're stopped just short of the tent's entrance.

Her chest rises and falls like she's self-soothing.

"You all right, there?" I ask, inspecting her dress, making sure she's okay before we join the party. "Still perfect."

Her bright brown eyes snap to mine.

But then, slowly, she squares her shoulders to me, and closes the distance between us.

Our proximity hits me head-on, and I'm frozen.

"Thank you," she says, quietly.

Before I know what's happening, she reaches up and straightens my tie, and I'm blindsided.

A woman who isn't my wife—ex-wife—is touching me.

I don't know how to respond, or if I should.

But my body does.

On an instinctual level, every inch of my body reacts. I'm unnerved by the intimacy of Avery's touch, and she's only adjusting my tie. I'm zeroed in on the ease with which she moves. How comfortable she is as she smooths her hands along the lapels and shoulders of my suit jacket as if she's done this a million times. As if each slow drag of delicate fingers over the invisible wrinkles doesn't set my skin ablaze through the taut fabric.

My breathing shallows, coming in tiny staccato gasps as I scrutinize the soft curves of her face.

I didn't make any hard and fast vows to "never date another woman again." Honestly, I'm still coming to terms with the fact that my marriage failed. My confidence is knocked. I've been out of the dating game so long. Do I even remember how to approach women? Will they want me when my divorce is so recent? What if I get rejected? What if I don't have the stamina? Jesus, what if gray hair is an instant deal-breaker?

I don't have all the answers yet, but I know I don't want to spend the rest of my life pretending it doesn't feel good to have a beautiful woman's hands on me.

"Listen, Stefano." Avery steps back, her gaze softening, searching. "I know you've got a lot going on personally...."

"Healing from a divorce while your ex is moving on can't be easy, Stefano, but..."

My neck and jaw stiffen.

I'm dying to know what comes after that *but*. I'm waiting with bated breath to hear what sunny silver lining she'll tack on the end of that bruised sentence to make my life all better.

But then she surprises me.

"Today can't be about you, though," she says.

The mild irritation I felt seconds ago grows to full-blown annoyance.

"You think I don't know it's my mother's birthday? I'm just curious, why do you think I was sitting in my car while my siblings help celebrate her big day?" I tap my fingers to my temples and explode them.

But Avery doesn't respond to my gesture.

"That was a lot of words from you all at once," she quips. "Are you sure you're feeling okay?"

"Not that I owe you an explanation, but I was trying to spare her my mess. I figured if I stayed away long enough, maybe those vultures in there"—I fan my hand toward the Gossip Set in the tent—"would find something else to talk about other than my divorce or who the hell they can fix me up with now that my ex-wife apparently found herself a replacement." I step back, fuming and needing air to breathe.

Why am I telling her all of this?

"That's not what I meant," she reasons, quietly.

I don't know if it's her soft tone or the fact that she seems so unaffected while I'm agitated, but it grates on my nerves.

"Well, what did you mean because obviously, I'm aware today can't be about me."

Like she senses I'm done, determination darkens Avery's stare, and she erases the distance between us.

"I'm sure you look at me and think I'm some pushover you can control, Stefano Fortemani. But what you don't know about me, is I don't take shit. Not from anyone." She stabs her bright pink fingernail into my chest, pausing for a beat. "Because you seem to have missed it, I was being empathetic to your situation, but I think you should be aware. The whole brooding, edgy silver-fox thing you've got going on, it comes off as cold and antisocial. Something else you might want to work on during your self-improvement journey along with all the sex and dating." She snickers.

Thanks for that, Johnny.

My cheeks heat but I swallow, determined to hear her out.

"Now, what I meant was, they've all been waiting for your arrival to get started. And while this is your mother's tea, it's my event, representing a business that supports my livelihood, and *people* I care about. I won't have you ruin this."

Everything around me muffles, and I feel like I'm wearing earplugs. We stare blankly, silently at an impasse, per usual, assessing each other.

"We're in full agreement," I finally say.

"Great. Then, do yourself a favor and smile, because your brother needs you."

Then, just like that, she flashes me a tight smile and storms away, and I'm left standing on the outside with my head still spinning.

What was that? What did she mean, my brother needs me? Which brother, and what in the National Geographic is a silver fox?

CHAPTER TWO
Stefano

AFTER AVERY LEAVES, I spend another five minutes outside the tent unwinding myself from her Jedi mind tricks.

So, if I'm understanding her correctly, today isn't about me, nor Mother...on *her* birthday. No, in a plot twist that frankly, I'm still wrapping my mind around, it's about one of my brothers who needs me. Which is why, the instant I walk inside, my plan is to pinpoint which brother, then get to the bottom of this elusive reason I'm needed. For now, though, I'm stuck on the Google results for "silver fox."

An attractive older man with mostly gray or white hair, huh?

A lightness blooms in my chest.

I don't know about the old part. Although, comparatively speaking, I'm guessing by her best friends' median ages and the fact that she regularly finds a corner to sit and nurse her glass of wine, Avery is around Dante's age, give or take. Easily, early to mid-thirties. In which case, I've likely got close to a decade on her.

That's just math.

It's the attractive part, though, that's got me standing taller as I run my hand through my hair, draw my shoulders back, let my arms relax, and duck into the tent.

Surprisingly, a sense of calm settles over me when every pair of eyes in the room snaps to me.

Including the assessing pair attached to one Avery Ellis.

A fresh rush of adrenaline zips through me.

The articles I skimmed referenced the likes of George Clooney and Idris Elba. They aren't fresh-faced actors with a light sprinkling of silver creeping in. These are bona fide, aged-to-perfection, black-and-gray-haired sex symbols that women go gaga over. They've each been named World's Sexiest Man Alive. The tinged gray scruff and silver waves of these well-groomed men who ooze charisma only makes them sexier.

Curiosity buzzes through me.

Does Avery Ellis think I'm attractive?

Halfway down the table, Marcello releases a booming laugh, stealing my attention. As usual, he's leaned back in his chair, long legs stretched out, hands back behind his head while he's steering a vibrant discussion.

I've got to be honest, I haven't seen Dante yet, but Marcello looks decidedly unbothered. Not at all like a man desperately in need of his big brother's support.

Glancing back at Avery, she flashes me a reassuring smile, and I feel my eyebrows drawing together.

While Avery and I have repeatedly clashed, do I hate the ego boost her word choice—*and* touch—has given me? Certainly not. Is the fact that the only empty chair at the table being located between her and Mother the reason I'm questioning her so-called brotherly emergency? Damn right.

Something else is at play here.

What game are you playing, Pollyanna?

My chin high, every inch of me puffed up, I train my attention on her, taking easy strides down the length of the table, greeting guests along the way.

Except, when I'm a quarter of the way down the table, Marcello bellows my name, waving me over.

"Stef! You made it, just in time."

He lowers his chair onto the grass again, slapping my hand before he tugs me down into a full bro hug.

"Had a few things to take care of first but what's up?" I ask, hoping his question might either give me insight into what I've missed or validate my suspicions about Avery hunting me down.

"Bet. That's just life sometimes. I know you wouldn't be late if it wasn't important." He nods a few times, reassuringly, before he circles back to his query. "Now, I could use your help. I'm trying to see something here."

Lay it on me.

Marcello looks me directly in the eye as he asks, "How many French fries is it cool for a friend to take before you're like, *nah*"—he slices his hand over his throat—"go order your own?"

A wave of laughter rolls over the surrounding guests. Noticeably, including an attractive young woman with angled and textured curls wearing a pale blue dress seated particularly close to Marcello.

I stare at him for a few seconds, wondering if wingman services qualify as "support."

Darting my gaze to Avery, who's suspiciously paying me zero attention, I scrub a hand over my face, chuckling before I return my focus to his fresh, stubble-free face.

Here I was thinking, could this be the question that clues me in on the need that's so important my brother sent Miss Sunshine USA to hunt me down? But no, this is just my charming, attention-seeking youngest brother, living his best life with a captive audience.

As the youngest, he's always employed unconventional ways of grabbing the spotlight. Spider-infested grape pranks, a "summer of fun" idea box next to the swear jar, creating his own Rosé Cabernet blends at the winery without putting it to a family vote because he claims his ideas are always dismissed. This French fry conundrum is just another example of Marcello finding a way to be seen.

"Yo, I'm dead serious," he presses me. "Be for real with me, Stef."

His eyes widen and flicker to the woman beside him, pleading with me not to make him look like a simp in front of her.

"I guess it depends on the size." I laugh, and almost snort because I know my brother's gutter-dwelling mind. Almost certainly, *that's what she said* is teetering on his tongue, so I clarify, stressing the food. "Are we talking a large or a regular serving of *French fries?*"

"Oh, here we go..." Marcello rolls his stark green eyes and groans, audibly annoyed.

"What?" I ask, struggling to comprehend whatever wingman cue I've somehow missed.

"Why do you always have to overthink everything?

Damn," he grumbles. "I'm not asking for the numbers guy who manages the finances for a conglomerate of family businesses, so get that out of your head. Just give me ball-park."

"Okay, let's see…" I nod, giving his silly question proper consideration, on the off chance he's responsible for the Sun Signal glowing across that sky that led Avery skipping to the rescue.

The woman, who I'm certain is the barely legal eighteen-year-old daughter of one of Mother's friends leans in, her knee brushing against Marcello's.

"I said, maybe ten…" She giggles and shrugs, flashing my brother a lip-biting smile.

Marcello spreads his legs wide, arms loose, assuming a relaxed pose that shamelessly draws attention to his family jewels.

She's a child. Not a good look, bro.

"For the sake of time and your overly analytical skills…" Marcello prefaces, playing to her. "Let's say it's large fries with one dipping sauce, no ketchup or salt packets, and no additional fries at the bottom of the bag."

Mentally, I take all these factors into account, estimating there's about fifty to ninety fries in a large, then I take ten percent off the top. Even further, taking that five to nine, I average again.

"Seven, max."

Marcello snaps his fingers five times in quick succession before he slaps the table victoriously. "What did I tell you? If you want ten fries, you're going to have to buy your own."

They fall into lively bickering and laughter as he whispers

suggestively, "Unless, we're on a date..."

Okay, then.

Evidently, my job here is done.

I continue down the table toward Mother. As I'm walking though, Avery lifts her chin, her gold-flecked brown eyes widened with urgency. I've got no clue what she's trying to communicate, my supportive services all but forgotten until she presses her fingers to her lips, pointing her forefinger to the left.

My gaze flits across the room, snagging on movement near the buffet tables.

Looking like he might pull his hair out if he didn't shave his to baby-butt bald, is Dante, in deep conversation with his best friend Marco.

Flashing Avery a reassuring glance, I change course, slowly, *carefully*, veering in their direction.

From the short distance, anyone would assume they were just two guys in suits, celebrating and shooting the shit. They're simply catching each other up on life's happenings.

But I know better.

With every step closer, I scrutinize the way they're huddled together, their closed-off postures as they whisper in hushed tones, going back and forth in quick succession. That's not all, though. It's almost imperceptible but the thing that's most telling is Dante's shaky hands.

Something indeed is happening.

Whatever it is, it isn't good.

Once they're in earshot, I clear my throat, announcing myself. "How are the English tea sandwiches?" I ask.

Their eyes flicker to the tiered tower in front of them like they've only just now registered they're standing beside the buffet.

"Stef, *damn*. You made it." Dante drags his hands over his scalp and wordlessly heaves a relieved sigh.

"I did."

But then it hits me that my brother is wearing a suit. And not *just* wearing a suit. It fits properly, which means it's been tailored. There's a tie and an ironed button-down to pair with matching black leather belt and Oxfords, and... *Is his beard scruff gone?*

He turns, further magnifying my suspicions when he finally meets my stare and whispers, "We don't have much time and I need to talk to you."

I ease in closer, my throat constricting as I join their huddle, replaying Avery's advice.

Smile, because your brother needs you.

Marco drags his hand over his mouth, down his chin until he pinches the skin at his throat.

Shit.

My mind graduates to full-blown panic. Is he sick? *Is Mom?*

Think.

Damn, that's why she skipped Bermuda for a high tea with friends and family. She's preparing. This could be the last time I see my mother, and I'm late because I was sitting in the car listening to a mediocre motivational speaker give pointers to the modern man on getting back in the game after divorce.

I'm a horrible, selfish person.

My attention shifts to his shaky hands, his slow, shallow

breaths. "Is Mother okay?"

"It's not that kind of emergency. Everyone in the family is fine," Dante says like he senses I'm one hop and a skip from going off the deep end.

He knows how tightly I'm holding on to what family we have left.

"Jesus, Dante." I close my eyes for a beat, shoving aside those unthinkable thoughts. "You can't make vague comments like that and expect me not to jump to terrible conclusions. Just tell me what the hell is going on."

Eyes lowered, he squares his shoulders to me.

"I need your support."

"Anything."

A few seconds pass as Dante stares at me like he expected pushback. The ease of it all not sitting well with him before he backtracks.

"First, tell me why you're late," he counters.

Nice deflection.

I huff out a laugh. "Let's not do this. Are you going to tell me or keep up this half-hatched guessing game?"

Dante shoots me a sidelong glance that pleads, *humor me*, but my nerves can't handle the suspense.

"Out with it, D."

But then he doubles down.

"Why were you late?"

"Why are you dodging the issue? We're not standing in the corner of this tent because you were concerned with my whereabouts."

Thankfully, Marco has my back.

He lifts a challenging eyebrow and taps his watch. "D, do

you really want to waste more time?"

"Yeah, tick tock," I say.

But Dante persists, and I'm not foolish enough to believe he won't hold out on principle.

"As if everyone doesn't already know." I shrug. "Carina posted a picture with her new boy toy."

Dante and Marco snicker.

"Oh, is that not manly enough for you two?" I shake my head. "Her sidepiece, fitness influencer boyfriend. Is that better?"

Marco presses a fist to his mouth, failing horribly at masking his laugh.

"Whatever."

Dante's eyebrows draw together curiously. "Sorry, Stef. So, you've been doing what…sulking?"

"In my car, listening to Johnny Timmons." Mortified, I cover my face with my hand, laughing with these two knuckleheads. "I know, it's pathetic."

They're bent over gasping for air, using each other to hold themselves upright.

"Ha ha. Get it all out." I chuckle. "I didn't want to up-stage Mother's big day. I hope this makes you feel better about whatever it is you were going to tell me because I'm leaving—"

Dante yanks me back into their huddle, still laughing, but his expression turns noticeably more pensive as he slips a small velvet box from his interior jacket pocket.

"What is that?" I ask, stupidly, knowing full well, my jeans and Timberlands brother in an impeccably tailored suit is a dead giveaway. "Are you and Morgan…now?"

Panic etches the lines of his face as he nervously darts his gaze past my shoulders. "Lord, keep it down."

Suddenly, I feel like we're in a time machine.

He isn't thirty-nine. He's nine—a few months from ten—and I'm fifteen, locked in his bedroom in the middle of the night. Tired, tear-stained eyes had peered back at me. He'd waited until the entire house was asleep to ask me how to make a girl like him. My initial annoyance faded quickly when I realized he hadn't asked Dad or Nono. Not Mother either. Chiara and Marcello were too young, but I was his choice.

Dante had chosen to confide his fears and ask advice from his big brother, who he'd watched like a hawk, emulated down to the tapered fade and spotless sneakers, trusted to guide him.

As the oldest of four, I've always set the example for my siblings. First to business school, marriage, homeownership…divorce. Now, he's about to follow in my footsteps down a muddied, heart-breaking path.

"You're going to ask her at Mother's birthday celebration?"

"Do you really think she's going to mind?" Dante counters. "She's on the phone talking to Morgan daily. *She* asked *me* what's taking so long."

That I believe.

She's all about growing her family. To say she was hurt when Carina and I told her about the divorce is putting it lightly. Carina was like a daughter to her, and I'm certain they've remained in touch.

"So, why now? What's the rush?" I ask, coaxing his stare

to meet mine. Maybe, I'll get a glimpse of what this is about. "Is she…"

"Asshole!"

"I was just asking."

"No, Morgan isn't pregnant. I *love* her." *If only that was enough.* "I want to spend the rest of my life with her. I want to start a fam—" He breaks off for my sake but the rest of that sentence barrels through my bruised and bandaged heart.

I want to start a family.

I scrub a hand over my face, familiar sorrow shredding my insides.

Marco's eyes widen, conspiratorially. "Not to insert myself but they haven't discussed whether they want kids yet…"

Dante tosses him a chastising *you're not helping* glance before he turns back to me.

Silence wedges between us.

"Say something," he prompts.

"How about four months?" I shrug, shaking my head.

He groans. "Say something else."

"What do you want me to say? It's June. You and Morgan met in February, and you're already living together. Now, you're proposing? I just don't understand what the rush is," I reason, wishing I could open his eyes for him, and make him see the glaring danger signs ahead. "You haven't had any drag-out, knock-down arguments that challenge the very foundation of your relationship. What about finances? You're living together, but she works in the city. How long before commuting gets old?"

"He's got a point there," Marco agrees. "Y'all need to

figure that out."

"Thank you." Dante sucks his teeth.

But I'm still hoping he'll listen. "My point is, you're thirty-nine. You haven't been trained yet to put things back in the fridge or dishes in the sink. You still leave wet towels on the floor." I huff out a laugh. "Do you even know you're not supposed to use her decorative hand towels?"

Marco shakes his head like this is Marriage 101.

"And he thinks he's ready for marriage." I pull in a lungful of air. "Yeah, okay. Like I said, it's too soon."

"Is it?" Marco chimes in again, seemingly realizing he's on the wrong side of his friendship.

I shoot him a warning stare, but Marco's comment feels like the fuel Dante was waiting on.

"Listen, I get that must be hard after Carina but please don't be that guy right now." Dante pulls in a long breath through his nose and slowly releases it through his mouth. He tilts his head to me without looking head-on. "I'm telling you I'm in love and about to make the biggest decision of my life."

"Think, Dante."

"Jesus, I don't want to think anymore. I've waited my whole life to feel this. My mind is made up."

I pinch the bridge of my nose, annoyed that he won't listen to reason.

My brother, better than most, knows heartbreak—familial and romantic. We both know. When it comes to love, though, he's never experienced the kind you can't walk away from clean. He's never felt, touched, given so deeply that love overflowed into a tiny soul whose unborn fingers

25

held the key to life, only to watch it slip away.

It's taken me over a decade to realize Carina's and my dream should've started with us.

"So, tell me again why I'm here if you already made your decision." My voice hardens.

"I don't have Dad or Nono. All I have is my stubborn, overly cautious older brother. I need your support," he says. "You're here because I want your goddamn blessing, you asshole." He laughs a defeated laugh.

Deep down, I want to ask why my marriage wasn't enough of a cautionary tale. How he could watch the years turn me into a shell of my old self, yet he's volunteering for the same torture.

Doesn't he get that whirlwind romances are just seeds? Love is a gradual process, not an instant one. You've still got to tend to the vines, water and harvest the best grapes. The crushing, pressure, and fermentation, that's where the real magic happens. When you dare to let them mature, that's when you really know what you're working with.

Love means taking your time.

Even still, it doesn't come with guarantees.

I flash him a tentative smile, though.

Above all, we're Fortemanis and brothers.

We stand together, always.

"Of course you've got my support."

He tugs me into a hug, thanking me. "I'll take it," he says as Marco joins in with a raucous laugh that gains us an audience.

Slowly, we pull apart to the tune of collective applause.

Then, like it was all the fuel he needed, Dante steps back

and straightens his tie. "Wish me luck," he tosses back, goofy grin in place as he rounds the buffet, moving toward the table with onlookers beaming back at him, ready for the show.

In an impressively smooth move, he swipes Marcello's empty water glass and spoon, halting the party. "First of all, I want to thank everyone for coming out today to celebrate Mom's sixty-fifth birthday—"

"Darling, hush," Mother interrupts him, feigning shock. "I don't know why people keep saying that. I'm sixty-five years *young*."

Another wave of laughter falls over the table.

"You don't look a day over thirty-five, Mom," Chiara adds, doing a great job of ensuring everyone's spirits are lifted for what's next.

"Victoria Fortemani, ladies and gentlemen." Dante heads off the applause. "Are you enjoying your big day?"

"Immensely, my darling," she replies, her eyes sparkling the way they always do when she's the center of attention.

Dante takes his cue, walking alongside the table until he stops behind Morgan. He rests his hands on her shoulders and leans down to kiss her forehead before he resumes his speech.

"Well, that's exactly what I want to hear because now I've got to follow it up with an apology." He scans the faces of each guest. "You see, part of my birthday gift requires me to hijack your party for selfish reasons…"

Soft gasps pinball around the room as everyone looks on expectantly.

As if on cue, in a coordinated sequence, the faint music

stops, Dante turns Morgan's chair, and tugs her to her feet.

Her hands in his, he swallows, then lowers himself on one knee.

Mother covers her heart with her hand. She's all shiny eyes over the smile of a proud parent whose family is growing.

My throat constricts.

The tent fills with sighs, swoons, and cheers.

Tears stream down Morgan's cheeks.

"From the moment I met you, my beautiful un-Valentine, Wonder Woman, I've never been more certain about anything in my life. I knew I wanted to be the croissant flakes on your lips." She laughs through her tears, fueling Dante to go on. "I wanted to talk about wine, life, family, friends, and business with you. And some may think I'm rushing in…"

He jabs thumb toward me, and I chuckle, looking around the table…

Is that?

On the other side of the table, mixed in with the high-backed chairs at a table full of specialty teas, homemade breads, and fruitcakes, I recognize Morgan's friends.

Avery, I get. She's an event planner. It makes sense. But why are Seneca, Valerie, and Monica are here? Which strikes me as odd because if this proposal is supposedly spontaneous, why would they be at my mother's birthday?

Morgan's friends wouldn't attend a sixty-five-year-old's party, unless…

I flit a glance at Avery.

On the table, there's a small fanny pack with a bulging

zipper, a thick pink book, and a long-lens camera perched and pointed in her hands as she captures this moment.

She planned this.

They all knew.

"Why wait when I've never been more certain that waking up and falling asleep with you in my arms is the only life I want to live?" Dante asks the room then meets Morgan's teary-eyed stare. "Marry me, Morgan Elaine Forster. Make me the happiest man on the planet."

"Yes!"

Dante scoops her up in his arms, twirling her around as the party erupts with joy.

For the second time in an hour, my head spins, sending all the pieces of this puzzle falling into place. This last-minute tea party, the change of travel plans, they were a cover for an engagement party. Everyone knew except for me, including Avery Ellis.

I won't have you ruin this.

Half of me is ecstatic that my brother has found a love that makes him feel so deeply. The other half, though, wouldn't put it past Pollyanna to persuade Dante to keep me in the dark. Can't have the rain blocking the sun, now, could she?

She knows I'd have convinced my brother to wait.

I didn't go through hell and back just to watch my brother repeat my mistakes.

"Buttering up the silver fox is all in a day's work, even for a sunshine warrior, huh, Pollyanna?" I say under my breath as we lock eyes across the room.

I match her smile with one of my own then put my

thumb and middle finger together, slip them between my lips, and unleash a hail of a whistle.

My brother needs me now more than ever.

CHAPTER THREE

Avery

M Y CLIENT, NICHELLE, whose completely over-the-top Hollywood glamour wedding I'm planning, squeals with delight.

"*Girl*, I feel like I'm famous!"

She's been glued to her phone, her long, clacky nails texting and scrolling the interwebs for the past twenty-two minutes—and thirteen seconds if, say, you were dog-tired and counting down until the end of your workday.

Usually, I don't care.

My appointments are my clients' time. We can spend it dreaming out loud about venues, linens, photo booths, and flowers. Or we can get full-on velvety, buttercream cake bites and bubbly. At the end of the day, my goal is to bring their biggest celebratory dreams to life in 3-D technicolor. I worry about the logistics, budgets, and suppliers, so they don't have to.

But today is Tuesday.

Most people live for weekends, but I work hard, Wednesday to Monday, so I can play even harder—sans my little guy, Ace, who spends the night with his granny—on

Turn-Up Tuesday with my Sister Circle. It's our standing weekly time to refuel, recharge, and unwind over wine and whatever we can find to pair with it.

After the past week and a half I've had…

Between the tea party, Morgan's engagement, and the resulting fifteen minutes of fame they've sponsored for my little event-planning company, Ellis Events, I'm exhausted. But then throw in a national holiday that condones overpricing five-second sparklers and sleepless, never-ending fireworks, all-nighters.

Bring on all the wine and unwinding.

"Lord, my cousin is on the bird app, telling anyone who'll listen that THE Avery Ellis is the mastermind behind my upcoming nuptials," Nichelle says. "I have never in my twenty-five years heard this woman utter a word with more than two syllables, now she's talking about nuptials?"

I giggle.

She is loving every minute of this.

To Nichelle, the residual fame she's experiencing because I'm *her* wedding planner, might as well be *Entertainment Tonight*, *E News*, and *TMZ* coverage combined.

"You were made for the spotlight!" I decree, peeking at the time above all the silenced notifications on my phone.

Four twenty-four.

Our appointment—and my workday—is over at five sharp.

"Yes, indeed. Shine all the light on me." Nichelle cackles. "I know how to amplify the hype."

I mumble my agreement.

"When I tell you these people are in my DMs clambering

for ceremony details…" She flits a quick disbelieving glance at me. "Meanwhile, I'm just over here, my mouth clamped shut like, I wish I would…" Her face scrunches up with amused and pure, unfiltered nope.

The way every town from Napa to the Bay is talking about Victoria Fortemani's birthday tea, and how that's somehow translated into me becoming this ungettable event planner everyone wants, simply amazes me. For me, it was another day working and playing hard. How was I supposed to know planning an elegant affair for a powerful woman with equally powerful guests would be game-changing?

I guess, who needs the philharmonic, or my uninspired last-minute Tea Time playlist continuously shuffling on low volume, when I can bippity-boppity-style turn a gathering into a magical engagement party for entertainment?

"*Puh-lease,*" Nichelle continues her animated rant, posturing for an invisible crowd. "The last thing Faison and I need is paparazzi staked out for pics of a private Avery Ellis event. No, ma'am. Not on my big day."

Warmth swells in my chest, copping a squat right between my bone-tired ribs.

"And not on my watch," I chime in.

Nichelle snaps her fingers, punctuating her agreement.

The flair for dramatics on this one…

I shake my head, laughing softly as we amble through the elegant Julia Morgan Ballroom where her reception will be held this coming winter. It's one of my most coveted venues. Gorgeous doesn't even begin to cover how stunning this place is. Timeless luxury, modern amenities, historically and architecturally breathtaking, all located in the heart of San

Francisco. And bonus—for me—it easily accommodates large guest lists, which is both rare and perfect for Nichelle's grand vision.

It's also why we're here now to review the food and logistics with their attentive, and *very* patient staff.

"Should we maybe work our way over—"

"Oh. My. *God*!" Nichelle interrupts with Sir Mix-a-Lot "Baby Got Back" levels of comedic seriousness.

"What?" I laugh, praying this will be a quick story.

"My book club has hijacked our group chat to discuss my wedding." Nichelle pauses for dramatic effect, I'm guessing, waiting for my reaction.

"That's awesome. Is Sydney going to be able to attend after all?" I ask, putting an upbeat, hopeful spin on whatever she says next.

What's one more book club member when we're still rearranging tables and adding place cards, before we give a final headcount to the staff?

Nichelle closes her eyes, centering herself before she seems to regroup.

"No, no, you don't understand what this means."

Lifting my chin, I give her my full attention.

Tired bones, wine, and all that.

"My book club? It's made up of the best that introverts have to offer, and they're talking about how you curated this classy, sophisticated high tea for Napa's upper crust," she explains, accurately assuming I'm still not following. "These women are not on the chatty, hot takes for breakfast, lunch, and dinner social media platforms. They're pretty curated bookish pictures, and mounting TBR lists. Now, suddenly, they're discussing which of those fine-ass Fortemani brothers are still on the market and lavish weddings..."

My brain stalls halfway through that last sentence.

Fine-ass Fortemani brothers?

I blink way too many times to be natural.

My pulse pounds in my neck, heat prickling over my skin, for two *very* good reasons.

First, why are these introverted insta-curators discussing Dante's brothers almost two weeks later? I thought all the buzz was about tea parties and weddings. Stefano and Marcello were guests. Secondly, and this part is truly baffling, is there really a competition between a young player and a tall, broody—albeit grumpy—silver fox with undeniably big, *um*...hands?

Why did I have to call him a silver fox?

Why did I walk up on him in that car listening to Johnny Timmons—who is problematic for so many reasons?

Every inch of me softened because here was this man dealing with his ex-wife's hot girl summer, and there he was looking for tips on getting back out there. Of course, the man's faith in marriage is shook.

He'd looked so adorably awkward, stammering, mortified that I'd heard the words "dating" and "sex."

Jesus, the way his eyes had darkened, and he'd frozen when I touched him.

Again, why did I jab my finger into his starched suit then recoil when I was met with steel?

He nearly had me fooled, too.

I get this overwhelming urge to grab Nichelle's phone, and tap a quick message to her bookish friends, telling them to move it along. The product packaging and branding is on point, but what's inside leaves so much to be desired.

But then I come to my senses, mumbling a decidedly ambivalent, "Aah, okay…"

Whatever that means.

The thing about Stefano Fortemani that's so infuriating is, physically speaking, he's appealing to the eye.

I never said he wasn't attractive.

Indisputably, the man is a striking, biologically designed specimen. If "chestnuts roasting on a mid-summer open fire" was a color, there would be his intense, penetrating eyes, stoking a fire straight through me. I'm talking broad-chested, clean-cut with soft silver curls, a square jaw, and ridiculously long eyelashes. Sadly, his entire wardrobe is relegated to suits in varying shades of black, gray, and navy, but he's well-dressed. Impeccably so, in tailored suits that mold to his thick frame in the most elegant, refined way that screams words like "expensive," "high-powered," "smart," "smells so good, I want to peel off every yard of fabric and thread with my teeth…"

And it's all true.

The problem?

As beautiful as he is, socially, emotionally—*shamefully*—he's just too dang serious.

Too bitter.

Which, there's a time and a place for everything. But not at your mother's sixty-fifth birthday. Certainly, not at your brother's—Napa's most eligible bachelors—impromptu engagement to my best friend who loves him purely and deeply.

Stefano Fortemani is like a pill warning label, telling you everything that could go wrong short of killing you, instead of celebrating the miracle that insurance covered the full deductible.

What's the rush?

The way I wanted to remind him that love can't be measured in time.

Whoever said there was a magic formula?

Yeah, sure, x months + x hours = true love.

No. It doesn't matter how long it takes if the feeling is real and irrefutable.

See, this is why I need Turn-Up Tuesday in the fiercest way. If only to deep-dive into Morgan's wedding dreams to drown out any lingering annoyance I've been harboring toward Stefano. The engagement was a success, and now, there's no reason for us to interact until the wedding.

Yes, that's it.

Relief floods through me.

Nichelle clears her throat and eyes me curiously like she senses she lost me somewhere. Then, wrongly pinpointing the source of my confusion, she clarifies, "TBR. To be read…"

"Ah, okay." I nod, shoving aside all thoughts of Mr. Sex and Dating.

"The point is," she continues, undeterred, "not only have they heard about your tea party and your friend's engagement, half of my friends and family—including guests who've yet to even RSVP—they've been texting and calling. Every one of them beside themselves with excitement that you're the event planner."

"I can't tell you how beyond grateful I am."

"Trust, this isn't a molehill-mountain situation, Avery." She takes my hand in hers, the pads of her fingertips brushing lightly over my skin. "I mean, yes, this is amazing for my Hollywood dreams, but this is *huge* for your bottom line. Ellis Events *is* the spotlight."

To her point, judging by the surge of followers on my social media and the big names on some of my missed calls, *Lifestyles of the Rich and Wedded* may not be too far-fetched.

Joy wells up in my heart.

"Isn't it something, though?" I muse.

"It's something, all right. Something mind-blowing and amazing." Nichelle switches back to scrolling through comments. "Girl, shut up and take all my money."

Inside, my exhausted little body rejoices.

"Okay, well, if we're going to live up to book club standards of fabulousness, we need to get this appointment underway."

Nichelle nods, wide-eyed and dead serious.

"Just a couple more minutes," I say, knowing she needs a reactionary moment to their comments before she'll officially move on. "We've got filet mignon waiting…"

I waft the air in her direction, hoping the aroma will entice her to gravitate back toward the table.

We're supposed to be finalizing linens and meeting with the staff for a food tasting. Yet, while we've lapped this lovely art deco ballroom with me admiring its lotus-shaped glass chandeliers and Gatsby-esque feel, we've yet to logisticize this wedding or take even a bite of the delicious-smelling, savory entrees sitting on the table getting cold.

"Lord knows, I could eat right now," Nichelle moans.

I glance over to the white-clothed table fully dressed and brimming with a feast fit for a bride and her famished wedding planner. Then up to the clock above the fireplace.

The events director catches my eye and shoots me an understanding smile.

A small giggle bubbles in my throat.

That look, it's one of sisterly and professional solidarity.

I swear she knows I'm secretly counting down until Nichelle's appointment is over. It's like she's subliminally cheering me on. *Girl, last appointment of the day. Get through this with a smile, and in a half hour, you'll be at Morgan's with your Sister Circle. Your mom is picking up Ace from daycare, so you'll be free to sip Pinot, gush about the engagement, and NOT jump the gun on planning her wedding that probably won't be for another year, but you can daydream…*

Silver linings.

Come on, five o'clock.

Because clearly the events director is amazing at her job, intuitive as all get-out, and giving compliments is like showering others with free happiness confetti, I point to my blouse then her satin floral dress and pantomime a chef's kiss.

Her expression softens with thanks.

Hmmm. Maybe I'll skip the Pinot for Prosecco. Making it through this day feels like a celebration.

My mood lifts at the enticing prospect of relaxing with my girls.

Walking a little taller and lighter on my feet, I tuck my planner bible under my arm and slip my phone from my skirt pocket, prepared to knock out a few more email responses.

As soon as the screen illuminates, my heart stops.

Four missed calls from Mommy.

"Fudge."

I pull in a lungful of air, determined not to get lost in the worst-case scenarios why she's called so many times when she usually picks him up closer to six.

Breathe, then call her.

Forcing a smile, I clear my throat to get Nichelle's attention. "Hey, I've got to make a quick call if you want to get started with the tasting before they begin cleanup," I say encouragingly.

"Sure, yeah. No problem."

She must register the slight worry etched between the lines on my face because she shoves her phone in her purse and steadies me with an intense stare.

Her eyebrows draw together. "Is everything okay? You seem upset."

"No, yeah, I'm fine." I shake my head, forcing a smile. "It's just my mom. I missed her calls, and she's picking up my son from daycare today," I explain. "I'm sure I probably just forgot his PJs or toothbrush."

Nichelle gives me one of those silent *it's always something* smiles before I tap Mommy's contact and walk briskly back toward the private bridal suites.

"Hey, what did I forget?" I ask when she picks up.

"Ooh, honey, I hate to do this to you when it's your girls' night, but I've gone and caught myself a stomach flu. Lord, when I tell you it's coming out both ways—"

"Please don't." Disgusted relief lifts my laugh. "Mommy, ew, just…TMI."

"*What?*"

I'm still cringing and laughing as I close my eyes against the dueling Doctor Mom urge to rush over and fix her up and the hourly life calendar barreling to the front of my mind.

"Do you need me to bring you some ginger ale and saltines?"

"Chile, I'm on an every-fifteen-minute-water-sip diet trying to stay hydrated, then I'll have some toast," she says. "Don't you dare worry about me. Go get my baby and tell him we'll do Disney and Hot Wheels as soon as I'm up and running again."

"Are you sure?"

She smacks her lips loudly in my ear. "Lord, if you don't go get my grandbaby so I'm not sitting up here worried on top of managing my insides…" Mommy warns.

"Okay," I laugh through my disappointment, switching gears to crisis-management mode.

On top of worrying about her, there's no way I'll be able to make it to Turn-Up Tuesday. By the time I pick up Ace, get home and call a sitter, the Sister Circle will be calling it a night.

I flip my wrist to check the time.

"I'm going to wrap up this appointment, then head straight to Mighty Les Enfants Academy."

"Let me know the second you've got him."

In record time, Nichelle and I knock out linens selections over mouthfuls of filet mignon, lobster, and lemon pepper chicken cooked to perfection. By the time she opts for elegant crimson red tablecloths and chair covers paired with warm cream napkins, table runners, and drapes, we're out of time, and I'm back in sneakers, sprinting toward the St. Mary's Square parking garage to beat traffic.

The good news is, I'm only four miles away.

The predictable bad news, with this standstill, my GPS is calculating thirty-three minutes.

"Let's get this over with."

Turning up my AC and turning down my music, I tap through my car's digital display screen until I find Morgan's name.

It rings twice before she picks up.

"Hey, girl, hey," she hums into the line.

Involuntarily, a sigh barrels out of me along with a sad, *"Hey."*

In seconds, the phone quiets before the volume magnifies the shuffle and swoosh of my girls, confirming they're present and accounted for—all four of them.

I'm on a group call.

"Spill," Monica, the no-nonsense mouthpiece of our Sister Circle commands. "Morgan said you did the sigh, so out with it."

My voice is weighted with every ounce of disappointment I feel. "Long story short, I'm not coming tonight."

"Girl, quit playing." Morgan cackles over my famous sigh. "We've got too much to talk about tonight. Valerie's over there falling for Fix-It Felix just because he flashed his forearms as he installed built-ins in her living room—"

"Okay, you didn't see his forearms," Valerie reasons.

Morgan continues listing all the gossip I'm dying to hear in person complete with animated facial expressions and wild hand gestures. "Seneca is contemplating quitting the bank. *Again...*"

We all laugh because it's become an every-other-week thing with her since she got her real estate license. Not that we don't all know it too well. That's how we met. Every one of us crossed paths, working at Regions West Bank over the years. Eventually, one by one, we left to start our own businesses—Morgan with Forster Business Consulting; Monica with Hard Core Pilates; Valerie's Estrada Realty; and me, with Ellis Events. All except, Seneca, who's still working up the nerve to leap in faith.

"Girl, it's okay, you'll leave *if* and when you're ready," I tell her.

"Thank you, Avery," Seneca says.

Ahead, the traffic moves a couple inches and I make it through the light, watching as my GPS estimated arrival time drops.

"*And...*" Morgan's whine commandeers my attention back to the conversation. I can practically see her pouting. "I was sorta hoping, since y'all aided and abetted Dante's proposal, we could recap the engagement and talk vineyard weddings..."

Everyone squees and swoons.

This circle has kissed dozens of frogs. We've talked about love and dating ad nauseam. But she's done. Our best friend is the first of us to get blissfully engaged to a man who fiercely loves and respects her.

"My *God,* I cannot wait to marry this man." Morgan

sighs. "Like, I want to travel and make a million plans together. I want to have kids—"

"You sure about that part?" I question, laughing. "If you and Dante feel the need to get in some non-procreational, PG-13 practice, Ace is available all week for your pre-parenting pleasure."

The traffic picks up to a slow crawl, and I weave into the right-hand lane, thanking my stars that I'm going to make it to Les Enfants on time, if we keep moving at this pace.

"I guess I should've said, *eventually*," Morgan adds.

But leave it to Seneca the sensible, head so far away from the clouds, practical line of reason that she is, she cuts straight to the chase, circling back to the subject at hand.

"Um, ma'am...we're going to need the long story long. You haven't missed a Turn-Up Tuesday since..." She breaks off guiltily, unwilling to finish that sentence even though I know that everyone is silently filling in that blank space for her.

I haven't missed our weekly get-together since my late husband, Justin, passed three years ago. He's the one who said it was a tradition he could get behind because he loved when I came home to him hopped up on wine and horny for him.

Hey, if all I've got to do is hang out with my son for a few hours to get you worked up, that's foreplay a man can't buy.

A somber laugh tickles the back of my throat.

He made sure I got to be with my girls every Tuesday. Then, Mommy kept it going while he deployed. It was supposed to be his last tour and he was getting out since his contract was up. But he didn't make it back, and my entire world shifted. Suddenly, I was a widow and single mom to a three-year-old, doing it all on my own. I couldn't just hold it together for Ace. I was solely responsible for creating the joy-filled world I wanted him to live in—even on Tuesday nights.

Then my girls brought the circle to me.

"Granny's gone and caught herself a stomach flu, so I'm inching my way to daycare to pick up Ace," I explain.

They all hum their understanding.

"But there's still a silver lining. I get to watch Disney movies with the cutest boy in town, so top that."

In the background, Dante calls out, "Baby, fifteen minutes…" While none of us are sure what he's referring to—the time before he leaves the house or how long to reheat a meal—it might as well be an alarm, clearing the room, because the Sister Circle is nothing if not assuming the dirtiest possibility.

"So, on that note…" Monica prefaces like we're not all thinking Dante and Morgan are trying to squeeze in a quickie before the girls get there.

After their abrupt "See you in twenty," to give the en-gaged lovebirds an extra ten minutes, Seneca, Monica, and Valerie rush off the phone.

I'm about a block from the daycare, prepared to end the call too, when Morgan asks me to wait.

"Give me two seconds," she says.

Then, in the background, I hear her talking to Dante. He says something about the last inning then before the line grows muffled, and Morgan is back.

"Okay, so, it's not what y'all were thinking with your

gutter minds." She laughs. "He's in the kitchen, on the phone with his brother, talking about some baseball game they're watching. Yet he insists he's ready to walk out the door."

"So, what's up?" I ask, hating the fact that of everything she said, I'm immediately curious which brother Dante's on the phone with.

"Oh, nothing crazy. I was just thinking... Since you can't make it tonight, how about we have dinner here, Friday night? You call a sitter, I'll grab a couple bottles of wine, we can watch that Tia Williams movie, and just chat about things."

A giggle teeters on my tongue.

Chat about things (i.e. Gush about Dante and their impending nuptials).

At the rate this week is going...

"That sounds perfect, actually," I say as I pull into the parking lot.

"Friday night, it is," Morgan singsongs cheerily.

Except, as I reach for the dashboard display to end the call, I hear Dante whisper, "Did you tell her?" just as the line disconnects.

CHAPTER FOUR

Stefano

B EFORE I REACH the vineyard staircase landing Friday evening, Dante is standing in the doorframe barefoot in jeans and a white T-shirt, grinning like a lovesick fool.

"So, your watch does work?" He laughs, pulling me up the last step into a brusque bro hug.

"Perhaps, if I'd been aware you were planning to propose, I might not have given so much weight to overshadowing Mother's party with talk of Carina's romantic trysts."

Dante barks out a robust laugh, stepping back. He shakes his head at me, pressing his hands along my suit jacket.

"Man, this is what I miss about you. Marcello never shows up to chill, dressed to impress, and using phrases like *romantic trysts.*"

"Glad to oblige."

He's still laughing at my expense but, secretly, I'm enjoying this exchange, too. We haven't had much time for casual dinners and easy conversation. Tonight, feels like an overdue occasion.

Dante smiles this over-the-top smarmy smile as he reaches up with his free hand to loosen my tie, a strange pride emanating from him. "Look at us, two brothers getting together to break bread on a Friday night, laughing, and talking about our lives…"

"Thank you for the invitation," I say, hoping his jovial attitude will stay the course of this evening.

He blows out an impressed breath then turns on his heel toward the door.

In the foyer, despite my refusal—multiple times—Dante insists on taking my jacket. After several minutes with him asserting, "You're seriously going to keep your jacket and tie on the entire time you're here? You know work ended hours ago, right?" I begrudgingly relent.

Mostly because I wouldn't put it past him to escalate to my shoes and slacks if I continue pressing him.

Taking his advice, I neatly hang my coat on the hook, pull off my tie, and stuff it in my pocket.

As he weaves through the living room to the formal dining room off the kitchen, I unbutton my top button, then work my way to my sleeves, rolling them up my forearms.

Except, when I look up, I come full stop in front of his pinewood table fully dressed with four place settings—two facing sets on either side.

My shoulders slump as I slowly drag my focus from the flatware to my guilty brother.

This week, I've made multiple follow-up calls, and left zero voicemails for the same reason I'm here tonight.

I want to talk to him.

Alone.

This is supposed to be a quick chat over a simple meal.

At the end of the night, we'll have eaten, and he'll have seen reason, leaving me to go back to worrying about the growth of our family businesses and whether jet-black hair dye is the ticket to getting back on the dating market.

Simple.

But before I can fix my mouth to ask any of the many questions barreling against the front of my mind, like who's joining us and why, Morgan bursts through the swinging kitchen door.

"Oh my gosh, I didn't realize you were here!" She sets a basket of sourdough bread in the center of the table and comes in for a full-body hug. "Thank you so much for coming. It really does mean a lot to us."

"Thanks for having me." I force a stilted smile as she bounces back on her heels, shoving her hands in the back pockets of her jeans.

She brightens, quick to fill the silence.

"Dante told me tortellini is your favorite, and I've got this amazing recipe from my mom…" She closes her eyes and moans. "Mm-mm-mm, I can't wait for you to taste it."

A smile tugs at the corners of my mouth.

"I know it will be delicious," I say, still salty, though slightly less annoyed that our twosome is doubling. Flashing her a quick smile, I flit a squinted glance to Dante. "I'm sure it'll be good enough to eat *two* plates."

He pokes his tongue into his cheek, inhaling.

As if on cue, the doorbell rings, and Morgan excuses herself to go welcome our mystery guest.

The second she's gone, though, I light into Dante.

"Are you serious?" I whisper. "I called you three times

this week to confirm we were meeting. I figured you knew I meant *alone*."

In the other room, Morgan's shrill scream is matched by a familiar feminine voice I can't quite place.

Then again, I'm not trying to.

My focus is centered on the way Dante's features tighten as if calming himself for what he'll say next, and I'm all ears. Because why not just invite me for dinner rather than let me believe it'd be just us?

"You're forgetting I know how you operate, Stef." Dante's tone hardens with challenge as his attention darts between me and the living room off the foyer. "Do you really think I don't know what you want to *discuss*?" He throws up air quotes.

"Look, I'm not against your engagement if that's what you're insinuating. Believe it or not, I'm happy for you."

"You could've fooled me," he scoffs.

"Well, I am." I stay the course, determined to get this out. "After what I've been through, is it so ridiculous that I'd want to protect you from suffering the same fate?"

"You don't know what you're talking about!" he snaps. "And contrary to what you think, you don't always know what's best for me."

I nod, giving him his moment.

How many times has he used some version of that statement with me, only to come pleading for advice later? *You've got a superiority complex; you don't know me...but how do I get her to notice me? Don't comment on my relationship...but she left me, and it hurts, so how do I get her back?*

I've got half a dozen years on him, and I've saved his ass

too many times to count. That's what I do. I look out for my family. I spare them by letting them learn from my mistakes.

"Don't I, though?" I chew the inside of my cheek. "Look, there's nothing wrong with an engagement. I'm simply saying take some time. Learn each other. Learn what's important to you as individuals and as a couple. Consider the benefits of giving yourselves the necessary time to embrace your union before the actual wedding day. That's all."

"That's all," he parrots.

Dante sighs, his frustration clearly mounting. "Jesus, can you just stop and listen to yourself for a second? A union? We're in a relationship."

I shrug. "Semantics."

"Whatever, you sound like some abstinence brochure listing the features and benefits of waiting. Time is an illusion." He scratches his temple. "Morgan and I have been through enough in life to understand the risks and value of what we have. We don't take it for granted."

"Again, that's not what I'm saying." I huff out a frustrated breath. "You're young."

"And therefore, inexperienced, right?" Dante scoffs. "You're not that much older than me."

The volume in the foyer grows louder.

Dante lowers his voice, leaning in. "Let's be clear, you're my brother, and like I said, I'd love your support. But if that's not something you can bring yourself to give—"

"Look what the San Francisco air blew in!" Morgan announces, breaking into my brother's unveiled threat as she ambles into the dining room with Avery Ellis on her heels.

Immediately, Avery sets her dark brown eyes on me, annoyance clouding over her mainstay sunny disposition.

"What are you doing here?" she asks, visibly as put out about my presence as I was by the fourth place setting. When I wordlessly fan out my hand to the table in explanation, she turns back to Morgan. "What is he doing here? I thought we were relaxing over wine and that Tia Williams movie while you catch me up on what I missed Tuesday…"

Ah yes, their weekly girls' night. How could she have passed up a wine-fueled happy hour to gossip?

The air is charged with tension.

Surprisingly, Morgan ignores her question and claps her hands together, pasting on a cheery smile instead.

"We will absolutely be doing the movie…*after* a nice sit-down dinner," she clarifies as if this was the plan all along.

Except, suddenly, I suspect it was.

Avery folds her arms across her orange-sweatshirt-clad chest. Her blonde ponytail is swept over one shoulder. She's in sneakers and matching sweatpants, dressed for comfort. She was lured in under the pretense of a relaxing night to unwind with her friend while Dante promised me food and a one-on-one, knowing I'd jump at the opportunity to reason with him.

They wanted us both here. Even if that meant keeping us in the dark about the reason.

What is really going on here?

Morgan playfully nudges Avery's shoulder with hers. "The more, the merrier, right?"

Avery darts an assessing gaze between Morgan and Dante then back to me like she's still chewing on this version of what's happening, and not the unabashed ambush we both know this is.

"Right," Avery cautiously agrees.

"Well, okay, then…" Morgan's wide-eyed gaze flickers not so subtly to Dante.

"Ah, yes." He clears his throat. "I hope you're hungry. My fiancée and I have been in the kitchen making tortellini, salad, and warm sourdough bread for you—from scratch." He looks at her lovingly. "We've also got some red blend wine to pair with it. Or a Riesling if you want white or sweet. A little music *and* we're hoping we can all enjoy some time together, and just…talk."

And there it is.

"Talk," I repeat, tasting the lie on my tongue.

"Yup, a little conversation over a home-cooked meal. A chance to catch up," Dante says vaguely.

There's definitely an agenda.

Quietly observing, I take note of the way Dante keeps rubbing the back of his neck, and Morgan's restlessness, her fluctuating pitch.

"Ms. Ellis." Dante takes a few steps back, sliding out a chair for Avery before pointing to the one beside hers. "Stef…"

As we both slowly walk toward the table, I briefly consider tonight could be a romantic setup.

His silver-fox brother, her wedding-obsessed best friend. It's textbook double-date matchmaking. The sort of thing that happened all the time in those romantic comedy movies Carina made me watch.

Except between our hosts' dips in and out of the dining

room to bring out the meal, my appraising glances at Avery aren't met with appreciation. After a stuttered scan of my shirt, she questions why I'm staring, scoots her chair another inch away from mine, and shoots me with a sidelong scowl.

I quickly toss out that theory.

Plus, I'm far more interested in what our hosts want to *talk* about.

So, once we're all seated with our plates and wineglasses full, and everyone has complimented the chefs, we dig in.

All of five minutes pass, the silence filled with clanking silverware and polite smiles, before Dante prefaces, "I gotta be honest here…" further ramping up my anticipation.

Avery steadies her fork halfway to her mouth, her attention, like mine, centered on my brother.

"I really want you two to be friends," he says.

"Omigod, yes," Morgan agrees.

Friendship is the reason they brought us here?

I feel my eyebrows dipping, and before I can stop myself, I ask, "Why?" I mean it to clarify Dante's intentions, but it comes out like I'd rather die before I consort with Avery Ellis.

Whether she's offended or not, she doesn't let on, though.

"Yes, is there a reason?" she asks, warmly.

It's strange, but I understand her approach. If Dante and Morgan have gone out of their way to bring us together when an email or text could've sufficed to put Avery and me in communication or a "friendship," their motivation feels like it stems from something grander.

It's Morgan who answers us.

"You've got so much in common, and we can't help wondering if you'd have found out on your own had the vineyard listing hoax never happened, you know?" The inflection in her voice lifts with the unspoken question.

Are you willing to give each other a chance for us?

Immediately, my answer is no.

Grudges are one thing. But keeping me out of the loop when it concerns my brother's engagement? It rubbed me all the way wrong. What's more, I'm convinced that Avery's rose-colored glasses are simply proof of youth and naiveté. She's unrealistically hopeful because she hasn't experienced enough of life's ups and downs. Not just about people but the choices we make that with age, we look back on in hindsight with so much clarity.

And that's fine, as long as you're not guiding someone else's decision that could leave him spiraling in grief and suffering.

"Maybe." I give a noncommittal nod, not wanting to come off too harsh with Avery again.

To my surprise, she quietly, stubbornly sips from her glass, sets it on the table, then twists to face me.

"She's absolutely right," Avery says with conviction. "That prank, 100 percent helped shape my view of you. Your role in that 'family ruse' could've left their relationship as collateral damage."

It's a matter of maturity, I reassure myself.

"I hear you, and I acknowledge your point," I respond. "For the record, my intention was never to hurt my brother or Morgan."

Good. Maintain your cool.

"Yes, this is why we're here tonight." Morgan weaves her fingers with Dante's, meeting Avery's blank stare. "We all want to move past this. He's my soon-to-be husband's brother. *My* brother-in-law." Then she turns to me. "And she's your soon-to-be sister-in-law's best friend."

Avery seeks out my stare again. "I know why *you're* here."

The accusation in her tone grates on my nerves.

Again, I remind myself this is what this generation does. They get hot-headed, venting and blowing things out of proportion. They point fingers first then ask questions later.

"Well then, by all means, please share it with the class, Pollyanna."

Shit, don't sink to her level.

"Pollyanna?" Avery releases a hysterical laugh. "See, you don't fool me. I see right through your over-starched suits and quiet judgment."

"I just meant that you've got such a warm personality."

Clearly, with everyone except for me.

"Yeah, I bet." She purses her full glossy lips. "Well, since we're talking about moving on and positivity, I thought I'd encourage you not to be such a rain cloud, stealing other people's sun just because you're going through a hard time."

"Okay..." Morgan interrupts. "Looks like maybe we should take over things from here."

But Avery is undeterred in her mission.

"So, your marriage is over and I'm sure that sucks rainbow cannonballs. But you know what? You're still here. You're still on this side of the grass. Why not celebrate life to the fullest while you're in your prime?"

At this, I've got to laugh.

She's somehow managed to insult both me and my marriage before she sprinkles me with confetti. Then she follows it up with a veiled compliment? *I'm in my prime, now, am I?*

I snicker. "Rainbow cannonballs, huh?"

"Yes, and I saw her post." She stays her course, hooking a hard turn into left field. Except, she says it so softly, so sympathetically, I almost miss it over the drumline pounding in my ears.

How did this become about me?

Carina's hand-holding post flashes across the front of my mind, jolting me back to Avery's soft gaze.

"By now, I'm sure everyone has," she reasons. "And so what if people are talking? It's time for you to start looking up and looking to your own future, not stifling everyone else's."

Heat climbs up my neck to my face, but I clamp my mouth shut.

Despite my mounting irritation, I don't want to exacerbate the situation. I keep my emotion in check. Lashing out won't benefit me. Adding water to a grease fire won't stop the burning.

"Okay, we've veering off on a tangent," Morgan warns.

But Avery holds up a finger.

"One last thing," she says before she drills in her final point. "Maybe you'd have friends if you stopped being a complete grump to everyone who knows and cares about you."

It's so absurd.

So preposterous that someone who knows literally nothing about me or my marriage—any marriage, for that matter—is commenting on how and at what speed I should move on.

Falling in love takes time. It's only logical that falling out of it should require the same.

I pull in a lungful of air, and pin Avery with a pointed stare. I'm prepared to impart some choice words on her but as I push my sleeves up my forearms, I register her attention shifting with my movements.

My gaze flickers to her flushed face.

Now, shockingly silent, her eyes burn a fiery amber hue, her lips parting as she watches me fold my arms across my chest and lean into the curve of my seat back.

Instantly, the curiosity I felt walking into that tent, my eyes searching her out, it surges to the surface of my mind.

Is she checking me out? Is she turned on…by my forearms?

No, couldn't be.

But just in case, I bend my arm, flexing my bicep as I question, "A complete grump?"

She leans forward, her focus lingering on the bulge of my muscle for a split second more before it snaps up to my eyes again.

"Are you seriously just going to k-keep repeating everything I say as a question?" she stammers.

Her breaths shallow.

Oh, yeah. Something is happening here.

"Maybe." I dart my tongue out, and trace my teeth over my lower lip, outright ogling her now.

Eager to continue testing my theory, I reach up, dragging my fingers over my lips.

Like she's under my spell, Avery mirrors my movement, pressing her fingers to her mouth, too, and it's beyond gratifying. It's unnerving how fast my pulse races.

Goddammit, it's an instant self-confidence boost.

Once upon a time, before I started dating Carina, women asked me out for drinks. I'd get phone numbers written on the side of my cup in cafés. I'd catch them staring. I had style and game. Twelve years of marriage, loss, and a divorce may have robbed me of my confidence to get back out there, but in this moment, I'm certain I've still got...something.

"What does that even mean? Maybe?" she asks.

"I just...I have so many questions, Miss Ellis." I lower my voice, playing up the bass. "First, I'm a silver fox, which, thank you. Then something about rainbow cannonballs... Now, I'm a grump?" I raise an eyebrow. "Which exactly is it?"

A light flush creeps over her cheeks.

She swings her legs back under the table and lowers her focus to the half-full wineglass in front of her.

Are we fighting or flirting, Pollyanna?

"Wait, you called him a silver fox?" Morgan asks, suddenly flooring it down that tangent. "I mean, I definitely see it but, what was the context?"

"It was nothing." Avery waves off the question.

I flash her a small smile when she glances in my direction, the temptation to unfasten more than just my top shirt button increasing exponentially.

But she doesn't circle back to her point.

In fact, no one says anything for a beat.

Fifteen minutes go by as we go back to stuffing tortellini

and bread in our mouths and washing it down with wine.

It's only when Morgan stacks her and Dante's plates to the side that I assume we'll circle back to the subject at hand. Maybe get to the real reason—beyond our age difference—that Avery and I can't be around each other two minutes before we clash. Maybe shed some light on why she can't get past the hoax or why she's only Pollyanna with everyone else.

Except, it's Dante who intertwines their fingers and meets our stares.

"Babe?" He gives Morgan the floor.

Nerves smooth the lines of her face as she sinks her fingers into her dark textured curls.

"We'd love for you to be our best man and maid of honor."

Avery gasps, pushing to her feet to walk around and hug Morgan. They squeal and fall into a tight hug with Morgan confessing that this past Tuesday, she'd already asked their friends to be bridesmaids.

I'd love to say I sprang to my feet to do the same with my brother.

I can't though.

Instead of laughing and screeching with them as they veer off into plans for "a dreamy outdoor wedding on the vineyard…" I'm fixated on the rest of that sentence.

"In September," she says.

As in less than three months from now?

Dante rounds the table, tapping my shoulder and snapping me to.

"So, what do you say? You down to be my best man?"

I push to my feet, forcing a smile. "You bet—" I break

off.

But he must sense the question in the lingering silence. He scratches his scalp, reluctantly tipping his chin to me.

"Next September, right?" I ask.

The women slowly turn to us, quietly assessing the situation before Morgan winces. It doesn't surprise me when Avery links hands with Morgan.

Friendship and loyalty.

She's the supportive best friend with no words of wisdom. Nothing to say. No sage wedding planner or friendly advice. Just leap and hope you fly, huh?

No help.

"So, it's safe to say there's no reasoning with you about a longer engagement." I nod, weighing how much I want to say. Then I figure, what the heck? "Not even a year? Seriously, why the rush?"

Avery comes to their defense.

"Because they're in love and nothing in life is guaranteed. I don't know, maybe because it's their decision. Or because they know if they wanted to get married tomorrow, I'll support them."

She reaches across the table, grabbing her glass and polishing off the remains of her wine.

"Of course, you would." I poke my tongue in my cheek, fed up with her little digs. "Life is nothing but a series of parties for you, right, Pollyanna?"

Quietly, Avery replaces her glass in front of her.

"As a matter of fact, it is."

"Figures."

Avery tugs at her sweatshirt sleeves, then stretches the

collar to pull it over her head without ruffling a single hair.

Dante shakes his head. "Look, we don't want to make things worse between you two. Let's just—"

"No, Stefano's got so much to say." Avery laughs as if now I'm not the one checking her out in a thin beige tank that exposes every smooth golden-brown inch of her skin and molds to her round breasts. "Have you ever thought maybe I'd rather spend my life celebrating the moments and breaths and wins and ups and good times? I've had my share—still have my share—of hardships. Not that I owe you any explanation. But I don't want to live in the shadows of grief."

She stretches, thrusting her chest forward, and a slow smile builds as she watches me watching her now.

I don't have the heart to tell her there's lettuce stuck in her teeth.

Dante settles on his chair again and clasps his hands on the table.

"When I thought we were losing the vineyard, it put so much in perspective for me, Stef." He pauses for a beat. "I don't want to wait on the right time. It feels right for us and what's important to our legacy."

Morgan and Avery return to their seats as well, like they too sense there's a few more kinks to hash out.

"With the on-site cabins finishing up next month, we thought it would be amazing to be the vineyard's first wedding," Morgan adds.

"Our ancestors walked on this land. They ran their fingers through that soil and those ribboning vines. Think of it as—"

Morgan cringes. "Oh, my Lord, please don't say it."

Dante laughs.

"Think of it as christening this land." He shrugs at the three of us chuckling and groaning our disapproval. "Whatever, maybe we'll do that, too. But to your point, marking a special first like this wouldn't hurt profits..."

The mood in the room noticeably lifts.

He waggles his eyebrows at me.

"Our guests will fill all the cabins. Then we'll still be able to help local lodging partners." Dante is on a roll, appealing to my business brain, and shamelessly, I'm listening. "Winery subscriptions will pick up. With the photos alone, adding them to our brochures and ad copy, wedding packages will be booked out for years."

Avery snaps her fingers.

"Ooh, and I've got a few magazine editor clients, too. Wedding features in *Vines + Vineyards*, *Visage*, *Blissful Bride*, and *Northern Living*... Look out world, wedding of the century loading."

I hate that it does indeed appeal to my financial outlook for our conglomerate of companies. We've got delis and restaurants to cater. We work with affiliate lodging partners to sleep overflow guests. We could feature the private label wines.

Frankly, a Fortemani wedding would be marketing we can't buy.

But couldn't it still be in a year? Or two?

"I'm in." Avery throws up spirit fingers before she bumps my shoulder with hers.

Her expression screams, *you know you want to celebrate,*

too.

I do.

"Listen, I agree. It all sounds amazing, and although I'll be honored to be your best man, you know where I stand on a longer engagement, and I think it's rushed." I shrug. "Vendors need time. Florists, photographers, bakeries—they need more than two and a half months to pull something like this off."

It's my final appeal to reason.

Which Morgan shoots down in one breath flat.

"Unless you're working with the dream team. With Avery as our wedding planner and you as her vineyard liaison, we'll make it work."

No, this won't make things worse between us.

Oh boy.

CHAPTER FIVE

Avery

THE SECOND MORGAN'S door closed behind me last night, I wanted to scream. For her and Dante's sake, I'd smiled *BIG* smiles. I'd geeked out over a vineyard wedding because that's what you do for your best friend. You put all personal hang-ups and complaining aside. You get on board with a full-fledged, high society wedding in the rolling hills of Napa less than three months out, even though you've got no idea how you're going to fit it into your overloaded schedule.

And you do it with a smile.

Then you arrive home and realize, in all the hustle and bustle to get away, you've forgotten to ask for your infuriating dream team co-member's phone and email.

I peek out of my home office into the living room where Ace is eating his chocolate pancakes and watching *Cars* for the third time this summery morning. He's reciting Lightning McQueen's lines verbatim, so I take that as my cue that he's occupied, and won't miss me while I make this, hopefully, five-minute call to Morgan.

A text would've been preferable but I can't risk the immediate and inevitable phone call that'll follow, and alert Ace that Mommy is doing something other than preparing his next snack.

Gently, I close the door, leaving it cracked, just in case.

My heart pounds against my ribs as I trek lightly over to my desk. Once I settle back into my chair and swivel just enough to slide my legs underneath, I take a deep breath.

"Lord…" With my right hand on my phone, I allow myself a tiny prayer that my best friend—bless her hopelessly in love heart—will simply give me Stefano's contact information without rehashing last night's dinner. "I'm asking for your grace and mercy this beautiful Saturday morning."

You can do this.

Morgan picks up after the first ring, her voice booming into the line.

"Ooh, you've caught me at the best time."

Instinctively, I glance at my watch, and immediately kick myself.

It's eleven o'clock.

Dammit.

"Hey!" I whisper to keep my voice down. "I'm just calling really quick to thank you and Dante for dinner."

But then a breeze whooshes in my ear followed by her footsteps loudly crunching over gravel, underscoring what I already know. She's on her daily trail hike through the vineyard, and she's got all the time in the world to chat.

"Girl, of course. You know you're welcome to grub with us anytime. But why are we whispering?"

"Ace is in there enjoying his happy little self, and I'm trying to sneak in some work."

She hums her understanding.

"Is he still obsessed with *Paw Patrol*?"

"Nope, we've graduated to the *Cars* phase." I laugh. "There is nothing cooler than this bigmouth, rookie red Corvette with decals for headlights."

Morgan giggles like she's about to give me the Wikipedia rundown on the movie then sideswipes me instead.

"Speaking of…" The exaggerated pause is purposeful, signaling she's about to spill the tea. *Or she wants me to.* As expected, she says, "You and Stefano were really going at each other."

It's bait.

I know exactly what she's doing, and which rabbit hole she's about to drag me down. At the table, she and Dante were sitting directly across from us. Undoubtedly, they witnessed the forearms display and the LL Cool J–worthy lip-lick hypnosis. Morgan knows good and well, I'm rarely ever hot, so my sweatshirt removal will be a topic of discussion, in addition to the silver-fox comment that will not die.

Except, little does she know, in saying his name, she's also given me the perfect out.

Snapping my fingers, I play up the dramatics.

"Shoot, Stefano." I suck my teeth. "I totally forgot to ask you for his cell and email, so we can get started planning your big day!"

"Uh-uh, nope, nope, and nope. Absolutely, not." Morgan's tone drips with *you are fooling no one.*

Still, I've got to play it off.

"What? I need to set up our first ChatVideo meeting, so we can get started planning on Monday."

The line grows silent for a beat, which tells me she's debating the truth in my answer. That's all I need because the second she gives me the information, Ace is suddenly going to need his Mommy, and I'm off the hook.

I bite my tongue to stifle my laugh.

Being a parent is a built-in *Get Out of Jail Free* card. Except, it also works for parties, dates, and unwanted conversations with a best friend on a mission to unearth gossip.

"Now, don't take this as me being ungrateful..." *Well, that's one hell of a preface.* "But I'm not giving it to you just yet."

"Why?" I all but whine.

"Isn't it the only fair thing that if you want information, I should get some in return?"

A groan claws its way from my throat.

The killer part is, I could wait until Monday. I could go to the Fortemani Vineyard & Winery website, tap over to the ABOUT US page, scroll down to Stefano's name, call the corporate number, and ask to be connected to him. It's that simple.

The only problem is that it would require levels of time and patience, which I currently don't have when I'm working on borrowed time.

If I'm going to schedule this ChatVideo meeting for the four of us on Monday, I need to prepare and send the invite this weekend to show up without my anxiety rioting in my chest.

That's just how I work.

Order, structure, details—they're all important for me to

function and feel ready to tackle whatever curveballs come up. A fact, which, unfortunately, Morgan is also privy to.

Thus, I bite the bullet.

Kicking off my fluffy slippers, I recline back against my chair, and prop my feet on the edge of my desk.

"What would you like to know in exchange for Stefano's contact?" I ask.

"Mm-mm, you really thought I was going to let you glaze over that silver-fox comment without checking in later?" She releases a truly wicked laugh.

"You're so lucky I can't yell at you right now."

She all-out cackles.

My friend is diabolical to the greatest power.

"Precisely." Her laugh tapers off, and I sense the other shoe about to drop. "Dante and I have been talking about this all night. Y'all sitting there, acting like you despise one another while undressing each other with your eyes like we weren't even there…"

"That is not what happened." *That is exactly what happened.* "Whatever, y'all are so underhanded. Instead of Moscato and movies, I was *forced*"—I emphasize the word for her benefit—"to endure an ambush dinner with an old-acting, too-serious, jaded man."

"Who just so happens to fit your type to a *T*," Morgan helpfully supplies.

"Shhh…"

My ear is stretched to the living room, where it's grown too quiet for a six-year-old hopped up on pancake syrup and Disney.

Slowly, quietly, I swing my legs off the desk and push to

my feet, inching toward my office door just as "Life is a Highway" blares through the speaker, giving me a mini heart attack.

Peeking through the door crack, I take one look and slap my hand over my mouth to keep from bursting at the seams.

"Girl…" I whisper. "This child has skipped back to his jam, and now he's in there singing into the remote."

Morgan joins in, crooning like a dog in heat.

Because my nerves are acting up, I sit on the edge of the desk to give my best friend a small chunk of my mind.

"Now, as far as Stefano Fortemani goes, much to yours and Dante's dismay, I'm sure, there's undeniably nothing there." Morgan snort-laughs at this, but she needs to get this out of her head. Quickly. "Can I appreciate his beauty? Absolutely, the man is fine as hell."

"Okay, let's hear this alleged but."

"Yes, *but*, he's grieving his marriage. *Hard*," I add to drill in my point. "And did I mention, the day of the tea party, this man was in the driveway listening to a freaking Johnny Timmons podcast? He was practically taking notes about sex and dating. Like, sir…be for real. *What are you doing?*" I shake my head way too many times. "*So* not my vibe."

Morgan quiets for a moment, and for a second, I think the call failed, but no such luck.

Not by the longest of shots.

In fact, when Morgan Elaine Forster, my closest friend, even more so than the entire Sister Circle, blindsides me with a whopper.

"I don't care if Stefano listens to Johnny Timmons while having sex, that man left here last night dazed and confused, like you reminded him he was fine." She blows out an amused sigh. "*Shoot,* he couldn't have been five miles down the road, and he's calling D to talk about you..."

Naturally, this is the moment Ace decides he wants to sneak into my office and ask for a grape juice box, which I decidedly do not allow on my beautiful cream carpet. So, at the literal worst moment of this conversation, I pause to pop into the kitchen for a spill-proof sippy cup, then get him settled back in his lap of stuffed animals and cars luxury.

At this point, once the door is shut, I need details.

Sitting is overrated.

"Okay, I'm back." I lean against the wall, my heart beating a million miles a minute. "So, you said Stefano called Dante to talk about me?"

Try as I may not to sound too eager, I'm failing miserably.

"Excuse me, but what happened to *I don't care about that old man?*"

"First of all, forty-anything is not old. I said old-acting," I clarify. "And second, I'm curious what he had to say about me. So, don't make a big thing about it."

She hums her disbelief but continues anyway.

"D and I immediately picked up the vibes y'all were throwing down at dinner."

"What we were throwing down?"

"Mm-hmm. We're convinced those schoolyard games you play—all the bickering, supposed resentment, and name-calling—all for show."

I've got to laugh because if my best friend is going to do one thing, it's support her claims with unfounded theories.

"Admit it, you're completely turned on by how much you supposedly hate each other."

"I never said I *hated* him. You are too much," I say, chuckling.

Her breathing shallows.

"Ooh, child, what I am is tired. I'm about to close this fitness ring, then climb my happy self right onto the couch and watch Netflix." Her laugh bellows through the line before it morphs into a loud, yodeling yawn.

Every bone in my body warns, *do not press her about what the guys discussed. Remind her about the contact information, then end this call. Quickly.* Knowing will only prove exactly what I already know.

Stefano and I are two wrongs that absolutely do not make a right.

Nothing's going to change that.

He'll still be a beautiful, pompous, self-important suit who thinks his opinion matters more than that of others. Schoolyard games or not, we'll continue to clash. More importantly, he'll still be the other half of the dream team, who I'll be working alongside in a spectacularly uncomfortable professional capacity.

Those are the facts.

It certainly doesn't matter that I haven't dated since I lost Justin, and Stefano's the first guy who's jumpstarted my…lower regions?

Damn.

I slide the tip of my fingernail between my teeth, tapping gently as I consider *maybe* my aversion to this man isn't as cut and dried as I'd thought. And now we're going to be stuck together almost three months, representing a wedding that could explode my business onto the event-planning scene.

We've got to keep it on the up and up.

Period.

But...

"*Ugh.* Okay, please don't make me regret this." I cringe, bracing myself for the backlash. "But what did Stefano say to Dante about me?"

At this point, this is no longer a want. I *need* to know what this man thinks about me.

"Shame, shame, shame, I know your name." Morgan feigns disappointment, but secretly, I know she's loving every second of torturing me.

"Yeah, yeah, what did he say?"

"In my book? Just know this is certified proof you're crushing hard on Stefano Fortemani, and the feeling is mutual."

Heat curls down my spine.

For the next five minutes, I cling to the phone like Morgan's words are my lifeblood.

Not only did she eavesdrop from the pantry where she could hear Dante chatting in the kitchen, but she took notes for my benefit.

I make a mental note to thank her when I can breathe.

Truly, this is the stuff on which lifelong friendships are built.

"Short story, long, their conversation was a brotherly one," Morgan segues, then gives me highlights that aid in my conclusion that it was about—shocker—dating and sex, the running theme of Stefano's new single life. Apparently, with his ex-wife debuting her new boyfriend, then seeing me watch him at dinner, somehow, he realized that maybe he wants to dip his toe back in the dating waters, too.

Lucky me.

All of which make him sound annoyingly more adorable and endearing than I'll ever admit.

I perk up, antsy for the rest.

But here's where I gasped and almost choked.

After Stefano told Dante he wasn't sure it was the best idea for us to team up because I'm, and I quote, "young, naive, and need more life experience." Which, to that I say, spend a week in my shoes. Still, Dante advised him to stay open to any relationship with me. Open, as in, even if I end up being just a friend, he should use our upcoming working relationship and wedding-planning interactions to get reacquainted with a woman who isn't his ex-wife (i.e., hello, my name is guinea pig!).

Now, obviously, he didn't say this to me, otherwise he'd live to regret it. But does he really think this is cool?

"He really said all that?" I ask, still reeling.

"Yes, but…" Morgan prefaces, and I suspect a silver lining caveat is loading. "It's all lip service. That man wants you, Avery."

I feel myself clamming up as I slide down the wall into a puddle of conflicting and frankly confusing emotions.

So, I'm immature and unexperienced, but I'm qualified to be the friend who reintroduces him to women?

Not to date or have sex with, but to befriend me.

He wants to study our interactions to gather data from

which he'll use to theorize some ridiculous hypothesis and test the results.

Every inch of me burns with humiliation.

This man doesn't even know me. He's never spent any real time with me, or else he'd know age doesn't equate to life experience.

What is nine years in the grand scheme of strife?

"Listen, Ace needs me, so I'm going to run now." Guilt consumes me the second the lie is out. "I'll check in with you later, but will you send me Stefano's contact information? That way, I can send out the ChatVideo invite to everyone before we meet on Monday."

"Damn, I'm such an idiot." Morgan pauses, and I sense she's scrambling. "Should I not have told you? I mean, I didn't want to upset you. He had no solid reasons, and Dante shut him down. It was so obvious Stefano didn't want to admit to his attraction, so he projected his anxieties as a divorced man onto Dante."

"No, I'm good."

Except, even as the words roll off my tongue, I feel myself slipping into business mode because this is what I do.

I hold it together.

I make decisions with everyone's best interest in mind. I set responsible examples and take my duties seriously. I worry, so they don't have to.

"Seriously, I thought we'd laugh at their warped thought process..." She breaks off. "Are you really good?"

I'm not.

But because I'm hearing this secondhand, damn right, I'm going to let this fuel my fire to prove him wrong.

"Great, actually," I say.

CHAPTER SIX
Stefano

H ERE'S THE WILDEST thing about life.
Mine has been about learning and climbing, always reaching for the next rung.

I've got decades of experience in management and winemaking. I know the vast, fascinating history of my family's vineyard grounds. From the acres of soil to every vine ribboning its way to the table. I was top of my class in business school. After twelve years of marriage, I knew my ex-wife's preference for yellow Starbursts. From her yawn/moan alone, I knew when she was up for more than sleep in our bed.

Used to know.

If the answers were in a book—or a podcast or audiobook—I could study and learn the ins and outs, read the details of processes and people.

But no one ever told me, book smarts and lived experience were mutually exclusive.

No one ever said, my story was interactive. That, all it takes is one setback to change the entire trajectory of my life. That on chapter forty-five, there'd be an unsolicited plot twist.

Instead of rebuilding after the storm, and finding my new normal, no I'm not doing that... No, suddenly, I'm spending my lunch, in a ChatVideo waiting room, bracing myself for an introductory shotgun-wedding-planning session with Dante, Morgan, and a woman with the dual superpower to get under my skin and remind me that I'm still a man with fire burning in my loins.

Jesus.

At least, I won't be alone with her.

Under my desk, my nerves work their way from the soles of my feet up through my bouncing knees.

Rubbing my sweaty hands down my pants legs to steady them, I close my eyes and pull in a long breath through my nose before I release it slowly from my mouth.

"This is no big deal. It's just like Dante said. Be receptive. Read her vibes. She doesn't know it's been a year since you've had sex."

My computer crackles to life, and when my eyes snap open, beside my dark square, there's a second one with a neon blue border around it, and Avery Ellis's name in the middle.

"Sorry, I thought I should tell you; you aren't on mute."

I flit a glance at the tiny microphone in the lower left corner, notably without the red line crossed through it.

This can't be happening.

I swallow over the lump in my throat. Fire swarms over my neck and ears, spreading to my cheeks.

Briefly, I consider clicking the Mute button, then quickly decide against it, knowing the change will reflect on my box.

It's fine, Dante and Morgan will be here any second. I can do this until they get here, I reassure myself.

Then the screen blinks, and there she is, smiling from ear to ear.

For a horribly humiliating beat, I stay unnaturally still, my attention drifting over this version of Avery Ellis displayed before me.

At Mother's tea, she was dressed in a bold yellow-and-white polka dot dress that suited her sunshine and rainbows personality—reserved for everyone but me, of course. Then at dinner Friday, she was dressed for comfort.

Today, though, it's not bright orange sweats.

She's effortlessly, undeniably beautiful.

Composed, in a burgundy blazer and a pale pink blouse. Light blush is dusted over her smooth, contoured golden skin paired with a deep-plum-colored lipstick, and her always penetrating brown gaze feels trained on me. Even her posture commands authority and respect whilst somehow maintaining every ounce of femininity.

Everything about her says, "Look at me, but don't dare underestimate me."

I never would.

However, while I've got no romantic interest in her based on our maturity and life experience—not to mention the almost decade I've got on her—she remains an attractive woman, who might identify my appealing qualities, and how to amplify them with women again.

Be open.

Like she senses me watching her on the screen, she clears

her throat now, signaling we need to get on with his meeting.

My pulse sprints.

Where are Dante and Morgan?

Reluctantly, I turn on my camera, forcing a smile and trying to laugh off my embarrassment when I'd love to yank out the cord, and throw my laptop out the window.

"Oh, yeah, no," I say, getting my lie together. "This woman, Elena. She's a travel photographer who works in the space a couple doors down from us, here in the Healdsburg office. She left, but she was at my door..."

It's a flaming-hot mess of an excuse, but it's the best I can do to save face, knowing she now knows how long it's been.

"Ah, I see. Of course." Avery nods but the corners of her mouth twitch. "Well, I'm sorry for the delay. I just got off the phone with Morgan."

"Let me guess, they're running late?" I laugh it off, grateful for the subject change.

But then, Avery's mouth presses into an unbending line.

"Actually, they got a flat tire on the freeway. They're not going to make it for this meeting."

Panic flares in my gut.

I nod, masking my concern, and searching for a reason—any reason at all—to postpone this meeting until they can join us.

Honestly, being in a room with Avery Ellis, virtual or not, it feels like trouble. I thought I could do this. Dante made it seem so simple: show up, listen, and take notes on the wedding stuff, yes, but also, on how Avery acts toward me. Read between the lines to the unspoken subtext between us.

It was supposed to be easy.

But now, they're not coming, and I'm stuck.

No, I can't do this.

Swallowing, I glance at my phone on the desk beside my laptop. "Maybe, I should check on them. You know, see if they need any help changing the tire. Dante might not remember how to use the—"

"Don't worry. Roadside assistance is on the way now."

"Right."

Out of objections, and at her mercy, I decide shutting up and taking her lead is my best course of action. Speak when spoken to. Listen and take notes.

I suck in a lungful of air.

But just as I reach for the Mute button, Avery tilts her head, stealing my attention.

"I realize this isn't ideal," she says. "However, we'll get through my meeting agenda much faster than anticipated. I'll run everything we discuss by Morgan and Dante later."

Faster is better.

"Silver lining," I say.

Avery starts to speak again, then she seems to reconsider. She lowers her chin briefly. "I always say that."

It's whisper-soft. Almost like us having anything in common gives her pause, too.

"Great minds," I muse.

That's the ticket. Just keep it short. One-to-two-word responses only.

Again, she stares at me like I'm a Rorschach inkblot, unsure of what she's looking at.

Whatever it is must be off-putting because a meeting agenda overtakes my screen. As she explains that she'd reconsidered canceling this meeting due to our wedding date time constraints, my attention drifts to the bullet points. To the words "logistics" and "timeline," before I come to a halt, my attention climbing back to the top.

"Icebreaker?" I ask.

For ten minutes?

All niceties, any hints of attraction, gone, Avery straightens, posture ramrod straight.

"Listen, I know you don't like me, but I'm a professional." Her tone takes on an impatient lilt. "Please don't disagree because your actions say otherwise that I'm some flighty, immature woman who plans flowery weddings, and couldn't possibly understand your protectiveness following your family's grief and your uncoupling."

Her full lips press together, pursing.

"Now, I have a short agenda prepared, and several meetings on my calendar following this one, so if it's all the same to you…"

"Of course."

I feel myself disengaging from the conversation when the document on the screen is replaced by a new one with a single world in large, bold black font at its center.

"Now, you mentioned the icebreaker. Since we'll be working together to bring this wedding to life for our families and businesses, I feel that it's pertinent for us to find some middle ground. So, I've reserved ten minutes for us to work through any lingering grievances that might be in the way of doing so. Here's how it's going to go…"

Over the following two minutes, she explains that she'll set a timer for ten minutes—no more, no less—during which we'll take turns asking anything on our hearts as fast and as honest as possible to clear our slates. Then, after she reiterates how much she values order and structure, and will protect it for the sake of her best friend and my brother, a clock appears in the top left corner of the screen.

The way she says, "I'll go first. Ready?" it feels like, *I can be a professional for the sake of our loved ones, can you?*

I lift my chin and nod.

Avery's fiery brown eyes narrow comically to slits, and as we stare into each other's digital boxes, I can't decide if this is a genius truce strategy or if she's just laid down some wedding-planning revenge gauntlet.

Then she starts the timer, and fires off the first question.

"You brought up Dante's marriage proposal no less than three times at dinner Friday night. What bothers you more, the fact that you weren't in on it? Or that he isn't taking your advice to prolong the engagement?"

All right, I guess we're getting right to it.

Game face in place, I reply, "Neither, actually," hoping my minimal response will still work.

This earns me a serious deadpan, so I figure I'd better elaborate as quickly and succinctly as possible.

"Rushing just feels ill-advised. Especially, for such an important life decision. But since we're on the subject, did you purposely keep the proposal a secret from me?"

"Yes."

It's her entire response.

Albeit simply stated and childish, it's an honest one.

Avery shrugs, like she, too, is annoyed that my family's secrets are at the crux of our mutual gripes. However, given the vineyard hoax, she's right to assume I'd have tried to reason with Dante, so I let the point rest.

Which, now I'm second-guessing.

Her expression tightens as if my silence is a full admission of guilt, and the crime should be sentenced accordingly. *So be it.*

I fan out my hand, signaling that it's her turn.

In the back of my mind, though, I don't know why I expect her natural progression would be to jump from the proposal to planning. Then again, we'll be getting to logistics and timeline shortly.

Avery squints like she's debating her next question before she asks, "So, why Johnny Timmons?"

"Why not Johnny Timmons?" I counter.

"If we answer questions with questions, this won't work." Avery stares pointedly.

"Fine." I trail my finger along my collar, emboldened when, yet again, her gaze follows. Although, I'm still unclear how this helps to clear our slate, I follow her honesty cue. "His podcast was a recommendation from Elena, the travel photographer down the hall. She recently remarried and said her husband—also his second marriage—swore that Timmons had helped lift him out of his rut."

This part is true.

Avery scratches her scalp, glancing at me sideways.

Google is free, but I'm eager to hear what makes her tick.

"Now, my question," I say, piggybacking on hers. "What

makes him *problematic?*"

Like she's rehearsed a rebuttal for just this moment, less than a minute is all it takes for her to list the reasons on her fingers.

"For starters, you might've heard about the so-called self-help guru's book being dropped by his publisher due to sexual misconduct. Beyond making advances on fans and staff, berating abuse victims, unfounded financial wealth-building claims, and general douchebaggery. Need I go on?"

Shit.

I blow out an impressed—and shamed—breath.

"Absolutely, not." A shaky laugh trembles over me. "Noted. I'll be sure, going forward, to complete my research before taking random self-help podcast recommendations." *How did I miss even a whiff of this?* I shake my head, then realize maybe being preoccupied with family loss, in every sense of the word, could have been a contributing factor.

"Yes, the man is reckless, to say the least, but you can doom-scroll about that later. We've got, what..." she glances to her left, I'm guessing at the clock that I've been vaguely watching count down "...six and a half minutes, give or take a few seconds. I'm next, so—"

I interrupt her. "Technically, it should be back on me. You asked if you should go on about Timmons. I answered."

If we had an instant replay of the past few minutes, the questions have been a two-way conversation. But suddenly, I feel like things are shifting in a direction I don't want to go, so I'm being a stickler.

The vein at Avery's temple twitches, like she knows this, too, but she's humoring me.

She drops her gaze briefly before it springs up, a storm raging her eyes. "You're right," she bites out between clenched teeth, her focus again flitting to the clock.

"Good girl."

Avery's attention snaps to me again as she stutters, "P-Please, ask away then."

From the instant she introduced this speed icebreaker, a barrage of questions have flooded my mind. *Why are you nice to everyone but me? Why a blonde wig? Why event planning? Do you honestly believe we'll pull off this wedding in two and a half months? What's your romantic type?* But then I settle on the one I'm most eager to learn.

"What is your gripe with me?" I ask.

Avery sits up, reenergized, like I've walked into her trap.

"Stefano, I honestly don't love the way you've inserted yourself, your opinions, and your personal baggage into Morgan and Dante's relationship. I'm concerned you haven't supported their relationship from the start."

It's so simply stated, but the accusation hits hard.

I feel my defenses rising.

Glancing at the time, I zero in on the final minute winding down.

"Is that so?" I bite out.

The muscles at my jaw harden and jut out at the sides.

She's accusing me of being a narcissist when all I've ever done is put my family first. If anything, I'm still putting my brother's happiness—his future—ahead of mine.

"For me, the disconnect lies in the fact that I suspect given the chance, rather than respect Dante's feelings and choices, you would've steered him away from proposing based on the results of *your* marriage."

Carefully, she chooses her words, avoiding technicality questions.

"Now, I won't comment on your marriage or your divorce."

"Sure you will."

A genuine smile quirks at her lips.

"You're right, in a roundabout way. I think it's worth noting that your ex has publicly moved on. My point in broaching the subject is that I'm sure you're not welcoming everyone's opinions about it."

Well, it's my brother and not people looking to gossip, so...

My pulse throbs.

We're down to seconds.

I listen to her go on about how family is important, but marriage is between two people.

All the while, it's on the tip of my tongue to shatter the ice completely.

I want to tell her how badly I'd like to back out of this silly dream team rather than spend my days with a woman who believes life is just a series of rainbow cannonballs and butterflies. Since we're willy-nilly doling out quick, unfounded judgments, I want to strongly encourage her to take her own baseless advice and keep her immature opinions to herself until she knows the hard work required *after* the vow exchanges and party cleanup.

But then she says, "It's just a thought."

A humorless laugh hurls out of me before I mumble under my breath, "It's interesting you've got such strong opinions about marriage..."

Avery's giggle snaps my attention back to the screen where the timer is counting down the final seconds.

True to the diabolical woman she is, she says, "Well, maybe that's because you're not the only one who has been in one," just as time runs out.

Wait, what?

The timer blares incessantly.

My head spins, and I'm dying to ask more questions but she's already flipping open a large pink book with fluorescent tabs sticking out of the pages.

She's married?

No, she said, "has been in one." Past tense. Even still, she's been married?

Suddenly, I'm wading through every interaction we've shared trying to remember if she ever mentioned a husband or if she was wearing a wedding ring.

Avery gives me no time to catch my bearings or get a glimpse of her left hand. Immediately, she jumps back to her agenda bullet points.

"Usually, I have twelve months to plan an event of his scale, but since this past Saturday marked eleven weeks to the wedding date, we've got to work fast and efficient. Divide and conquer." She taps around her keyboard until a whoosh echoes in her background. "Check your email."

A few seconds pass before my computer dings loudly.

In my mail folder is a message from Ellis Events with the subject line

12 MONTH WEDDING CHECKLIST AND PROJECT ASSIGNMENTS

Without waiting for me to open it, she proceeds, informing me that we'll treat the months as weeks.

"For instance, this week, we'll need to check off all the items for *12+ Months*, and as many as possible from the *10–*

11 Months list."

When I open the message, I'm pleased that she's assigned lodging, wine, catering, and event venue to me. It feels like we've got our bases covered when I the skim the checklist items for the week, and catalogue items like choose a date, select wedding party, budgets, rings, style, venue selection, and assembling a team of wedding pros.

"Now, let's get down to details," she says.

Over the next twenty minutes, she moves seamlessly through initial planning logistics—when and how often the dream team will meet, plus project assignments. We'll join ChatVideo meetings Monday and Thursday afternoons with periodic on-site meetings on Saturdays, as needed, until the September 30th ceremony and reception.

I'm still scanning items like compiling a guest list, browse dresses, and save-the-dates, that all fall under Avery's projects, when the swoosh zips through the air.

My email dings again.

"I just sent an invite for the Fortemani-Forster Wedding calendar. When you accept, you'll receive meeting alerts, one day and one hour before our scheduled meetings. This coming Thursday being our first official one."

Her work done, Avery stops sharing her screen, and it's us again.

No Dante and Morgan.

No clashing or clock.

Just me staring at her through a screen, both impressed and feeling like a complete ass for assuming I know the first thing about her. What's worse, I'm not only curious, but I'm also open to learning.

CHAPTER SEVEN

Avery

L AST NIGHT, THE stars aligned.
Well, first they were disordered chaos all over my dining room table. All week, Stefano's voice taunted me. *Rushing just feels ill-advised blah, blah, blah.*

Ugh, like nightmare fuel, first, my go-to florist—I'm talking flora-scape architect genius—tells me she's booked through January. Then, same with the deejay, who plays music from this century. Booked. When none of my photographers were available, I figured, *this is the worst of it.* I was forced to use Stefano's referral, and call Elena, the travel photographer down the hall from him who it turns out, isn't a made-up person, but a nice woman despite her husband's self-help podcast recommendations.

Taking his help, I thought I might die of humiliation because it felt like such an *I told you so.*

At least, sending a list of *un*problematic podcasts felt mildly redeeming. Temporarily, because of course, Stefano thanked me and said he's excited to listen, effectively stealing my joy.

But the real rotten cherry on top?

Three! Not one or two, but *THREE* of my key dress designers couldn't pull off a one-of-a-kind dream dress, ship it, and fit it in two months...

What is wrong with these people? Haven't they ever heard of wedding magic?

Low-key, I was starting to think, that uptight man put some kind of curmudgeon hex jinx on this ceremony.

Good girl.

He called me a good girl? Why was that so sexy?

Why am I letting this man get under my skin?

Alas, I pulled out my fix-it kit, and voilà! With finesse and the utmost professionalism, I tackled the obstacles with my list of backup vendors.

And my list of IOUs to call in favors.

The Napa bridal boutique with almost every dress Morgan pinned in stock, had "a cancellation."

The only dress appointment available for months, and they squeezed in Morgan in at eleven o'clock Thursday morning.

Immediately, I called the Sister Circle, begged them to rearrange their schedules, call in sick. Heck, fake a stomachache if necessary.

They needed to be there.

As the thrilled maid of honor and wedding planner, I offered to hand-deliver Morgan to the boutique. After they agreed and Morgan invited her mom and Victoria, I was set to mark my calendar when I realized Ace had a dentist appointment today.

This is my life.

A special blend of highs, lows, and pillow screams, before

I play Tetris with my already crammed schedule.

Of course, all to the soundtrack of *Cars*, playing from the back seat where my little guy is excitedly chomping on mini carrots and enjoying this impromptu field trip.

"Less than three minutes until Auntie Mo comes flying down the steps to give you some sugar," I say, peeking at him in the rearview mirror.

My heart leaps the way it does every time he Macaulay Culkin–style slaps his hands over his squishy cheeks.

Thank you, YouTube shorts, for that one.

There's a quiet moment as I flip on my left indicator and slow at a STOP sign, feeling grateful he'll get to see me working.

As I accelerate through, making a right onto the vineyard's gravelly lane, I call Morgan on Bluetooth.

"I'm here," I say when she answers.

"Hey, can you come in for a couple minutes?" she asks. "We've got a full hour. I want to give you a list of the changes Dante and I made..."

I flit a glance at the time on the dash, mentally calculating drive time and lunch hour traffic.

"Can you email it to me?"

"Can you afford to pass up a potty break?" she quips, bypassing me for my baby. "Hey, my little Ace with flying colors."

A couple minutes and a timely stop at the big-boy toilet later, I'm standing in Morgan and Dante's office with my camera hanging from my neck while she rummages through her Pendaflex.

"Here it is!" Victoriously, she tugs a sheet of paper free.

"It just a handful of changes." She passes it to me.

Oh, no big deal.

No, capping the guest list at fifty when Victoria's list has 250 people on standby, isn't wildly unrealistic. Then again, it'll be like a Venn diagram riddle seating chart when there's a column beside each name, detailing who, by no means, can be seated next to them. Naturally, they'll all want to have unobstructed views of the wedding party pairs, each making special entrances with original, never-before-seen dances.

I shoot Morgan a confused glare.

Then I read the last item.

Victoria has requested an invite to Stefano's ex, Carina.

My attention snaps to Morgan.

"Why would she want her here?" I ask. "That seems so…fudged up," I say for Ace's sake. Not that he's listening to anyone besides the great Lightning McQueen.

Morgan shrugs. "Dante said she still considers her family."

I consider this for a moment, wondering how his mother doesn't see how having his ex around might not be conducive to Stefano moving on with his life after the divorce.

Shoving the thought aside—because that man isn't my business—I ask Morgan to watch Ace for a few minutes while I take some photos of the main lawn and the terrace.

I'm gone, *maybe*, ten minutes. *Maybe.*

When I get back to the office, though, it's empty.

Halfway down the hall, I spot my best friend, frantically opening and closing doors, and whispering Ace's name.

"Where are you? This isn't funny, hiding from Auntie Mo."

"Yes, baby, how did you get away from workaholic Auntie Mo if she was watching so closely?"

Morgan whips around.

"Omigod, I checked my email for two seconds," she explains. "Then I turned around and he was gone."

Together, we double-team the rest of the rooms before we pour out the front door. In no time, we're rushing down the entry steps toward the main lawn. My nerves are all over the place, and I'm about to start yelling his name, when Morgan throws out a crowbar arm, halting me.

When I meet her wide-eyed stare, she presses her forefinger to her lips, then taps her ear.

We grow still, listening.

Soon, Stefano's deep chortle fills the air.

My immediate instinct is to U-turn, and sprint back to the house. I can't handle another run-in with Stefano Fortemani. I should be searching for my son who could be playing with table spiders on a trail somewhere or drunk off dirty grapes.

But then, Stefano asks, "Where are your parents?"

Immediately my body slow-motion, zips around, my ears perked toward his voice.

Is Stefano talking to Ace?

"I don't have a dad." My son's clear, high-pitched voice fills the air, and my heart lurches.

I want to jump out from behind this bush, and tell him, "You have a dad, who gave his life for us and this country. Just because he can't be with us now, that doesn't mean he's not looking down on you, proud as the day you were born."

Instead, I cover my heart with my hand, heat stinging at

the corners of my eyes as I listen.

"Well, is your mom here?"

Somehow, I feel like I need to hear this. I've been so busy shielding him, filling his life with so much joy, I don't think I realized he may feel Justin's void as much as I do.

Emotion clogs in my throat.

He's not too young to understand.

"She's taking pictures. We're on a field trip. You can come, too, but you have to ask my Auntie Mo," Ace says, sweetly.

A small, sad laugh tugs at my heartstrings.

"Oh, well thank you for inviting me. Should we go look for your mom and auntie?"

I pull in a deep breath, prepared to make my way back to the steps to wait for them, but it seems Ace is in no rush to find me yet. Not until he asks his burning question, first.

"What's your favorite car?" he asks.

As I pry the tiny branches apart, taking in Stefano's long limbs and rigid posture in a cobalt suit, I expect him to give Ace some perfunctory answer and quickly hunt me down.

But Stefano's dark eyes dart to the sky then to Ace's tiny Lightning McQueen corvette in his hand.

To my utter shock, he smiles warmly, and it's like he's pulled an Uno Reverse card on me.

"Phew, that's a serious question." He scrubs a hand over his beard scruff, comically feigning deep concentration, though I sense this isn't, in fact, a hard one. He squints at Ace. "Do you know what a Ferrari 250 GTO is?"

Warmth floods through me, watching him smile and humor my baby with a thoughtful answer.

"Is it a Corvette? My favorite car is a red Corvette just like Lightning McQueen," Ace supplies.

No shocker there.

Which only makes me feel slightly better about all the money I've spent on a car bed, themed sheets, and toys.

Morgan slaps a hand over her mouth, and I've got to bite my tongue not to laugh. Even though our drive home will center on talking to strangers again, I can't discount how adorable this conversation is.

Stefano chuckles.

"Well, I can see how you might be confused. They both come in cherry red, like your friend, here. The Ferrari is an Italian race car, though. Luxurious, elegant, perfect for a gentleman who appreciates and dreams of owning a handsome vehicle."

My shoulders shake with stifled laughter, though, to Morgan, I still ask the question, niggling at me.

"What's Stefano doing here?" I whisper.

We crouch down, inching closer to spy on them behind a bush, while she quickly brings me up to speed on his hours-long visit to the vineyard. He's been down by the guest cabins, inspecting the progression of the project to ensure they'll be ready by September.

I don't know why this surprises me.

By all accounts, he's a skilled businessman. A reliable, structured, overly cautious overachiever who rarely steps out of his comfort zone. Everything about him exudes type A, straight and narrow living.

His presence on the property today makes complete sense. He's concerned about the vineyard's lodging partners, and what the eventual photos in brochures will do for the bottom line.

Why wouldn't he take his assigned lodging project and immediately go to task?

Also, why is it shocking that he hasn't given me pushback about planning a wedding he doesn't agree with?

"He's ninety-five and he has stickers," Ace adds, snapping me out my thoughts. Apparently, much to Stefano's amusement.

As I pry the tiny branches apart, taking in Stefano's long limbs and rigid posture in a cobalt suit—on another sweltering hot summer day. He's smiling and talking to my baby with animated hands. I'm dumbfounded by his duplicity.

Nothing about what I'm looking at meshes with the person I've built up in my head.

Stefano releases an impressed chuckle. "Whoa! A ninety-five-year-old Corvette, huh?"

Ace is tickled pink, like an almost centenarian car is both unfathomable and the funniest thing he's ever heard. My son lets loose an infectious, musical laugh that warms my insides.

"No, silly," he says. "That's his number. He's a race car."

"*Ohhhhh...*"

Adrenaline rushes through me, and I'm secondhand elated.

"God, he's so good with kids," I whisper to Morgan.

It was an observation. Really, just me, musing about how easily Stefano is getting along with my son.

But my best friend doesn't miss the opportunity to help me reconsider a friendship with him.

"Well, you know he and Carina tried..." To have babies,

she means. "Dante said they miscarried twice, and it took a huge toll on them. IVF and adoption weren't part of their plan either."

My throat tightens, as I put two and two together.

"Do you think fertility was at the root of their divorce?"

"Girl, you never know what happens in people's marriages, but I'm sure it didn't help."

I cover my heart with my hand, now, inching closer still. I'm overwhelmed with emotion for a man who I thought I'd figured out. He's been through the depths of hell, his heart broken repeatedly. Of course, he's concerned for his brother. Of course, he's holding on to what family he's got left.

I look again at this man with his impeccable grooming and a full head of salt-and-pepper curls. His intense brown eyes seem softer the way he's engaging with Ace.

Suddenly, I'm overwhelmed with a harrowing realization.

We go about it differently, but Stefano Fortemani and I want the same thing. We want to shield our loved one from the pain we've experienced.

I get a light, floaty feeling in my chest.

Ace clearly has no clue what Stefano's talking about, but Ace looks up at him like a car-loving god, evidently eager to add value to the subject when he contributes, an excellent point that, "Sally is a blue car. She's Lightning McQueen's girlfriend."

Evidently, enjoying this conversation more than he might've imagined, Stefano masks his snickers.

"Sally, you say?"

Naturally, Ace fishes out a happy blue miniature car with

big cartoon eyes from his pocket.

"Ah, a Porsche." Stefano's eyes light up. "I've got a black one parked at my house, not too far from here, in Healdsburg. If you ever come back to visit, I'll bring my car."

Ace's shoulders sag at his sides. "I live in Fracisco."

Morgan shoots me a chastising glare. "You really need to teach your kid not to tell all y'all's business to strangers."

"That's the thing, he normally wouldn't," I say. "He usually runs from strangers."

Wistfully, I watch them together, two guys discussing cars, the way I'll likely never be able to. And I know this might just be a phase, but I realize Ace needs strong male role models in his life to answer all the questions I can't.

"How about this?" Stefano claps his hands. "Let me help you find your mom. I'm sure she's worried sick about you. Then if she's okay with it, we'll get you back out here for a ride with Sally."

Ace's bright brown eyes sparkle with excitement.

Morgan and I barely make it to the steps before they wander up the path.

"Mom, the man has Sally locked in his garage!" Ace announces.

Stefano plants himself beside Morgan and throws up his hands in surrender. "Guilty as charged." He chuckles but I don't miss the searching glance he darts to Ace before he meets my stare. "Hello, Avery."

His dark brown gaze bores into me as he straightens his tie.

"Hey, thanks so much for bringing back the little explorer." I tuck a flyaway hair behind my ear, unsure how to troubleshoot the errors I might've made with him. "This is Ace, by the way, my son."

His brow furrows slightly.

I don't miss the quick glance he flits to my left hand.

After our ChatVideo meeting on Monday following my marriage bomb-drop, I knew he'd had more questions about my husband and my bare ring finger. Still, I pressed on with the meeting, determined to prove I wasn't too young and naive to run a business. Maturity isn't determined by age or time. Not that we were ever in a position to share personal details about our lives.

But now, I've got a son, too?

He must have a million questions.

Graciously, though, he doesn't broach any of them now.

Stefano's expression softens.

"Nice to meet you, Ace. I'm Stefano." He gives him a hardy handshake. "Your Auntie Mo…" He flashes Morgan a confirming glance, waiting for her nod before he continues. "She's marrying my brother."

My son is uninterested until I add, "They're together like Lightning and Sally," without realizing, it might be a dead giveaway that I'd eavesdropped on their conversation.

After Ace hugs his Auntie, Morgan takes him inside for one more bathroom stop before we get on the road for her dress-shopping appointment.

Then, I'm alone with Stefano.

Silence thickens between us for an awkward beat.

Neither of us knows what to say. We're so used to bickering, proving our loyalty to Morgan and Dante. How should we act when we're not at each other's throats?

Or when the other has just shown your son a considerable kindness when he thought no one was looking?

He straightens his tie again. Then he looks at me thoughtfully.

I feel him scrutinizing my face.

A prickling sensation scatters along the back of my neck. My thoughts race, urging me to regain control of the situation before I spiral down the *good girl* fantasy hole.

"I hear it's going to be a full house at the bridal boutique." He flashes me a smile that might as well be an olive branch, the way I latch on to it.

I'm the first to break eye contact.

"Oh, yeah." I exaggerate a sigh, glancing up to the house. "Both mothers, the Sister Circle, plus Ace. Let's pray there's champagne on the premises."

Our combined laughter is stilted and careful, like we're both holding back for the other's sake.

I get this unrelenting urge to get this weight off my chest.

"Listen, Stefano, I know we've got another ChatVideo meeting this afternoon, but I just want to take a second and tell you how much I appreciate you talking cars with Ace."

When he looks at me, I search his eyes, hoping my words feels as genuine as I intend them to be.

"He's a great kid."

"Thanks. That means a lot."

A few seconds later, Morgan and Ace come bounding back down the steps to wait by the car.

Stalling, I shoot Stefano another glance. "Don't let me forget to go over them when we meet at two, but Morgan gave me a list of *requests…*" I drag the word out for dramatic effect.

The corner of his mouth kicks up. "Do I even want to know?"

I cover my face with my hand. "Oh God, no. Think choreographed pairs dances as we enter the ceremony…"

"Sadly, I'm prepared for worst-case scenarios concerning my brother, so I might be equipped to help."

Equipped? Really?

It's absolutely corny. A totally, fittingly and unknowingly dirty innuendo, and so comically him.

Inside I'm cracking up because it's not friendship or aligning stars, but somehow, laughter and comfort feel like a step in the right direction between us.

Just then, Morgan reminds me of the time, and as I tell Stefano I'll see him in a few hours, climb into the car, and pull onto the main road, my breath catches in my throat.

I'm more looking forward to our meeting than dress shopping with my best friend.

CHAPTER EIGHT
Avery

WE MAKE IT to Bridal Bliss with ten minutes to spare, and thankfully, everyone else is already here.

Corralling our group to the right of the entrance, I clear my throat to grab everyone's attention.

"Before Shanice calls us in for the dress appointment, let's take a moment to go over some ground rules," I say, fishing out dual-purpose judging/paddle fans from my tote, instructing the ladies to, "Take one then pass the stack to the next person."

Morgan giggles as she reads, "Love it! I say yes to this dress," then turns it over, scanning the "Hmm…it's a no from me" on the flip side.

Functional, fabulous, and a fan, in case things get heated. Logistically speaking, I've come prepared.

By no stretch of the imagination do I believe eight strong-willed women won't have as many opinions about Morgan's wedding attire. Including the bride, we've got four Sister Circle members, Chiara (honorary Sister Circle status), Victoria Fortemani, and Morgan's mom, Georgia. Ace is here too, but wedding gowns aren't exactly his thing. Order and structure are nonnegotiables.

"Now, I know we're all super excited to be a part of this beautiful tradition. I'm sure no one has been creating Pinterest boards and leafing through bridal magazines..." Everyone laughs, guiltily. "However, in the interest of saving time, and to keep Morgan's decision at the forefront, once we're seated, you'll each have twenty minutes to browse through exclusive designer collections for a dress—that's singular—for our bride to try on."

"Ooh, I love this idea." Valerie smiles warmly.

Chiara squees excitedly with her.

I don't miss Victoria and Georgia sharing an impressed glance either.

Even though I'm a smidge salty that Victoria callously, thoughtlessly wants to invite Stefano's ex-wife to his brother's wedding, even though she's clearly basking in "greener pastures," I'm so glad they're here supporting Morgan.

"Think of this as a front-row seat at an extremely condensed fashion show. Two hours. Eight dresses. Three bottles of champagne!"

Monica and Seneca quietly hoot and holler.

This is still a business establishment.

When Shanice finally ushers us into the viewing area, everyone—except for Morgan—claims their seats around the raised platform. After I settle Ace on the floor next to my chair with his iPad, earbuds, and cars, the ladies are raring to go. Then, just like that, we drop off our belongings, and it's a veritable tulle and lace free-for-all.

Monica runs roughshod toward an A-line number with a cinched waist and diamond-encrusted bodice. Seneca,

Chiara, and Valerie get lost in tea-length. Georgia is drowning in ball gowns. *Both of which are distinctly not Morgan's taste nor her vibe.* But Victoria and I rightly find our way to modern mermaid and trumpet cuts.

By the time we've selected our dresses, hung them in Morgan's dressing room, and we settle in our seats again, it feels like curtain-up.

"Dress number one…"

Morgan sashays out of the dressing room. She's wearing a cream-colored, boatneck tea-length dress. Valerie's choice, which makes her look like she's ready to time-travel back to the 1950s rather than down the aisle.

It's classically beautiful, but *so* mismatched with her vision.

Seven "Hmm… It's a no from me" fans fly into the air.

A negatory consensus.

Brutal.

"Look, I thought it was really cute." Valerie defends her selection, but she's no match for Monica.

"What woman do you know who wants to be cute on her wedding day? Beautiful, stunning, glowing, drop-dead gorgeous, yes," she reasons. "We need Dante teary-eyed that he gets to spend his life with her."

At her left, Seneca rests a calming hand on Monica's forearm. Since I'm on her right, I flap my fan at her, sending a cool breeze in her direction.

Yeah, only seven more to go.

In a twist of instant Karma, Monica's diamond-encrusted A-line doesn't even make it to the platform before the fans go up, shutting it down.

After two no's, I excuse myself to the dressing room to check on Morgan. After a double knock, I enter and find her struggling with the ball gown tulle snagged on her ring.

"Here, let me," I say, gently unravelling the fabric.

When I meet Morgan's wandering stare in the mirror, she deflates into a sigh. Mostly, because it's her mother's selection.

Saying no to a scalloped-neckline Cinderella monstrosity is one thing when it's a friend's dress choice. But how do you tell your mother that she's picked the one gown that makes your face turn with disgust?

"It's hideous." Morgan's shoulders shake with defeated laughter.

"Girl, the second I saw Georgia pick that one, I was like, *Oh, no. This is going to end badly.* That's why I'm here."

I squeeze her shoulders and flash her a megawatt smile.

But then she twists in my arms to face me with her brows drawn together.

"Um, do you really expect me to believe that's why you're hiding in here with me?" She blinks a good dozen times. "I know your busy brain has settled long enough, and you're thinking about Stefano..."

Wow.

There's no point denying it.

When Morgan, Ace, and I stepped foot into Bridal Bliss, I figured I'd leave all thoughts of Stefano on the doormat. Just throw myself into helping my best friend find the perfect wedding gown to exchange vows with the love of her life. In my mind, all eight of us would make joyful, teary-eyed toasts—if even I'm a lightweight drunk and champagne makes me horny. It wouldn't matter though because we'd be celebrating Morgan and Dante's eternal love.

Then my brain and touchy-feely heart promptly reminded me that I'm an empath.

The thing is, I know loss.

But after Morgan told me about Stefano's situation, I haven't been able to stop thinking about how harshly I judged him. And based on what? His suits? A family effort to rouse Dante from the same unimaginable grief that Stefano is likely still grappling with himself?

Imagine, in so many years losing your father, grandfather, at least two babies, plus the dream of having kids at all. Then the cherry on top is a finalized divorce.

And yet, he stood there talking to Ace with so much compassion. Laughing and really talking to him, man to man. Rather, man to incredibly adorable boy.

All I wanted to do was hug this broken man and help him put all the pieces back together.

"It's so bad." I shake my head. Disappointment sags through me. "Do you think I like being this way? Trust me, it's one thing to be highly attuned to other's emotions and energies. I listen; I understand on the deepest level. People get to feel seen and heard. But it's mentally straining, to say the least. It's like, hello burnout, come on in."

Morgan laughs. "That's all good and fine, but this isn't just about emotional broadcasting, friend. I stood right there watching you feverishly fawn all over this man because he was talking about cartoon cars with your son." She cocks her head, every atom of her calling my bluff.

At this I've got to laugh.

"My *God*... He's so damn fine. I can't even deny it."

"And single."

I wave her off because truly, the last thing I need in my chaotic life right now is romance. Sex, maybe. But certainly not a candy-coated man with a gooey center to sap my empathetic heart dry.

"I'm so serious when I tell you, I'm just window-shopping with no immediate intentions to purchase."

Morgan is bent over cackling in that tulle tumbleweed draped around her body.

"Just so you know, you're fooling no one." She gasps for air, still breathlessly laughing at me.

But I've got to nip this in the butt right here and now.

"Honestly, that's the whole truth." *THE LIES!* "Absolutely, I'm looking forward to our ChatVideo meeting at two, and I fully expect you and Dante to be there."

"Uh..."

"It's not why you'd think, though." Positioning myself behind Morgan, I busy myself, fastening the two dozen buttons trailing along her spine. "I feel like utter shit, holding the vineyard hoax against him, judging him, thinking I know the first thing about him when he's been through hell and back."

"Child, that man has been through the wringer."

"I *know*..." I heave a shameful sigh. "Morgan, I've got to smooth things over with him, let him see a different side of me."

Morgan tosses me a suggestive stare over her shoulder.

I swat her arm.

"My *Lord*, relax. I'm not trying to hook up with Stefano

Fortemani—"

"Yet," she creatively supplies, as if I don't know her mind has a second home in the gutter. Plus, fairy tales are my territory. Mine might've been cut short, but that doesn't mean I can't help other people find theirs.

"What I'm saying is, we've got this meeting coming up. I'm thinking…*maybe* I'll ask him to show up early. Share my story about Justin, you know? Encourage him to share his, so it sinks in how much we've got in common."

She inhales sharply.

"Wait a doggone minute." Morgan hikes up the hem of her dress and twists around. Her expression is all open-mouthed fire and ice as she stares at me in disbelief. "Avery Ellis, are you, by chance, saying that Dante and I were right and you two should be friends?"

I let out a howl of a laugh straight from my gut.

Here I'm thinking I've said something wrong, and she's just being dramatic to deliver that unspoken *I told you so*.

Except, the howl alerts the rest of our pack.

Next thing I know, Seneca, Valerie, and Monica are squishing themselves into this sardine-can dressing room with us and the fluffiest dress from hell.

"Why are y'all hiding in here and leaving us out?" Monica asks. "We want to know what all the whispering is about?"

"Is it Victoria?" Seneca asks.

"*Girl*, I was thinking the same thing. What if you want to wear a sexy, second-skin dress?" Valerie's lip curls as she tilts her head examining the ball gown. "Not when Dante's mother might think you're some uncultured floozy… And who picked this hideous tissue wad?"

We all fall out into a fit of giggles, shushing and holding on to each other.

"Shh… that's Georgia's pick," Seneca explains.

Valerie's eyes go wide as saucers. "Ooh, mama, no."

"I *know*. I don't want to hurt her feelings though, so somebody is gonna have to say yes to this dress." She dips her chin. "But only one or two."

Let's not get carried away.

It's Monica who circles back to why we're in here.

"So, dress number three is a bust, too, but again, what's all the hush-hush whispering about?"

I shoot Morgan a pleading stare.

But it's too late.

"We caught Ace and Stefano talking at the vineyard, and now Miss Wedding Planner of the Year is crushing on Stefano."

"No, that is absolutely ridiculous," I say emphatically.

I'm met with four deadpan stares, daring me to lie in a room full of mirrors.

The Sister Circle are my mirrors, constantly reflecting.

An exasperated sigh huffs out of me.

"Lord, have mercy, I just thought he seemed sweet." I shrug. "Plus, why would I even bother when he's fresh out of a marriage, and his mother is inviting his ex-wife to the wedding, hmm?"

"If you like him and want to pursue it, I can go to Dante and see about him uninviting Carina," Morgan adds.

"It's not about liking him; I'm empathizing with him."

Even if he's got archaic ideas about maturity and age. Well, about most things. He'd rather go with a full orchestra instead of a deejay. He wants them to jump the broom AND cut a log in half with a double-headed saw. Like, who brings a weapon to a wedding?

I let my shoulders sag at my sides.

"Here we go with the empath stuff." Seneca flicks her gaze skyward and laughs.

Valerie, the queen of online dating zeroes in on me, though. "Ma'am, he's divorced, and she's got a new boo, so I'd say that's over. And sweet is how it starts. Why do you think I get my steps in at the park twice daily? All the single dads, The *zaddies…mmm.*"

My face twists.

Surprisingly, no one else seems grossed out.

"She's not wrong," Seneca says. "Women of child-bearing age are hard-wired for men who seem responsible enough to take care of their family. I thought it was a myth but stick Will with his baby cousin or his sister's puppy in front of me, and my ovaries practically weep with joy."

"Will needs to shit or get off the pot." Valerie says what we've all thought at least a dozen times about Seneca's complacent, live-in boyfriend, even if I'd have gone with a less vulgar saying. "Why should he marry you when you already treat him like a husband?"

"*Anyway…*" Seneca ignores her. "Like I was saying, a man being sweet to your kid is like sexual catnip."

Monica flashes her a side-eye.

"Look, I don't know about all that, but Stefano is fine as hell, single, and the silver-fox thing is sexy as all get-out. He can call me a good girl and spank me anytime."

"Mon?!" I stumble back, laughing and letting the wall hold me up just as a knock sounds at the door.

"Is everything okay with the dress?"

Shanice.

It's pin-drop silent.

We're locked in a group stare like it's not super suspicious and rude that we've been in here for Lord knows how long.

Plus, there's a foot-long gap under the dressing room door, so I know she sees five pairs of feet. Well, four since Morgan's are resting in peace under Georgia's *Bridgerton* ball gown.

"Uh... The dress was giving Morgan a hard time, so we were helping her, but we finally got it now. We'll be out in two shakes," I say.

Three minutes later, the Sister Circle is seated again. Ace is sitting on Chiara's lap with his iPad. The champagne glasses are topped off, and resting on a silver platter, and Monica and I with our fans in hand, are poised and ready to say yes.

As planned, sadly, dress three is a no-go. Which, as it turns out, so are dresses four through six. Chiara and Seneca don't seem surprised, considering tea-length has already been established as not the best fit for this occasion. But dress five was Morgan's ace in the hole. The regal, high-neck lacy dress, a la Beyoncé and baby Blue Ivy for *Vogue*? It was supposed to be her failsafe worth seven other nos.

THE dress.

Except it's giving tissue caught in a net.

Morgan's lips quiver as she turns on the platform.

I catch her glassy stare.

"We've still got two more," I say, encouragingly. "I don't want to toot our horns or anything, but Victoria and I are known for our style."

Chiara giggles.

"Darling, you'd be beautiful in anything," Victoria says. "However, Avery has made a great point. There are two beautiful gowns left. All you need is one."

Morgan nods obligingly.

As Shanice helps with the train, back to the dressing room, I fish out my phone.

Shoot, twelve forty-five, already.

At the rate this two-hour appointment is going, even if somehow, the next dress is "the one," it'll be one o'clock. What am I going to do, say, "Hooray, you found a wedding gown, now wrap it up because I've got to get Ace some lunch, and get you home for a ChatVideo with Stefano at two?" What if she doesn't find one? *Tough luck. Let's go. Time's a-ticking.*

I've got to push back the meeting with him.

Hi Stefano, I'm still at the dress-shopping appointment, and I've got to grab lunch for Ace and get Morgan back. I'm worried I'll be late for our 2:00 meeting. Are you available later this afternoon or tonight? I could do 4:00 or 6:30. Let me know. Thanks.

In my periphery, Morgan sashays toward the platform in the sweeping, strapless, white lace and organza trumpet dress that Victoria selected. It looks amazing on her, sculpting her curves, and against her rich brown skin… She's a goddess.

If anything, Georgia's teetering cry-face should be the

dead giveaway.

"There's the smile I've come to know and love." Victoria beams.

Except, tears are contagious.

The fans raise in quick succession. As do the happy waterworks.

"*Yasss!*" Monica croons, teary-eyed. "We love it, and we say yes to that dress, queen! You know you better..."

Shanice helps Morgan onto the platform.

Beneath her big watery brown eyes, we're graced with a full-tooth grin, her trademark red lips stretched from ear to ear.

Soon, Seneca has her phone out with Lil' Mo's song, "4Ever" blasting through the speaker. Champagne glasses in hand, Monica and Valerie start dancing. Then Chiara takes Ace by the hand and joins them, and it finally feels like a celebration.

Even Victoria and Georgia push to their feet, choked up but joyous.

"I love it!" Morgan yells, respectfully low. "Yes, to this dress!"

Again, a place of business with other customers.

"Our girl is making it official..." Seneca belts out, dropping her hips and swaying with her glass lifted in the air.

"I know you all better bring this much energy for your pairs entrance dances at the ceremony," Morgan says.

I'm just about to join them when my phone pings somewhere at the bottom of my purse.

"Oh, you know, Marcello and I are coming with the fire." Monica sips her champagne.

I laugh as I rummage around the bottom of my bag, weaving my hand past my computer, my fix-it kit, keys, and planner bible.

"Where is it?" I grumble.

Not to be one-upped by Monica, Seneca adds, "Hey, I don't know what Dante's friend Mike is working with, but best believe, I will be spinning circles around y'all, so…"

"Jameson and I have known each other since we were kids," Chiara boasts. "We lived for every slide, two-step, and shuffle."

I'm over here cackling when Valerie, who couldn't care less about competitive pairs dances because all she wants to know is if Dante's other groomsmen and college friend, Everett, is single.

Briefly, I wonder what kind of music Stefano likes.

What if he can't dance? *What if he can?*

Every nerve ending on my body stirs and tingles.

Shaking my thoughts loose, I remember closing my phone inside the pages of my planner after I'd texted Stefano. Finally, spotting it, I slip it free.

On the screen, there's a notification from Stefano, but before I get a glimpse, Chiara dances over to me.

"Come groove with us." She pulls me to my feet, bumping her hip against mine. "Victoria made lunch reservations at one of their local restaurants, Bramoso. She said they've got these white truffles to die for."

"I was just texting your brother to see about postponing our meeting for a few hours."

"Oh, that's right. Stef is your *vineyard liaison.*" She rolls her eyes and laugh. "The dream team can wait until we feast on fabulous Italian."

I glance at my phone, lifting my chin to the screen to unlock it. It opens on Stefano's last message.

> Don't worry about it. Enjoy yourself. We can meet tomorrow.

"See, no big deal." Chiara's shoulders lift and fall. "Now, come dance, be happy, drink champagne, and cry ugly tears with us."

A hardness settles in my gut.

Why did I say anything? It would've been rushed, but I could've made the appointment.

I smile nervously at Chiara, before I focus on his text again, ignoring the disappointment sagging through me.

"Give me one sec to reschedule," I say.

As Chiara shrugs and rejoins the group, I tap out a quick response.

> It's really no problem. Late meetings are a regular thing for me.

My fingers are on the keys when the three tiny ellipses pop up. He's sending another message, so I erase my rambling apology, and wait.

> Unfortunately, I've got other plans this evening, but let's follow up tomorrow. Have a great time.

A heaviness weighs down my body as I tuck my phone away and try to perk up to join my friends.

Chiara tips her chin to me. "All good?"

I nod a bunch of times, forcing a smile.

"He's got other plans tonight, so we're going to meet up sometime tomorrow."

She does a double take. "I'm sorry, my brother, Stefano Fortemani, has other plans tonight?" Disbelief twists the lines of her face. Then, if I wasn't looking, I might've missed it but Chiara shoots Victoria a look of... *What does that look mean?*

I'm staring at them trying to break the secret code but Ace tugs on my dress.

"Why are you sad, Mommy?"

Before I can answer, he places his small red car in my hand "to make me feel better." Which, had he given it to me before we got to the vineyard this morning, it might've.

But now, looking at its big cartoon eyes and bold racer number on its sides, I can't stop thinking about Stefano. My mind zigzags from him talking to Ace, to Sally locked in his garage, and the babies he and Carina never got to love on, like I love Ace.

Worst, what are Stefano's plans?

I take Chiara's glass and down the rest of her champagne. Lightweight or not, bring on the hangover.

CHAPTER NINE

Stefano

"LISTEN MAN, I'VE given you space. We need to talk..."
My best friend Dylan heaves an exaggerated sigh into
the line.

I've known him since we were kids, popping wheelies on
our bikes through the Napa hills. All the way up until he
moved junior year in high school, then reunited in college,
we've been thick as thieves. Even though he lives in Chi-
town with his wife, son, and daughter, we'd plan family
vacations together, and send holiday cards.

Still, whenever we reached out, it's always like no time
has passed.

*Even when those vacations had become fewer and farther
between as Carina and I found it harder to watch their family
grow.*

In those time gaps, though, there's always social media
keeping him in the loop.

"Nah, I'm good," I say, downplaying Carina's romantic
update.

Mainly, I'd rather forget that she's jumped back in with
two feet. But I've also got back-to-back virtual meetings over

the next three hours. One of which is with Avery, and I'd prefer not to be in my feelings this time.

So, nonchalantly, I add, "From the looks of things, it seems she's good, too."

There's a slight pause, during which I sense my guy choosing his next words wisely.

Looks like we're doing this.

Swiping out of the "Let Yourself Grieve" podcast episode that Avery recommended, I set down my phone alongside my keyboard and half-eaten turkey sub.

"Honestly, Paula and I... I mean, you've been talking about the love slipping away for years, but we always thought you guys would climb out of this rough patch, the way you've climbed out of every other valley life has thrown at you. So, it's been a shock to us, too."

"Yeah, I know..."

"Just remember you've still got us," he adds.

An email notification drops from the top of my computer screen. It's from my next client, a family friend, West Woodworks, who I'm scheduled to meet within a half hour.

I toggle over to the mail app, and relief immediately works its way through me, loosening my limbs.

A meeting cancellation on a Friday?

Thank you.

My ears perk up at a low whisper in Dylan's background, that I'm assuming belongs to Paula, eager for an update on me, too. As close as Dylan and I are, our wives forged a friendship that veered neck and neck with ours.

"If you need advice or want to vent, say as little or as much as you're comfortable sharing," he urges me.

We both know that means hold nothing back.

But since I suspect that sharing nothing will only lead to Dylan pushing harder, I bend.

Reclining in my desk chair, I clasp my hands behind my head.

"Carina looks happier than I've seen her in years. And after everything we've been through, losing Dad and Nono, then two babies... She deserves every ounce of joy."

"Yeah, man." Dylan pauses briefly, and I sense the other shoe about to drop. "And you, how are you doing?"

A calendar alert darts out from the edge of my computer screen, reminding me of my 1:30 appointment with Dante, Morgan, and Avery. Immediately, my mind drifts back to the vineyard. Back to Ace and his mom, who, by her bare ring finger, might understand divorce firsthand.

"Me? I'm uh..."

I blow out a long breath, staring at my calendar.

The entire time chatting with Ace, I got this eerie, déjà vu feeling. Like I knew him despite never having met. Then, I turned the corner off the path, spotting Morgan and Avery, and it clicked.

The same bright, sparkly brown eyes and golden-brown skin. The tiny round nose. The endless questions cued and ready to fire.

As much as I was struck by their resemblance, though, I was blindsided by how little I know about Avery Ellis.

How could this woman look at the world with rose-colored glasses when Ace himself claimed he didn't have a dad? Which means, not only has she surrounded herself with reasons to celebrate life, but she's also doing it with the weight of shaping a tiny human being squarely on her shoulders.

How could I complain when I only have to take care of me?

Even still, she could stand there, having overheard me talking with her son, and look at me with kind eyes? She could thank me for selfishly shooting the fan about cars with a kid because I never got the chance with my son?

I was wholly unnerved.

She was lowering her guards for me, absolving me of a guilt I rightly deserved to feel, and I was greedily softening to her.

"I'm not going to lie: divorce is for the birds." I laugh. "But all in all, I'm finding silver linings here and there."

"Oh yeah?"

Briefly, I wonder if Avery listened to all the podcasts that she recommended to find her silver linings. Did she need the reminders to forgive and physically take care of herself? Is that how her friends became family? How she reclaimed her own identity? Dove into event planning?

I shove the questions aside, circling back.

"Believe it or not, I'm actually calling to see if you and the family have any plans to visit your dad this September?"

Dylan huffs a little laugh. "That's really specific. Is there a reason that we should?"

By the time I bring him up to speed on Dante's shotgun wedding to a woman they didn't know existed before now, they've booked flights, a stay at one of our lodging partner's small B&Bs, opted in for all the yet-to-be-determined wedding festivities, and volunteered his four-year-old daughter, Danielle, as the flower girl.

Because my guy is hell-bent on circling back to my "well-being," he waits until Paula leaves the room before he whispers, "All right, she's gone. Now, hurry up and spill because that long-ass pause when I asked how you were doing spoke volumes."

I bark out a laugh.

"How long have we known each other?" Dylan asks. "You hesitated, and as far as I'm concerned, the way you were in college... Shoot, you might be back to your player ways."

"I'm glad you have so much confidence in me." I chuckle. "But I've just been listening to some great self-help podcasts and wrapping my mind around moving on when my divorce was finalized last month, you know? There's not really anyone."

Just because a woman who's previously made it known that she loathes me is suddenly nice, it doesn't mean there's more to it.

Dylan huffs an amused laugh.

"Not really anyone, huh? That's what we're going with?" The line swishes like he's settling in for a deep dive. "Who is she?"

"Who is who?" I feign confusion, knowing, over the years, we've been down this road too many times to count. I'll give a little, and he'll pull the rest out of me.

"Let me guess, she's some supplier for the winery?" Then he snaps his fingers. "No, no, she's probably one of Morgan's sisters?" Sister Circle, but close. *Shit.* "Tell me I'm wrong."

I inhale sharply.

My phone pings with a text notification from Avery asking to meet thirty minutes early before Dante and Morgan join. As I tap out a quick affirmative reply, hoping it'll get me out of this interrogation, Dylan correctly interprets my silence as a confession.

"I'm proud of you, man," he intones. "You deserve to find happiness again. I want you to be open to meeting someone and enjoying her company. If only to look long enough to fuel the spank bank."

"Okay, thanks for that—"

My line beeps, and my sister couldn't have more perfect timing. I take the out. "Listen Dylan, this is Chiara calling on the other line. She's been trying to reach me since last night. I've got to run but I'll talk to you soon."

"Look at you, being soft." Dylan snorts. "But it's cool. Call me when you want to man up and talk about this."

The second he ends the call, my line clicks over, and I breathe a relieved sigh.

Except, in my rush to get off with Dylan, thinking, somehow, I'd been saved, I forgot this is my annoying little sister, thirteen years my junior.

If she's calling, she wants something.

"Hey, Stef," she croons into the line like her reaching out to me is a regular occurrence rather than a shock to my system.

"Good afternoon, Chiara. Everything all right? Did you need anything?" I rush to ask. "I've got another meeting here shortly."

Considering she's an honorary member of Morgan's Sister Circle, I purposely leave out that it's with Avery. The last thing I need, going into this meeting, is my sister adding to

Dylan's and Dante's gospel to get me to be open. *Nor more images to add to my mental collection for later self-pleasure.*

I lower my legs and push to my feet, ducking out of the office into the hallway toward the vending machine.

It's too early for wine, but at this rate, chocolate will have to be a substitute to get me through this day.

"No, I don't need anything..." She trails off, her silence prickling with subtext. "I'm just trying to figure out why you lied to Avery yesterday. You haven't had plans since 19—"

"Thank you." The muscle at my jaw hardens. "I'm so glad I answered your call. Really, we should have these riveting chats more often." Sarcasm bleeds into my hardened tone.

"Wow, that wasn't an overreaction or anything."

I huff out a sigh.

"Again, I've got a meeting so..."

"So, why lie to Avery?" she presses. "Is there something else going on? You can tell me."

Okay, sure.

"What is it with everyone latching on to this subject? Avery and I are working together on *our* brother's wedding. That's it," I bite out. "First, Dante and Dylan, now, you're doing what? Faulting me for opting for a meeting during business hours?"

Chiara's laugh is loud and wicked like this is too easy, I've seen myself into her trap.

"Be for real with me, Stef."

She's calling my bluff.

It would be so easy, to brush this conversation off as my nosy little sister, digging for dirt on my nonexistent love life.

Now, though, that's a valid description. Unless I use this opportunity to get a woman's perspective regarding what women think of me. *After the vineyard, what fueled Avery's sudden eagerness to meet. Maybe, get some insight on her. Or ask about her divorce from Ace's dad...*

I shove my hand in my pocket for my wallet, slipping it free as I scour the brightly colored metallic packaged chocolate bar selection in the vending machine.

When I don't answer, Chiara tries a different tactic.

"Would these plans happen to include ordering takeout and watching television on your couch?"

I let my head fall back onto my shoulders.

"You're the worst, you know that?"

"Yes."

At least she knows it.

"I stayed home. Is that what you want to hear?" I groan. "I spent my Thursday night touring an online dating app." *Trying not to think about the way Ace's mother looked at me at the vineyard.* "I created an empty profile, which I immediately canceled when I saw how morally confused these people are who claim they're looking for love."

Chiara giggles. "My *God*, you didn't!"

Oh, I did.

"You're in for the rudest awakening."

"Discouraged, I was hoping to glean a tiny morsel of insight about dating nowadays, and I ended up watching *Door-to-Door Dates*—"

I barely get the show name out before Chiara jumps in excitedly.

"Oh my gosh, I've watched all twenty seasons. What did

you think?"

"Surprisingly, it wasn't half-bad."

She's fully invested now, and I'm not sure if it's a mistake getting her hyped about dating.

"And your conclusion about the current state of romance in the world was..."

Slipping a five-dollar bill into the machine, I press a letter-number combo, my mouth watering for the Snickers that plunks down. After I scoop my hand in to grab it, then my change, I rip the brown packaging off, and take a large bite.

"Can I get back to you on that? I'm still traumatized."

We both laugh.

I've got to admit, I don't hate the lightness filling my chest.

Dating is certainly not for the faint of heart.

Or the bold.

Really, I haven't figured out who it's for, but I'm steering clear.

"Lord, you've been single for two seconds," Chiara says. "Imagine how I felt before I found Lamar."

I don't have to since I, along with the rest of the family, was there—on multiple occasions—mopping up endless tears and reassuring her she's amazing and worthy of love.

Guess I should start taking my own advice.

Taking another bite of chocolaty, nougaty goodness, I let the sugar surge through my veins. I take wide strides back to my office, and plop down onto my chair.

"To answer the question that I know you're itching to ask, no, I'm not ready to date or secretly fawning over Avery." *That much.* "Between throwing myself into work, cleaning up the Healdsburg house, and spending the next two months on wedding liaison duties, that's enough."

"Sooo…"

"I'm not ready to date, but I want to be organized and prepared when the time comes," I say, hoping we can change the subject now.

She releases a disappointed sigh.

For the life of me, I don't know why I don't see the curveball coming when my sister winds me up, only to completely throw me.

"Anyway," she says. "If you were available, you should've just met up with Avery instead of lying. She seemed really disappointed when you canceled on her…"

Wait, what?

My body posture perks up.

"Disappointed?"

I'm straining to hear even the slightest hitch in her breath. *Was Avery really upset that I canceled? Or is Chiara just baiting me?*

My pulse surges as I wait impatiently.

"Yeah, we were all at the bridal salon yesterday, dancing and drinking champagne when y'all rescheduled for today. She was the only one sitting hunched over, looking around in confusion like she had somewhere else she wanted to be…"

No, this is ridiculous.

Avery Ellis is a young, beautiful woman with a great kid, a thriving business, and sunny outlook on life. Men are probably beating down her door for a date with her. Her ex-husband's got to be kicking himself that he let her go.

I let out an exasperated huff.

The very notion that Avery Ellis wanted to see me seems preposterous, except...

I glance at my watch.

Avery and I are meeting early.

In five minutes.

One of which passes while I rush Chiara off the phone. Which, in hindsight feels like a mistake.

I'm left nervously staring at my reflection in my computer screen, and dissecting the nano-scopic possibility that Avery might have a small thing for me.

The instant her picture appears, I straighten, tipping my head, angling my good side to her.

"Hi!" I say, way too cheery. And loud, considering this latest addition to my newly minted spank bank.

Involuntarily, I survey her sheer black, short-sleeve blouse, her Beyoncé-esque blonde wig twisted up with a pencil, those warm brown eyes, and the sexy smile stretching her full lips.

My pulse races.

"Hey, thanks so much for joining early." She shakes her head and blows out an amused sigh. "And for understanding yesterday. I got the date for Ace's dental appointment mixed up, and it threw off my entire day. I was trying to squeeze everything in, but I shouldn't've assumed your evening would be free to reschedule. Obviously, you've got a life." She lets out a shaky laugh.

"It's no problem, really. It's fine," I say, mesmerized by her slow, surveying glance.

"Okay, so..." She takes a deep breath. "It's been a hectic

week, but we made it."

Despite myself, I inch to the edge of my seat.

"Celebrate the wins, right?" I say.

"Exactly." Avery blinks a handful of time before she clears her throat. "Now, before we begin the meeting, I'd really love to start over with you."

Breath bottles up in my chest, and I'm staring wordlessly. It's so vague.

What does she mean? Let's introduce ourselves as if for the first time? Or pretend my brother and her best friend aren't engaged, and I'll ask her out on a date?

"What did you have in mind?" I ask.

Avery lowers her chin to her chest, giggling. When she meets my stare again, she brightens, and I can't discount the hope fluttering in my chest like an army of caged butterflies.

"*God,* Morgan and Dante will never let me live this down but..." She winces. "I was thinking maybe they're right and we should clear the slate. You know, get to know each other on our own terms, or whatever?"

She inhales sharply.

It's that last word that I cling to, though, as she goes on about how much we've got in common.

Whatever.

Avery didn't say date or be friends or even let's simply be cordial to each other. She wants us to build something new. That *whatever* is more than enough for me. We get to decide.

"At the end of the day, I hate that I misjudged you." She shakes her head, like she's physically dislodging the thought. "I've been thinking a lot about our icebreaker, and how I sorta dropped that bomb on you about my marriage. Then you meet Ace at the vineyard, and he tells you he doesn't have a father, which isn't exactly true."

"It's okay, you don't have to explain," I say, even though I'm holding my breath and hoping she will.

She nods to herself as she pulls in a long breath.

"I want to, though." Avery reassures me. Then, like there's no screen between us, she fixes me with a stare so intense, so confusingly familiar. In the space of a breath, she rewrites every page I thought I knew about her as she softly adds, "I'm a widow."

My heart bottoms out.

I was prepared for Avery to tell me about a messy marriage. About the complications that go with severing ties and years of promises and vows. In my mind, I'd already filled in blanks about financial woes and an ugly custody battle because how could I look at this woman, Pollyanna with her ever-present smile as she solves the world's problems, and imagine she's been masking an unthinkable hurt?

Of all the things she could've said, I never in a million years would've expected she'd lost her ex.

The parties, the overcompensating cheeriness, she doesn't want to bring others down. She's sunshine because she must be to block out the darkness.

"Avery, I'm so sorry."

She waves me off, but I know loss. After Dad and Nono, I struggled to find my footing. Grief and devastation touched every aspect of my life, including my marriage. And while death and divorce are nowhere near the same—I might still bump into Carina; I know she's still around, living her life, but Avery will never see her husband again—that sort of pain, bereavement, it's real and unrelenting.

"It's been three years since I lost Justin." Her voice drifts as she lowers her gaze. "It still doesn't feel real."

God, part of me wishes I could reach through the screen and take her hand in mine, say something sympathetic and profound. Tell her everything is going to be okay. But deep down, I know it won't. Time will pass, and that wound will heal, but the scar, the proof of that pain, just underneath the surface, will always be there.

I smile solemnly, encouraging Avery to continue.

"He was on his last tour. His contract was up, he was getting out, and we were finally going to have a big reception since we'd gone down to the courthouse initially." She laughs absently. "After watching me watch *Say Yes to the Dress* a bazillion times, Justin was so thrilled knowing Ellis Events was taking off."

"I'll bet." I smile over the lump in my throat.

Avery shrugs.

"Anyway, I don't want to go too deep. My point in telling you all this is that we've gotten to know each other in snippets through Morgan and Dante, and strangely…from the Gossip Set." She giggles. "I'd love for us to connect without the middle people. I'm hoping, in sharing real pieces of myself, maybe we'll *both* be inclined to do so…"

Before I get the words out to tell her, "Of course, yes, I want a clean slate," I hear her repeatedly muttering *please* under her breath.

Something like joy jolts through me as we circle back to her question.

"I'd love you." I gasp, quickly correcting myself. "I meant I'd love to get to know each other on our terms. Or whatever…"

She deflates into a fit of giggles.

"This is too good. Serious Stefano the suit with a slip of the tongue…" Avery presses a hand to her heart, her shoulders shaking. "Who would've thought we'd ever see the day?"

"Come on, Pollyanna… You're making fun of my suits again when you're carrying around that gigantic pink flower-power planner in this digital age?"

We both shake our heads.

We're both shocked to be enjoying this exchange more than we could've imagined.

"You laugh but analog doesn't run out of battery or overheat in the sun." Avery holds up her hands in mock surrender. A permanent smile is etched on her face as she seems to regroup. "All jokes aside, I'm happy. This has been weighing on me since yesterday."

"Me too."

Avery radiates with relief as she segues to how full her heart was watching me talk with Ace. Naturally, we fall into a full-blown *Cars* conversation before she recaps the dress-shopping shenanigans, and how much she loves the tight relationship my family shares. In the same way, her mother, Ace, and the Sister Circle keep her lifted and light.

Not some new man.

Sometime after she details the ins and outs of her flourishing business and a Hollywood glamor wedding she's currently planning. I realize that there's a great chance I'm enamored with Avery Ellis. Whether I'm ready or not, I want to know this woman who loves her friends fiercely, forgives easily, and smiles through chaotic days.

The air settles for all of five seconds.

Then Avery pops back up, leaning close to her screen.

"But there's something you should know about me." In her background, her phone rings, and she silences it before centering her attention on me again. "I'm super competitive, so if you really want to prove how cool we are, we *must* have the best pairs entrance dance at the ceremony."

Only slightly concerned what other requests Morgan gave Avery yesterday, I lean in, too.

"Say less."

If we're forging *whatever* together, it's got to be the best.

Avery slaps her hands on her desk, her face beaming before she can't contain it any longer.

Her infectious laugh sets the tone for the rest of the meeting. She tells me Ace can't stop talking about me, and that he's named one of his cars Stefano, which makes my whole heart ache. Then we make plans to meet next Saturday at my place in the city—hers is a little tight and has toys bursting from its seams. We'll lay the groundwork, pick a song while wine-tasting for the wedding menu, and practice our dance before the Champagne Sip.

Yes, yet another wedding festivity that Avery's added to our calendar since we last spoke.

The first weekend in August, the wedding party will meet at a champagne bar, as sort of a mixer, to get to know each other before they're—not Avery and me—thrown into the dancing deep end to choreograph a show-stopping routine.

All in all, I'm excited about the turn our whatever is taking.

I love how talkative and free, comfortable she is with me. I love that we're about to make up some silly, lighthearted dance. More than that, I love that, during this singular meeting, I've felt more like myself than I have in nearly a year.

WHEN MORGAN AND Dante finally enter the ChatVideo room, Avery shares the agenda on her screen.

AGENDA
PROJECT COMPLETIONS FROM LAST WEEK
THIS WEEK'S PROJECTS (10–8 MONTHS ITEMS)
BRIDE AND GROOM ADDITIONAL REQUESTS
QUESTIONS

As Avery speaks, the PowerPoint page turns to a checklist of last week's projects. All business, she checks off choose a date, wedding style, venue selection, assembling a team of wedding pros, and select a fairy-tale wedding dress.

Avery and Morgan break out into squeals and happy clapping.

Dante and I share an exhausted glance.

"So, before we switch to Stefano's projects, Morgan, we've got a jeweler appointment this coming Tuesday to purchase Dante's ring, save-the-dates and invitations have been designed, and..." She pulls in a small breath, then sags on the desk. "Look, I know we're not on your additional requests yet, but guys, if you're really going for fifty guests, we need to do some serious cutting and send the save-the-dates this week, *Dante*..."

Oof!

Avery shoots daggers at him through the screen.

Morgan elbows him, and whispers out the side of her mouth, I'm guessing reminding him what we're discussing.

He groans.

As expected, the guest list is evidently a point of contention.

"Yeah, I'll talk to Mom this week," he says.

"Great, now, I want to confirm the wedding party members." Avery reads from her huge pink planner, "On the bride's side, we've got Monica, Valerie, Seneca, Chiara, and me, for a total of five. On the groom's, there's Stefano, Marcello, Mike, Everett, and..." She glances over her notes. "Looks like, Jameson, also, for a grand total of five."

"Dante, seriously?" I ask.

"What?" My brother's head pops up again guiltily from his phone where I'm sure he's been sneaking to watch baseball.

"Jameson for a groomsman?" I ask. "What are you trying to do?"

He shrugs.

Apparently, it's no big deal to include—and partner—a guy who grew up with our sister and who abruptly ended their friendship without explanation.

"Does Chiara know?" I ask.

"Should Chiara care when she's dating his best friend?"

Dante counters.

A long silence ensues.

Luckily, Avery stays her course, confirming Ace will be ring bearer, while I chime in, rounding out the wedding party and officially naming Dylan's daughter, Danielle, as flower girl.

Honestly, we really are the dream team.

After she passes me the project baton, the PowerPoint pages turns again, and I check off my completed lodging and catering projects. In no time, we divvy up this week's tasks: wedding party attire (Avery); book officiant (my cousin, Enzo); mail save-the-dates (Avery); bridal undergarments (not touching that one with a ten-foot pole), and registries (Avery). With Avery's business, she's already secured a photographer, videographer, deejay, and florist. She's even reached out to her bridal magazine editor clients about featuring the wedding.

I'm feeling like a slacker.

The page turns on the screen, and BRIDE AND GROOM ADDITIONAL REQUESTS is in bold at the center.

Avery closes her planner.

"Down to our last order of business..." She quirks a small smile. "We've covered the entrances dances and the smaller guest list, but I wanted to bring this last one to Stefano's attention."

"Sure, let me know how I can help," I say, eager to pull my weight. *Even if my mind has time-traveled to next Saturday, picturing Avery and me swaying to the beat.*

"Well, it seems Victoria requested to invite Carina."

Shit.

CHAPTER TEN
Avery

THE FOLLOWING SATURDAY afternoon, I pull up to Stefano's ultra-chic high-rise building on the edge of Lower Nob Hill. A swift and friendly valet takes the keys from my hands, and a bright-eyed doorman directs me to a grand marble concierge desk, where I'm currently shaking like a leaf behind a grocery delivery guy loaded up with bags hanging from his arms.

I pull in a long breath, strangely nervous to see Stefano.

As I slowly release it, the sleek, raven-haired concierge in a pristine red suit waves him over.

"Hello, again, friend." She smiles and hovers her fingers over the keyboard. "Twice in one day, huh? Who've we got this time?"

"Let's see, it's got to be…" The guy tugs around one of the bags to scan the sticker affixed to the side. Surprise etches the lines of his forehead. "Ah, shoot. It's Fortemani."

I've got no idea why a grocery delivery would elicit this level of shock from them, but it does.

The woman's confused gaze darts briefly to his strained arms as he hinges his weight onto the desk. Her brows braided together, she turns, picking up the phone and resting it on her ear before she presses a few buttons.

"Hello, Mr. Fortemani, we've got a gentleman here in the lobby with a grocery pickup for you... Uh-huh, yes. I'll send him right up."

When she ends the call, the man quickly thanks her, going on about the size of the pickup this go-around. Then he hikes up the bags again and shrugs with a *see you later*, and he walks away.

But now I've got questions, too.

Is it simply that he rarely uses grocery delivery services?

The guy recognized his name, though. So, maybe, it's the contents of his order. But what strange things could he have purchased for a casual Dream Team night to pick music and choreograph a dance? Worse yet—and this is really reaching, based solely on out-of-context reactions from two people I don't know—but what if his plans the night of the dress shopping appointment were with a woman? Not just any woman. What if she's Carina, and Stefano's giving their marriage another shot?

The way Stefano clammed up when I told him Victoria wants to invite Carina to the wedding—the way he hasn't brought it up since—my early arrival could easily be cutting into their dinner date.

Shoot, shoot, shoot, shoot.

I turn on my heel toward the smiling doorman just as the woman swivels forward, glancing directly at me.

"I can help you here," she says.

I swallow and turn back.

"Hi...yes, I'm here to see him, too. Mr. Fortemani," I

say. "I'm a little early so I can come back—"

"Your name, miss?"

"Uh, Avery Fortemani," I say, slapping a hand over my face, cringing at my error. "Sorry, I'm Avery *Ellis*, here to see Stefano *Fortemani*."

The woman flashes me a wide, knowing smile that, if I'm reading this correctly, says, *if you didn't want it to be a date then why did you try on five outfits? Why are you sweating and shaking? Why did you awkwardly sit through multiple Chat-Videos with him and shamelessly google his address to prepare for "dance practice?" And for the love of God, WHY are you slapping this barely divorced man's last name onto yours, and standing there with a personalized gift, if you aren't shamelessly hoping for a date, hmm?*

Obviously, her smile is nosy.

And correct.

I've been a nervous wreck because I thought I felt a shift between us. One day, we were at each other's throats. Then I caught him with Ace, and we cleared the slate. I went and overshared about Justin. Now, instead of funny jokes and verbal jabs about his starched suits and my planner bible, I've started looking forward to seeing him, digitally or otherwise.

Suddenly, I'm noticing how nice his smile is and how large his hands are. Which, *okay*... They're big, so of course, my mind pours right down the drain to the gutter, imagining what else might be as big on him.

One week of niceties.

That's all it took, and now I'm naively standing here holding a bag full of personalized gifts.

I've got a dang prickly pear cactus with a tiny card that

says, "Big Prick Energy. Thanks for inviting me over."

Ugh. I thought it was cute.

But now, it just feels like overkill.

"It's no problem for me to come back in an hour."

I force a small smile as she glances back to her screen and taps over the keys. "Ah, here you are. You're right, he isn't expecting you for an hour, but I'm sure it'll be a pleasant surprise."

For whom?

The nosy smile stretches wide on her red lips.

She fans out her hand across the lobby to the elevator bank where the grocery guy is waiting, too.

After I thank her, I rush over, just as the doors open, and the man nearly drops one of the bags.

"Here, let me help, you," I say, hooking my tote over my shoulder, and leaning down to take one armful of bags from him.

As we step inside the spacious mirrored elevator, he releases a long breath.

"Thank you, sis. I thought this one was a goner." An appreciative smile twists the lines of his rich brown skin. "I tell you, this guy must be having a fancy party, all the stuff he bought."

Heat creeps up from my neck to my cheeks.

The entire way up to the twelfth floor and down the elegantly finished hallway to Stefano's door, I'm silently praying I'm not crashing his second-chance romance. As the guy, who turns out to be super talkative and nice, knocks on the door, I hold my breath until I'm light-headed.

Then the door swings open on the picture of a certified

bachelor with baseball blaring from the television.

A gasp escapes my lips.

Suddenly, my nerves and conclusion hopping make perfect sense. I've been to his family functions. His mother is like my new best friend. I planned his brother's secret proposal to my best friend, and we've sat through several ChatVideos together now. But other than a couple glimpses of him listening to freaking Johnny Timmons in his car and talking to Ace, I've never witnessed Stefano Fortemani without his armor.

Not in any real way, at least.

But this version…

This shields-down, in-his-element, easy black T-shirt and jeans silver fox in his ultra-chic den?

Good God this is what a grown-up crush feels like.

Forget teenage dreams and bad boys. I want a sexy-ass full-grown man who owns real estate, a vineyard, and state-of-the-art, wildly expensive vacuum cleaners. I want to wind down with wine and cheese with the backdrop of sweeping city views in all directions. I want to memorize the sharp angles and lines of his obscenely beautiful face, run my hand through his messy salt-and-pepper curls while I gaze into his depthless dark eyes. For all that's good and holy in this world, I just want this man who makes a costume change feel like foreplay.

"Avery?"

Shoot, I'm staring.

He presses his hands down his jeans, hanging loosely, appetizingly low around his strong hips.

My lungs constrict and my heart stutters, but I force myself to focus on his soft gaze.

"I carried some bags," I say, but it lands with as much conviction as Baby carrying a watermelon before Johnny Castle banned her from corners.

Speaking of corners, the edges of his mouth lift.

He doesn't even bother hiding his smile.

What am I going to do though? I sound like a complete idiot.

A laugh trickles pathetically out me as Stefano steps back to allow us inside to drop off the bags.

As he tips the delivery guy and walks him to the door, I briefly take in his space.

Heaped mahogany bookshelves and stately furniture fuse a warm palette with fine finishes and cool blues and grays. Natural light filters through floor-to-ceiling windows onto gray oak floors and two-tone area rugs. It's modern-age luxury, single living meets timeless comfort and escape.

It's him.

The door slams shut behind me.

"So, you carried bags?" He raises an amused eyebrow.

"Look, I did my good deed for the day. Can you say the same?"

He brushes his gaze down over my black Vans and leggings, before he registers the oversized gray DREAM TEAM shirt I made.

"Is that—"

"A custom shirt I designed special for this occasion?" I nod, eagerly reaching into my purse. "And did I make a matching one for you? Why yes. Yes, I did."

"Oh, well in that case." Stefano chuckles.

"Morgan and I were at the jeweler picking out Dante's ring on Tuesday. She did a great job, by the way. And anyway, I got to thinking about dancing today, and I wasn't sure you owned anything other than suits, so…"

He barks out a deep, throaty laugh.

Taking his DREAM TEAM shirt by the collar, I flounce it out, then flip it over. "And that's not all…" I say, tickled as he reads the bold black writing sprawled across the back.

I DON'T ALWAYS WEAR SUITS BUT WHEN
I…WAIT…YES I DO.

He snickers.

"Well, this didn't hold up."

"Don't feel bad," I say, angling my back to him so he can read mine.

I DON'T ALWAYS HAUL AROUND A GIANT PINK
PLANNER BIBLE BUT WHEN I…WAIT…YES, I DO.

Stefano tucks his lips between his teeth and nods.

I laugh.

"Okay, I don't actually have it with me either, but the thought was there." I playfully swat his arm. "Look, if you're not nice to me as a first-time guest, I'm not going to give you the other gift I brought for you."

He covers his heart with his hand. "So there really is more."

"And not just a dope wedding-themed playlist…"

On the TV someone hits a home run, and the commentator yells, "Let's go! This ain't Denny's but that's a *GRAND SLAM!*"

The crowd goes wild with cheers.

We stare a beat too long.

Thankfully, Stefano breaks eye contact first. Every inch of my body is tingling as I follow him away from the foyer, bickering about the benefits of a deejay versus the orchestra as we enter the spacious chef's kitchen where we double-team unloading the grocery bags. Which, funny enough, includes vegetable and deli platters, a party sub, two king-size Snickers, and about five drink options.

"I didn't know what you might be hungry for," he says.

All at once, I realize this large order isn't his norm.

My heart rams against my ribs.

"You ordered all of this for me?" I ask.

He shrugs. "Figured the least I could do is feed you if you're coming here with music, moves, and custom DREAM TEAM shirts."

The moment feels light as a rock.

"All right, then." I peel off the plastic film on the veggie platter, dip a celery stick in the ranch dressing, and stick it in my mouth. "Grab your dancing shoes, point me to the Bluetooth handle for your speaker, and let's pick a song."

Twenty minutes zip by with us feasting on ranch-drenched vegetables and sipping Prosecco as he vetoes ninety percent of my playlist.

"What about Dinah Washington? A little 'September in the Rain' or 'Time of My Life' from *Dirty Dancing*?" he suggests randomly.

I about fall out, laughing.

"Sir, we're not about to be foxtrotting and tangoing into this wedding ceremony." I go back to searching through my music library. "At this point, I just need to make sure you can dance?"

I try—and immediately fail—not to look at his lips.

"Are you questioning my moves?"

He has the nerve to look adorably offended.

Then he's rounding the kitchen island and tugging me up off my barstool. He guides me with his large, firm hand at the small of my back until we're in the middle of the living room for all of Major League Baseball to see us. In a total GQ move, he taps and swipes through his phone, silencing the television, before a dramatic succession of drums, violins, and bandoneons fill the air.

My right hand is gripped in his left as he glides his other lower. With seamless movements, he guides me all over his condo.

I feel like a rag doll.

A hot-and-bothered one whose anatomically correct parts are currently throbbing with need.

Lord, give me the strength.

Suddenly, we're back in the open.

In a quick and firm move, he twirls me out, and snaps me back until my body is molded to his. My leg is hooked over his hip, my chin nestled in the crook of his neck, our chests pressed flush and heaving against each other.

If he calls me good girl, I'm a goner.

As we slowly pull back, the look in his eyes dares me to be ashamed of my apparent newfound silver-fox fetish.

Why I thought this man could possibly have no moves is beyond me. I was sorely mistaken, and whatever that was... I want to do it again, faster and horizontal.

That's where my mind is, descending to gutter levels when Stefano withdraws. Not all the way, just enough so that our faces are a breath apart and we're staring achingly into each other's hungry eyes.

I should pull away.

I should be the level-headed one here, considering we're both healing from the worst kind of loss, and anything between us would only be hormones and flesh. But Stefano's arm feels so good banded protectively around my waist. And I haven't been held by a man, felt so precious in his grasp in…far too long.

So, when Stefano leans in and slants his mouth over mine, waiting for me to reciprocate, I do. I eagerly part my lips, giving him access to deepen the kiss. To taste my moans and feel how much my body craves him.

Like a switch flip, we go from torturously holding back to a mess of needy hands in gorgeous silver-lined curls—his, not mine—and breathless whimpers.

Good God, every inch of him invades my senses. He smells so good. Sweet and clean. Expensive. And his body is so warm and solid. So hard.

He's all man.

It's been so long since I've been kissed properly, and I don't want it to end.

God, please don't let this end.

But as soon as my prayer up in the air, as I lower my hands to Stefano's waist and slip them under the hem of his shirt, dragging my nails subliminally over his back, telling him I want more, that I need more than kissing, he steps back. His chest rises and falls with shallow breaths, and I see the apology in his dark, penetrating brown eyes.

"I'm sorry."

A war wages in my head between *what the hell just happened* and *please, please let's go back to doing it.*

My entire body throbs, aches for him, and he's apologizing.

"*Okayyy*," I say, stepping back and swiping my phone off the kitchen island. "I think it's safe to say the tango is off the table."

Stefano drags a hand over his face.

I'm humiliated with regret swarming inside me, yet he's visibly relieved.

Averting my gaze, my focus snags.

It's while I'm staring at the tan line on his finger, utterly confused why he stopped the kiss that my mind mercifully pivots.

"That's it!" The song barges through my hazy embarrassment and lightbulbs in my mind. "Jagged Edge. 'Let's Get Married' with Rev Run!"

Despite the awkwardness, Stefano nods and smiles. "It's perfect."

"Right?! It's upbeat, wedding-themed, danceable," I list, getting excited about our—*hopefully* limited touching—routine, rather than my libido raging wildly against me.

I've been physically rejected and I'm horny as hell, but we've got a song!

Silver linings.

With the music pumping from his word-class entertainment center, I scarf down a sandwich, polish off my champagne, and we put together some semblance of four eight-counts that, with practice, should gain us the crown.

Eventually, I gather my things to leave, tucking the tiny cactus in the crook of his couch to discover later. Stefano walks me to the door, and with a terribly awkward side hug, I step out into the hall.

Only when I hear the door snick closed, I can't whip my phone out fast enough.

SISTER CIRCLE CHAT

Avery
911!!!

The entire drive home, I bring my girls up to speed on the Stefano saga—minus the kiss because I'm the only one allowed to freak out, right now. Deep down, the second he pulled back, I sensed his mental combat, so I'm only half relieved when Monica contends that our emotions are running high and that I shouldn't draw any conclusions just yet. So, I'm going to take my cue from him, we all agree.

Real simple.

It's not like my emotions—and now, my libido—are involved or anything.

CHAPTER ELEVEN
Stefano

A WEEK LATER, the wedding party erupts in applause as I enter the private wine-tasting room at Il Sapore.

"Ayyy! There he is. The man, the myth…" Dante, up off his chair, and striding toward me, beams like I'm the man of the hour as he slaps a heavy-handed arm over my shoulder and fist-pumps the air "…the legend!"

More cheers.

It's a bit much, if you ask me, but I play along.

For the past twenty minutes, I've been circling the block looking for parking. Not surprising, I've learned my lesson that arriving last means I'll be in the spotlight.

"Thank you for the warm welcome." I chuckle, waving to the group as I scan the white-clothed twelve-seater table for the only empty chair.

I'm placed beside Avery. Initially, the seating arrangement doesn't strike me as odd.

Starting at the head of the table closest to the door, Chiara is next to her paired groomsmen Jameson at her left. Beside him, Seneca and Mike. Then Valerie and Everett. Dante's at the opposite end of the table, with Morgan at his left, followed by Avery, which leaves me between Marcello and Monica to round out the group.

Makes perfect sense.

But then Marcello, my loudest, most opinionated— craves the center of attention—younger brother shoots me a quick glance before tearing his focus away.

Now, I've seen this *you've done it this time* expression too many times. It's his best and worst quality because his face tells on him.

So, when Dante obnoxiously announces, "Let the Champagne Sip begin!" I amble down the right side of the table, muttering hellos, and squeeze Marcello's shoulder before I settle in between him and Avery.

Only, this time, he wordlessly tips his chin to me.

My face contorts.

Whatever is bothering him, it's much worse than I initially thought.

Naturally, it's this moment that Dante throws his head back, laughing loudly, at the other end of the table.

When I turn, Avery nudges my shoulder with hers. Reluctantly, I hazard a look at her.

"Hey. Good to see you," she whispers.

"You too. You too," I repeat, nervously as her eyes rake appreciatively over me. "I tell you, parking in this city is brutal." I flash her a small smile, still wary how we're going to get this runaway lust train back on the track after that tongue tango.

But this is a great start.

Suffice to say, I'm hoping for an easy, casual, *slow* getting to know each other period. Even if, unbidden, images of

Avery in my arms, my lips pressed to hers, insist on filling my head.

I scratch at my beard scruff.

"Oh, I meant to tell you, we got the magazine feature." She squeals.

Excitement zips through me.

"Wow, that's amazing."

"Yeah, *Vines + Vineyards* is going to do a full-page spread." She nods. "*Blissful Bride* and *Northern Living* agreed to list it in their spring issues next year, too."

At her side, Morgan elbows her.

"Oh, one sec," she says.

As soon as she turns away, though, I steal another quick glance at Marcello. But I don't get the chance to lean in and chat. No, because this is an Avery Ellis event.

On cue, she clinks her water glass with a fork to stop the chatter.

"Now, that everyone is here, I'm thrilled to kick off The Fortemani-Forster Champagne Sip." Immediately, she deep-dives into the night's agenda. Of course, there's a structured plan for how this evening is going to go.

I suppress a laugh.

Over the next ten minutes, she outlines the plan. First, we'll enjoy a variety of champagne (graciously, she's request-ed the Fortemani brand sparkling wine) and light fare (flatbreads, cheese, and meat charcuterie boards). Responsi-bly, she pauses to highlight the availability of local rideshare options afterward for safe driving. Then she bullet points mixing and music in breakout pairs, giving us a chance to introduce ourselves, discuss wedding attire and theme, as well as—and I suspect this is the ulterior motive—the ceremony entrance dances.

"Now, Stefano and I've got this in the bag…" She giggles. "But we welcome your best efforts in this dance-off."

Laughter lifts the room.

"We'll see about that." Chiara elbows Jameson.

My sister was on dance teams from elementary to college. Their "team" is likely our biggest competition, so I know she'll be gunning for us.

"Nothing like starting off a life together with a little competitive spirit," Seneca quips.

As I glance over to Dante to see his reaction, I'm surprised he isn't laughing.

Nor is Morgan.

In fact, they're not even paying attention. He and Morgan are huddled close, whispering.

Shit.

Surveying Marcello in my periphery, I have a feeling my brothers know something I don't.

Just then, the door to our private room opens and a line of servers festively file in, setting the food, champagne flutes, and chilled bottles along the center of the table. A server pops the champagne, and suddenly there's music and the hum of excited chatter, jumpstarting the party. An upbeat, soulful classic buzzes on low while the group picks and grazes from the boards and platters. Me? I'm reading the liveliness of the room, wondering why my brothers' distracted demeanors don't match.

"Oh my God, everything looks amazing," Avery hums.

She twists to chat with the manager beside her, going on

and on about how gorgeous the place is and how much she loves the idea of music and good company coupled with great wine and food.

She'll be talking for five minutes, bare minimum.

It feels like my opening.

Except, as I angle my body toward Marcello, he beats me to the chase. With his attention centered across the table on Mike, he shifts slightly in my direction.

Out of the side of his mouth, he discreetly, quietly asks, "Are you good?"

I almost laugh. He looks like he's just declared self-imposed celibacy, and he's asking if I'm all right?

"Yeah, of course. I'm the best man, right?" I snort, tossing him another searching glance. "I ended up parking two blocks away but at least I doubled my step goal."

This is his chance.

If nothing is wrong, Marcello should relax. He'll slouch into the bend of his chair, sigh, then pop a cheesy bruschetta bite into his mouth. He'll pour himself a generous glass of champagne and brush off his worries because that's what my unaffected thirty-two-year-old brother would do.

But Marcello crinkles his brow.

His posture is ramrod straight as he scrapes a hand over his mouth and slowly drags it down his neck.

Aw, hell.

A toxic combination of curiosity and worry get the best of me, and I'm forced to take the bait.

"Why wouldn't I be good?" I counter.

I notice Avery's attention dart between Marcello to me, and I hedge my body toward him, leaning closer.

What's going on? I mouth.

Almost like he doesn't want to draw any attention to us, he slightly averts his gaze. In the back of my mind, I'm banking on this being about something low-energy fixable. A girl who rejected him, or Mother still not trusting him to take on clients without Dante's or my help. He's been vying for more responsibility since he was born.

Neither would be out of the ordinary.

But then he scans the room, slides his phone off the table and opens Instagram to Carina's profile. Then he drops his voice a notch.

"Read the caption," he says.

Then I do.

Like bile, hurt and shame lodge in my throat.

Painstakingly slow, I guide my thumb over a picture of my ex-wife's hand curved to the mural of faint stretch marks adorning her fleshy stomach.

This is joy.
#Newlife #Comingsoon

My cheeks burn with humiliation as Avery stands beside me.

"Okay, it's time for breakouts. You can stay here or go out to the main restaurant. Wherever you want but take your time. Ask the hard questions like what music do they like? What sort of person are they? Should you stare longingly into each other's eyes as you sashay down the aisle?" She giggles. "Make it your own, but make it work!"

Panic rushes over me as the room stirs.

As soon as the others move to find a corner to talk, I

scoot back my chair, nearly tipping it over.

"Is everything okay?" Avery's attention flits to my phone.

My heart pounds in my ears.

I don't have the resolve to quietly grin and bear it in front of a room full of people, though.

"Uh, I…I just need a minute," I say, standing and rushing the door.

Hanging a left out of the private room, away from the restaurant's main seating area, I hurry toward the employee exit at the end of the hall.

A manic energy races through me as I burst through the door into the alley.

My fingers twitch around the cool, tempered glass of my phone. Then I unlock the screen.

For so long, I stare at Carina's photo.

It's not that I'm jealous or that I want her back. This has nothing to do with her new relationship, or even, God willing, a baby. As much as it hurts feeling like my dream of love and family is out of reach, this right now, has everything to do with me.

Why haven't I felt ready to move on?

Why have I been holding back like it's too soon after the divorce?

Clearly, she's got no qualms about it.

At the core, though, I hate not knowing *how* to start over. There's no book or instruction manual for this. I'm struggling just to kiss another woman, who's gorgeous and fun-loving, and who clearly wanted me as much as I wanted her, and for what? Some arbitrary emotional hump that I need to get over? Because my ego is bruised by the optics?

I hold my breath.

Twelve years of marriage plus three more dating, now we're divorced and she's pregnant with another man's child. Meanwhile, I'm putting in hours at the gym and the winery, living the only life I've known? Anticipating more disappointment when I find someone new?

"Dammit."

My stare is fixed on my phone, preparing to block Carina, so I flinch when Avery barges through the door looking like a beautiful flame.

Fire burns in her blazing brown eyes. Her chest swells with steam as she grimaces, taking in the dark, narrow space, bricked in on either side of us.

Then her focus crashes onto me.

"Why are you like this, Stefano Fortemani?" She's fuming mad, but her voice wavers.

"I'm sorry, I didn't mean to—"

"God, I don't know why I even care." She scoffs and flicks her gaze upward. "I guess, I just want to understand all the mixed signals. Obviously, you're just regaining your footing after the divorce. That part, I get. But one second, we're at each other's throats nonstop, then you kissed me... I figured, even if it was baby steps then—"

I clear my throat.

I don't want to invalidate her feelings, but I don't want to hear the rest of that wholly untrue, conditional statement.

"Avery, this isn't about you," I say, sharply.

"Oh, well, in that case, please continue confusing the hell out of me." She releases a scornful laugh. "Yes, let's play tug-o-war with my emotions since this is all a game to you, and you're the only one involved with feelings."

She arches an eyebrow.

Still, I inch closer.

"Please don't deny it." She frowns. "I saw the looks you and Dante exchanged, and the whispering with Marcello. You've barely strung together two words to talk to me. Even now, it's killing you being *alone* with me out here."

Her shoulders relax.

Every cell on my body tingles with the urge to tell her how wrong she is. How the last time we were together, I had to physically restrain myself from reaching for her because how could something that felt so right, be wrong? How could I say I loved my ex-wife, then jump so quickly, willingly into another woman's arms?

But I don't say any of that.

Avery shakes her head, disappointment underscoring her sigh.

"Not that it matters to you, but I knew from the second you pulled back..." She breaks off, emotion steeping her silence. "When I left, I called my girls, and the first thing Monica said was to take my cues from you. Well, I've been paying attention. All the signs are telling me not to care. Not to make excuses. I should be running..."

But she doesn't run.

Like her feet are rooted to the ground, she's completely still, and I'm the one moved.

Strangely, my world shifts into focus.

Something I've done upset her. Affected her. Shouldn't I be paying attention to the people, the *person*, fighting for space in my life?

Hell, I've been giving Dante shit about delaying his engagement, but maybe he's got the right idea. Maybe, I should just screw all the podcasts telling me not to rush into a relationship. Maybe, time, maturity, age, none of it matters.

I tuck my phone away, step closer, and take her hand in mine, lifting it to my chest, so she can feel what she does to me.

"Don't run," I plead, quietly.

Avery looks like she's going to protest then thinks better of it. Her eyes brighten to a firework display of ambers and golden browns as she slowly registers the undeniable, racing evidence of my nerves.

Surveying me with caution, she softly asks, "Why?"

My voice, gruff with desperation, cuts against my own ears.

"Because I'd be a fool not to tear down every emotional and physical barrier for you, Avery Ellis. Because it's been a while, and I'm learning how to start over. Because I'd be the luckiest man alive to have the chance to try with you...*if* you're willing to be patient with a grumpy silver fox with 'Big Prick Energy'."

"You know that little cactus is the cutest thing you've ever seen." Avery giggles.

"Hey, people say we've got a lot in common."

She smiles sweetly. "Are you ever going to let me live the silver-fox thing down?"

"Not a chance, Pollyanna."

Tracing her teeth over her lower lip, she crawls her fingers over the taut slopes of my chest, like fuel, driving me wild.

"You should know that name has a very 'yes, daddy, I've been a bad, *bad* girl,' feel to it." Avery giggles again, like she didn't, with a single sentence, harden every muscle in my body.

My Adam's apple bobs. "I'm sorry. I'm a little out of practice."

"Oh, don't go selling yourself short. If you play your cards right, I might let you bend me over your knee…"

Is she for real?

Almost like she hears the questions flashing across my mind, Avery tugs me down by my tie, holding me a breath apart. Scanning the empty alley, she lowers her voice. "How bad do you want me, Stefano?"

Damn.

All the humor ebbs, before a tidal wave of desire flows over me.

Carefully, wordlessly and with purpose, I cradle her beautiful face in my hands. My breaths come fast and shallow as I let my mouth collide with hers. With her needy hands skating over the tense muscles of my back. With each brush of our lips, I inhale deeply, sinking into the soft swell of her lips until she clings to me.

But then she stumbles back, guiding me toward the arch of the boarded-off doorframe neighboring Il Sapore.

Her back to the wall, she tilts her pelvis into me, and instantly I know I don't stand a chance of going slow.

Closing my eyes against the sudden, insatiable, carnal need to feel her flesh to flesh, I deepen the kiss. I let my body absorb the feel of her round breasts pressing into me.

Again, she mouths into the kiss, "How bad do you want me, Stefano?"

Fire sears my back beneath her fingertips as she trembles and wilts in my arms.

Except, Carina's photo flashes in my head, making me feel like I'm being reactionary.

If Avery and I do this, I need to know it's intentional. I need to ensure we both want this for the right reasons.

Breaking the kiss, I withdraw just enough to see search her eyes. "Avery, what are you saying?"

She drags my fingertips up her thigh until her dress rides up. "Tear down the physical barrier," she says, confusing me by the turn of phrase. Until I realize they're my words applied seamlessly, interchangeably to us. "Start over with me. *Try* with me." *Make me feel wanted again.*

And that's what we do.

In the most uninhibited, unguarded and vulnerable way, we kiss deliberately, coaxing whimpers and moans from each other, the way I imagine we've long yearned for from a lover. As I drag up her dress hem and tear away her panties, she unfastens my pants, dipping her warm fingers over the waistband. With my full length hardening in her hands, and my mouth trailing along her neck, down to the curves of her breasts, her hip, hooked over mine, we edge further.

I'm aching to be inside her. I've never wanted anything so bad in my life.

Shit.

"I don't have anything." Condoms, I mean, which in hindsight, maybe it would've been smarter to mention this earlier. I swallow. "We should stop now…"

But Avery, continues working me in long, fast strokes, readying me. Then she presses her body flush to my chest, and it feels too good. *And it's been too damn long.*

"Uh, my last test…" She pants, giggling at my tongue in her ear. "It was three years ago, but it was clear, and as you can tell, I haven't been with anyone."

"Mine was a year ago." I huff out a laugh. "Clear here, too."

"I remember." Her lips curve, and heats swarm my cheeks, remembering that first ChatVideo log-in when I'd unknowingly announced how long it's been since I had sex. "So, pull-out, then?" Avery cringes.

I drop my head on her chest, amused and horrified that I'm single again, weighing the trustworthiness of the pull-out method and the dire need to bed a woman who has my knees weak for her.

We both burst out laughing.

"What?" Avery giggles again. "My boob is on your forehead and your hand is dangerously close to my inner thigh. My very bare inner goods are out here because my panties are tattered and on the ground. And if you think you're getting this wooden log back into those pants…"

"A log?"

Her eyes sparkle with amusement. "Neither one of us should go back in there without getting this out of our systems."

"So, we're really doing this?" I ask, my desperation indirectly growing with my waning restraint.

"Preferably, quickly," she quips. "Let's have fun until it isn't anymore."

Now, we're both laughing uncontrollably as we refocus our stroking and kissing. I lift her by the waist, and she centers my erection between her very bare thighs.

Opening for me, Avery arches, slowly taking me whole.

"Are you okay?" I ask.

She's clinging to me, her body molded to mine. "Um, you're…a little bigger than I'm used to."

"Do you want to stop?"

Avery shakes her head. She wants more.

So, I take it slow, careful not to hurt her as she arches again, meeting my first thrust. We move like this, easy with long strokes until she's used to me. Soon, we wilt into the fit and feel, relishing the mind-numbing pleasure.

"Jesus, it's been so long," I groan.

Every breath on her neck and gasp in my ear. Every touch. We're synchronized, tailored for each other. We're lighthearted and heady while we cling to each other, inching toward ecstasy, and it's perfectly us. Clashing, delicious friction, joy, vulnerably kissing and pleasing one another, in—*this falsely secluded*—public, no less…

My God, I want to try this, and *so* much more with Avery Ellis.

That's what scares me, though.

I'm the one who advised my brother against rushing in. I know the glaring danger signs ahead, and I don't care.

CHAPTER TWELVE
Avery

"DON'T YOU SLEEP?" Stefano groans underneath my pillow as I snuggle into his big spoon.

"Listen, I don't know what you want from me…" I'm only half-joking as I venture, "Do you know how long it's been since I woke up to a handsome, sweet, certifiably funny, attentive, virile, strong, sexy—"

He takes the bait.

Peeking out his sleepy head, Stefano squints at the light streaming through the blinds, his voice thick with sleep as he instructs me to, "Please continue."

"…Hard-nosed, no-nonsense, stoic, austere, quietly assessing, broody, intense man in my bed?"

Stefano deflates onto the pillow.

"Don't forget smart." He chuckles, gliding his large warm hand over my waist. He tugs me flush to his strong, hard frame, and my *Lord*… It feels so good waking to this.

Heat dances over my skin, sending tingles down my spine, and I, shamelessly giddy, arch my back into him.

"Hey, when I say every single one of those words turns me on…" I'm not surprised by the truth in my admission, despite the whiplash roller coaster we've been on to get here.

Stefano nuzzles into the curve of my neck, kissing along my nape.

A soft moan spills out of me.

I glance at the clock on the wall, calculating how many more times we can realistically have sex before Mommy drops off Ace this afternoon.

An hour and a half is plenty, so I reach back, fumbling for him. I'm laughing, not even bothering to hide my amusement when I tease him.

"I still can't believe what you did last night."

Effortlessly, he flips me over to face his shocked smile. "Avery, stop joking about it."

"Sir, it's not my fault you did what you did to me. In an alley, no less, with all our friends and loved ones ten feet away, on the other side of a single brick wall…"

Stefano's mouth falls comically open.

I can practically see his brain short-circuiting.

We said we wouldn't tell anyone, even though our friends and his siblings, probably know us better than our parents. Yet, last night, we walked our happy selves back into Il Sapore, and played Oscar-worthy roles.

We should've been celebrating my best friend and his brother, mixing and mingling. Yet, we spent the rest of the evening stealing glances we had no business taking.

And the champagne?

BIG MISTAKE!

Magnifying the senses when we were still fresh on the skin? When I could smell him on me, us on me? *Feel him moving with purpose inside me?*

I just know he's still figuring how he's going to spin this. He's inwardly berating himself for acting out of character and doing what we did then walking back in that room looking guilty as all get-out. Predictably, this devastatingly handsome man who recharged my batteries is likely still worried about what Dante and Morgan will think, after he went on and on about an extended engagement.

"Jesus, Avery." He rubs his face. "Please stop saying it like that."

I hesitate, then nod.

Reaching my hand up, I run my fingers through his hair, kiss his nose.

A heavy sigh spills out of me.

The air electrifies.

"God, I love your curls."

"Yeah?" He seems shocked. "Even with the gray? Because I was thinking about dyeing it—"

"No, it's the perfect mix of black and silver, and…" My insides ache with need. "Just…leave it."

"Okay, I will." A calm smile smooths his expression.

I can tell he's turning over something in his head. Then his gaze flits briefly to my hair.

To my wig.

"I know you're probably wondering how my hair always looks this fabulous…" I jest.

"Actually, I love your hair. I just wondered if maybe, there was a story behind it."

I roll onto my back, letting my sigh plume out of me.

"Would it make sense to you if I said it's about control?"

"Your choice," he reasons.

Tossing Stefano a sidelong glance, I see the genuine interest in his eyes. He wants to understand, and based on the hurt he's been through, he might be the only person I know who might.

"It was after I lost Justin." That familiar pang of sadness stirs in my gut. "I felt like my life was spinning out. I was a widow and single mom. I was struggling to understand the legalities of moving on without him, looking for signs of him everywhere, then feeling more alone when there were none."

"That must've been so hard."

I chew the inside of my cheek, forcing myself to continue. "I spent so much time in bed, listening to self-help podcasts, and holding on to his clothes because it made me feel closer to him." I shrug, feeling exposed, now that he knows what sparked my thorough list. "Then I hated the guilt I had for accepting so much help from Mommy with Ace or enjoying myself while doing *anything*. Slowly trying to put the pieces of my life back together…it was overwhelming."

Tears prick at my eyes, and Stefano pulls me closer, holding me to his chest, coaxing me to let it out.

"I changed my hair a million times. Cuts, colors, styles, I did it all." My heart wrenches. "I was stuck while the world was moving on. Every day felt like losing him again. Then, one day, I tried a wig, and something clicked. I had so many emotions swirling inside my head that I couldn't get a handle on, couldn't control. But at least I could control what was *on* my head, you know?"

Stefano turns me back to face him. For so long, he stares at me, searching my eyes like he's watching the pictures scrolling across my mind.

"I'm so amazed by you, Avery Ellis."

"I'll be here all week." I flick my gaze upward, hoping to lighten the mood. "So, anyway, relax. We don't have to tell anyone what we did. Or what we want to do," I say, suggestively. "If we want to christen this city...shoot, the entire state of California, that's our business, right?"

I flash him a reassuring smile.

A hot flush washes over my face when he doesn't immediately volunteer for fun, wild Californication with me.

"Yeah," Stefano says, absently. "No one has to know."

And the empath strikes again.

I'm ruining this.

One question—about my *WIG*—and now, I'm emotionally involved.

The thing is, last night no one could've told me a thing about getting freaky on the side of a building, in a sketchy-looking alleyway, where anyone could've happened upon us.

After the way life has cranked us through the wringer...

We rightly deserve to throw caution to the wind. We were living guilt-free in the moment. It wasn't about Justin or Carina. We were just two consenting adults, baring it all for one another. We were in control of our destiny. However, temporary.

Just us having fun.

But after we fixed our clothes and smoothed each other's hair. After he outlined my lips with his thumb, and pressed a final, petal-soft kiss to them, my heart stuttered.

All I wanted was to do it again.

Ten other people were in the room talking and laughing,

but Stefano's voice was the only one I heard. Instead of getting him out of my system, I'd let him in. I forgot what it felt like to be lusted after. For every inch of me to tingle with awareness. I forgot how intoxicating it was to have a man cherish my body, as rough and as tender as I needed.

I'd messed up.

I knew it then, and I feel it now.

Sex aside, I forgot how opening up to a man who genuinely wants to understand me on a deeper level can leave me vulnerable.

I'm not in my twenties, clubbing and hooking up for fun.

That ship has sailed.

I know firsthand what marriage and kids entails. *I know* he's *fragile, too.* So how do I explain forgetting that I never could do one-night stands?

Never.

One word: empath.

I feel. I am feelings. Worst of all, I'm other people's feelings.

My head swims.

I don't know what more to say. We tore down the physical barrier, and now I really want to try this—dating and getting to know each other on a deeper level. Even if we've got to do it in secret. He's lying in my bed in all his naked glory, exposed and beautiful.

But does he want to try with me?

"Say something," I whisper.

As I let my head rest back on my pillow with my insecurities lodged in my throat, Stefano lowers his head onto my chest. Slowly, tenderly he skates his fingertips over the curve of my hip. Then he replaces them with his mouth, brushing fire over my tender skin.

Desire coils low and tight in my belly.

Tossing away the covers, Stefano scoots down, centering himself between my thighs again.

"Look at me," he commands.

It's one ask, one tell, and it changes the entire mood.

He wants to see me as we learn each other intimately. It's loud and playful, switching positions, discovering uncharted erogenous zones, and trying not to laugh as we crash over the edge.

Far be it from me to deny him.

For now, a Sunday practicing our dancing routine, watching *Love & Basketball* in bed as we eat cereal like kids, exploring each other intimately—emotionally dumping on him, however one-sided—it feels like enough.

Until my phone pings with a text from Mommy, informing me she's dropping off my kid in less than five minutes.

"Crap! Get up!" I panic, staring wide-eyed at Stefano as I rush to my closet to grab an easy sundress. "Hurry, put your clothes on. My mom is dropping off Ace, like now."

To his credit, he looks horrified.

Stefano jolts out of bed and yanks on his slacks and dress shirt. I kick over his tie and shoes, for the first time grateful he's a suit-and-tie guy. Nothing like a man who my son and my mother will suspect I've been repeatedly doing the nasty with.

Nope, he simply dropped by after a riveting Sunday morning church sermon to...

"I'm going to go put two coffee mugs on the counter." I gnaw on my fingernail, my mind still whirling around ideas. "Let's say you dropped by to discuss wedding plans. Which…we need to go over the catering and wine, so yes, that's perfect…"

He's fully dressed, now.

Unaffected and put together as we rush into my kitchen.

After I grab the mugs and set them on the counter in front of the barstools, I spin around, expectantly.

"How do I look?" I ask.

"As beautiful as you did the moment we woke up." He chuckles, stepping closer to unravel my twisted bra strap. But then he traces his teeth over his bottom lip and slips his hand under my dress. Sliding his hand between my thighs, he dips his fingers into my panties and inside me like he knows I'm shamefully, mentally calculating if we've got time. *Again.*

I'm halfway considering it, too, when a car door slams shut outside.

"You are trouble." Guiltily jerking away, I rush over to the front window, and yup, it's them.

Close call.

Stefano settles on a barstool looking like a sexy cologne ad. Totally cavalier with his easy smile and endless charm, he flits a glance between the two empty mugs and my dusty Keurig.

"Should I make us some coffee, or…"

"No time."

After smoothing my hands down my dress, I settle one hand on the doorknob.

The second the bell rings, I swing the door open.

"There's my Ace of hearts."

He drops his cars and backpack on the floor, and rushes into my arms like it's been months since we've seen each other instead of yesterday afternoon.

"Grandma got me ice cream!"

"She did?" I shoot Mommy a chastising stare.

She knows what she's doing hopping him up on sugar before she brings him home, so he'll be bouncing off my walls.

But then Stefano laughs, and it's like a theatrical spotlight shifting as he enters stage right.

Half an hour passes, and I might as well not even be in the room.

Mommy and Ace aim and shoot rapid-fire questions at him. How's the wedding planning? How was the Champagne Sip? Did anything "eventful" happen?

I don't miss the sidelong glance Mommy gives our coffee-less mugs.

Even as Stefano responds impressively quick, I know we're doomed, the second I spot the misaligned buttons on his shirt.

That's what it's come down to.

One missed button, and boom! Mommy knows I've been doing the horizontal tango.

Soon, she and her conspiracy eyes go home. By the time Stefano stands to leave, too, I'm fighting back a horrible case of feeling-shaped things. For a moment, I allow myself to get lost in the fantasy. This gorgeous man, falling head over heels in love with me and my son. Us, growing together. Them, bonding over cars and attending Dads and Donuts together at daycare. Our families and friends blending seamlessly. *How can I not fall for him? Then again, who falls for the first person they connect with after marriage ends—one way or another?*

Stefano grins.

"Thanks for the coffee," he says loud enough for Ace to hear in his room.

We both laugh quietly.

But then Stefano pulls in a long breath through his nose and slowly releases it from his mouth, signaling his exit.

My inner voice and my gut perk up at his soft, downcast gaze.

Reading his energy, I expect a sneaky kiss or sly thigh graze before he invites me for a real cup of Joe later. Or, maybe, to ask if we can meet in person this Monday, instead of video chatting. Anything.

So, when he grabs his wallet off the hearth beside Justin's shadow-boxed burial flag, pulls me in for a side hug, and leaves without asking to see me again, it feels like a gut punch.

I know this is me, over-feeling. The man runs a conglomerate of companies; he could have a ton of work on his plate. I've, for sure, piled on planning projects. Who knows? It could be any one of a million reasons, but after last night and this morning, I was hopeful I'd be one.

But maybe it's for the best. Maybe, we just needed to have fun, and get it out of our systems. Maybe, neither of us is ready, and we should focus on the wedding. That way, no one gets hurt.

My heart recoils.

Theoretically.

Ten minutes later, *Cars* is queued up, and I'm back in the kitchen, scrolling through Instagram to quiet my loud insecurities as I make a strong cup of coffee for real.

Out of curiosity, I search for Stefano's profile.

Hey, I'm a glutton for punishment.

It's nothing more than a bunch of goal-slaying, work-ethic quotes and pictures of the Fortemani Vineyard & Winery. Except for one, two years ago, which I gingerly expand with my thumb and forefinger, careful not to like it, lest this man think I'm now a new-age cyberstalking fatal attraction villain.

In the photo, he and Carina are standing side by side, smiling. But it's hard not to notice the canyon-sized gap between them.

Like it's any of my business, now I'm wondering why he didn't post about her. Did he value work more? Or maybe privacy is important to him. Maybe, social media wasn't his thing. Maybe, he loves deep and out loud but doesn't need external validation.

Naturally, my busy brain needs answers.

Sugar and French vanilla creamer swirling in my steaming cup, it feels like go-time.

Now, being the thorough detective that I am, of course, I must tap Carina's profile for more pictures to corroborate my ridiculous—*extremely nosy*—interest in Stefano's marriage.

"Oh my *God*!" I gasp.

Ace comes zipping out of his room, immediately taking inventory of his lined row of cars, like that's the bomb-drop shock that almost made me scald my hand.

"What happened, Mommy?"

"I accidentally spilled my coffee. It was hot." My rudimentary explanation satisfies my kid, but I'm still unable to close my mouth as I take in Carina's Instagram post.

She's already pregnant by that fitness model?

Lord.

I'm all set to make an emergency Sister Circle call to gossip, when I zero on the time she posted.

Yesterday.

Like a *Back to the Future* rewind, scenes from the Champagne Sip, domino-style and in sequential order, fall across my mind.

Carina's post.

Marcello unnaturally quiet and whispering with Stefano before he ducked out into the alley.

The hurt and shame smeared across his face as he tucked his phone away when I walked out.

Us, in that dark doorway, working out his stress. Having fun...

It makes perfect sense.

Stefano wasn't just nervous about being with me. We didn't release weeks' worth of sexual tension. He was trying to forget about his ex-wife's baby news.

Keep it casual so no one gets hurt, right?

I guess I stand corrected.

CHAPTER THIRTEEN
Stefano

A VERY HAS SPENT the past week avoiding me.
Initially, when she canceled our Monday and
Thursday ChatVideo meetings, and sent detailed emails
instead, marking our planning progress, I figured she was
simply busy. She's an event planner. Dante and Morgan's
wedding obviously isn't her sole account.

Understandable.

But now, I'm surrounded by my brother and the
groomsmen, sitting on a cushy leather chesterfield in a
tuxedo shop, mentally recounting another polite and professional, novel-length email that came this morning, and I
know I've screwed myself.

At this point, I can't even deny that I miss Avery. I've
listened to all her podcast recommendations. I made a
Nineties R&B wedding playlist. I've practiced our dance
moves to the point I could lead a boy band. My Web
searches consist of bridal planners to replace her archaic pink
monstrosity, and every brand of toy cars there is. I'm now
officially a *Cars* and Lightning McQueen merch expert.

Disney should hire me.

The worst of it, though?

I'm now sleeping with a stuffed prickly pear cactus whose tiny "Big Prick Energy" card brings me an inordinate amount of joy, daily. When I'm not cursing my fears, of course.

So, yes. I've got feelings for Avery Ellis.

Plain and simple.

Right out the gate, I'm crushing on the first woman I've spent any real time with after my divorce, which is just ridiculous. I'm supposed to be dipping my toe back in the dating waters. Open, as in, to women. Plural. Having *fun until it isn't anymore*, right?

But how can I even think of another woman when, daily, I'm waking up to X-rated reels of us behind Il Sapore? How, when I want to be back at her place in bed with that sexy smile teetering on her full lips every time that I touched her?

Dante snaps his fingers next to my ears, jolting me out of my thoughts. He and the other groomsmen are on their feet, staring at me expectantly like they've called my name a few times.

"Yeah?"

My brother's eyebrows crinkle and he shakes his head. "Space cadet. Let's go."

Shoot, get your head in the game, Stefano.

I scratch my temple, still dazed as I push to my feet and follow them back toward the changing rooms for our tuxedo fittings.

"No, I was just thinking about, uh…" *Avery's raspy, musical laugh, taunting my ears. Her breath on my skin, her fingers in my hair, the heady feeling of her tight body pinned beneath me.*

Shit.

Dante tosses back an impatient glance. "What was that?"

I should spare him the lies.

I'm doing a terrible job of selling them to a guy who knows me inside and out. I'm a person who says what I mean, and with conviction. I don't stutter. For damn sure, I don't space out in front of room full of guys who witnessed me slink back into the Champagne Sip looking like I got bodied.

They know.

I know they know, but Avery and I agreed to keep it under wraps.

If nothing else, I'm a man who *may* have screwed up the best thing I've got going, worrying what our hookup meant going forward, but I keep my word.

"Right, I was saying, we could really elevate this look with matching socks and pocket squares."

Up ahead, Jameson cackles. "Tell me your style is dated without telling me your style is dated." He shoots me a chastising glance over his shoulder. "D, your brother is going to have us looking corny as hell."

Mike and Everett choose nonviolence, giving zero input. Both are married, and probably remember there's always one knucklehead groomsmen who thinks weddings are hookup opportunities masked as fashion shows.

Dante snickers. "Could be a nice personal touch…"

The sales associate smirks as he passes us our tuxes and directs us to our assigned changing room.

"What about suspenders, Stef?" Jameson calls out from behind the curtain.

My brother, steadies my arm, shaking his head.

"I wouldn't hurt him," I say. "Not too bad, anyway."

Dante chuckles.

But after Everett and Mike enter their rooms, my brother pulls me out to the main lobby. In a hushed tone, he asks, "What's really going on with you?"

"What do you mean?"

He tilts his head. "Really? You've been zoned out since you arrived, and now you're letting Jameson get under your skin over socks and suspenders? Come on, be for real with me, Stef. Something's on your mind."

I swallow, debating how to go about this without breaking Avery's trust.

I've tried *not* to think about her.

There's only so many balance sheets to juggle and miles to run on a treadmill when Avery is in my inbox, on my phone, and in my thoughts. I can't stop thinking about her. That story behind her wig hit me harder than playing with her son, for Chrissakes. Even her mother—though, I suspect she knew what we'd been up to—she made me feel comfortable and welcome, no questions asked. It only made me love Avery's and my dynamic more.

Until I freaked out.

Dante must know I'm conflicted because he adds, "Hypothetically speaking. If you can't tell me exactly what's going on, then tell me in broad strokes."

Nodding, I rub my hand over my face.

This could work.

"So, remember when we talked about me being open?"

"Yeah."

"Well, let's just say, I kicked the damn door down."

A ghost of a proud smile plays on his face. "So, you've met someone?"

"Man..." I sigh. "This woman is..." I was going to say something like lightning in a bottle, or magic. But I need to say this in terms that we know like the backs of our hands. "Okay, imagine you've got a bottle of Sauvignon Blanc or Rosé, right?"

Dante shifts on his feet, folding his arms across his chest with an invested smile stretched from ear to ear.

"So, she's young."

See, this is a language we know.

"Mm-hmm. Not too young but aged to perfection. The elements haven't been good to her, but now she's open and ready to enjoy. Ready to be at the center of celebrations..." I slowly dip my chin, my eyebrows rising. *Hint hint.*

Immediately, Dante picks up what I'm putting down.

"Oh shit."

My shoulders sag at my sides. "I know. It's not ideal, and to tell you the truth, I didn't even think she'd...agree with my palate."

His shoulders bounce. "Honestly, I had a feeling. You never really know whether you're immediately going to love it or if it'll clash with what you've...okay, can we skip the wine, and just talk freely, now? Hypothetically, about this woman?"

I chuckle and nod. "You've got to admit, that metaphor was on point, though."

"I'll give it to you. But to *my* point, it doesn't matter what you thought it'd be like with her. What matters is, how's your chemistry? Are you thinking about her constantly, can't get her off your mind?"

"It's ridiculous. I can't work, go to the gym, watch movies, nothing." My cheeks burn with embarrassment. "I just don't understand how it's this bad so fast, but there are...feelings involved."

He nods solemnly, contemplatively.

"What are your reservations?"

Our sales associate, tosses us a quick smile, subliminally telling us we can talk all we want *after* our appointment, so I'm inclined to get to the crux of my issue.

"Here's the kicker—I might've fucked it up." I pull my lips between my teeth, inwardly berating myself for being an idiot.

Dante arches an eyebrow.

"Let's just say, she comes as a package deal, and I got spooked by the kid." I drop my head into my hand. "And the irony isn't lost on me, that he is the coolest little guy. Like, I genuinely could hang out with him and have the best time. He's everything I dreamed about when Carina and I were trying."

"But?"

"I don't know, I just got it in my head that, maybe I was never meant to have kids—"

"With. Carina." He punctuates each word like he wants it to sink in.

I'm not as religious as I am spiritual, but I believe in a higher power. I believe in action and prayer. With Carina, I did both until my hands, back, and knees hurt.

But maybe, this is everything happening for a reason.

What if Carina's pregnancy is further proof of Dante's point? What if kids weren't in the plan for our union?

"Stef, you're thinking too much, and I know this is what you do. You're logic and learning, but there's no how-to book with the answers for this." Dante glances over to the guys standing in their black-and-white penguin suits, watching us, and he holds up a finger. "Listen, this is still new. You don't know how this is going to go, so just have fun."

My heart races as I think about what he's saying means for me. For me, with Avery.

"Action plus prayer. Both are required to heal. Do the work. Get to know *her*. And her kid. Stop thinking logically. Follow your feelings instead of thinking about how much time has passed, rushing in, and what other people will think. There's only two people in this relationship."

I hold up a finger. "Technically, it's three people. And I wouldn't call it a relationship."

Dante chuckles. "Whatever. Just give it a chance. If she makes you feel like the best version of yourself, and you have fun, and you look forward to every day...that's the good stuff. Don't let it go."

"But what if I build this connection with her and her son, and it doesn't work out? What if I don't have what it takes to be a father? I don't want to hurt the kid." *As it is, Avery and I have been hurt enough from our past marriages.*

"The fact that you're worried about that at all, tells me you're already better than you think."

I toss him a questioning glance and he nods, reassuringly.

"Anyway..." Dante swipes his hand over his freshly shaven head. "If you're really into her…" He grins. "Consider talking to Mom about uninviting Carina. Bring this full-bodied Rosé instead. It's hard to move on if your family's still living in the past."

With that nugget of wisdom, he dashes back to the changing room.

Quickly, I tap out a text to Avery.

Hey, everything is looking good on this end with the tux fitting. My cousin Enzo got back to me, and he's down to be the officiant. Dante's working on his vows, too. Wondering if this Thursday, we can meet at the winery to finalize the catering menu and playlist for the deejay.

Just in case, I add another option.

I'm open Saturday, too, if that works better for you. Let me know.

Then, before I can overthink it, I follow it up with…

I'd love to see you.

My mind is heavy as I put my phone away, but I quickly shove aside my worries and insecurities, regretful that I've managed to make this male bonding experience for my brother, about me.

Once we've all donned our tuxes, and we're standing still so we don't get poked by needles, the fitting shenanigans are underway, and I start feeling like myself. Or, at least not wound up with anxiety.

"On a real note, Stef, these pocket squares aren't half-bad," Jameson begrudgingly admits.

I raise my hands, smiling though refusing to take the bait.

But I've known this guy for years, so it doesn't shock me when he starts fishing for details about my conversation with Dante.

"So, y'all are all good, then?" He darts a fishing glance at me in the mirror then to Dante, brows raised as if concerned.

I'm not buying it for a second.

Mike and Everett share a pointed look, suppressing their laughter.

I huff out a sigh. "Ask what you all want to know."

Dante shuts us down though. "Who's up for drinks after this? There's an upscale bar that just opened down the street, and I've been meaning to check it out."

A wave of collective laughter rushes over the guys.

"Drinks at a new bar?" Everett shoots him an impressed look.

"You're not rushing home to Morgan?" Mike guffaws. "It's been two hours. Will y'all survive being apart this long?"

Dante isn't having it.

He immediately lights into Mike and Everett. "I know you two aren't calling me whipped. Let me check your phones. I'll bet you've texted your wives in the last ten minutes."

They both laugh guiltily.

"Shoot, I was going to pay for the first round and have Stef give you details about the bachelor party, but since you've got jokes..." Dante shoots daggers at them in the mirror.

Mike moves to turn to him, and howls from getting poked.

"Instant karma," Jameson says. "Every one of y'all are whipped and thinking about your women." He throws up his hand, fingers splayed wide. "If I'm lying, drop a finger right now, then show me your phone..."

Dante, Mike, and Everett are bent over laughing, guilty as all get-out.

As timely as ever, my phone pings.

I'd love to say I don't know why, but in this moment, every pair of eyes in the room shifts to me.

The corners of my mouth twitch tellingly.

Without a doubt, I know it's Avery responding to my text. Even if it's not, now I'm thinking about her again.

Jameson smirks.

"Yup, that's what I thought," he says.

CHAPTER FOURTEEN

Avery

"**I**F YOU THINK that was delicious, wait until you taste our fall flavors." Our *pâtissier* beams as she strides toward the table where Morgan, Dante, and I are still scraping the buttercream remnants off the last platter of cake bites.

"Why is this so good?"

She laughs.

Immediately, the three of us go to work, loading our plates with spice, carrot, and salted caramel cakes like we didn't scarf down every morsel of the white chocolate and red velvet slices she set down, not even five minutes ago.

I found this little French bakery, by chance, while going back and forth from the city to Napa to visit Morgan.

Blame my sweet tooth.

Thank God for Google Places. By the number of highly rated reviews, apparently, everyone and their mamas knew about this place: Gâteaux Sucrés.

Sweet cakes.

It's tucked on the outskirts of Sonoma, so it's not too far off the beaten path. Two birds, one stone, I knocked out my craving, and booked an over-the-top cake for Nichelle's Hollywood glamour wedding.

When I told her about Morgan and Dante, rushing to be the first wedding on his late grandfather's vineyard, the pâtissier was a sentimental mess, and fit us in.

Downside: the cake won't be an elaborate confectionary tower of flour and buttercream.

Upside: it'll be delicious with an understated elegance.

Win-win.

Morgan stuffs the salted caramel bite into her mouth, and immediately moans her approval. "What did you put in this? It's ridiculously good."

"It's just wrong." Dante shakes his head, his cheek bulging as he slouches back in the chair. "Sorry, babe, I can't marry you. I'm marrying this salted caramel piece of heaven."

An alarm chirps on his phone.

"Shoot, I've got to get back to the vineyard." He stands, shoveling another bite into his mouth. "I've got that meeting with the inspector for the cabins, but my vote is for the caramel."

She winks like, *I've got this, baby.*

They lean in for a chaste kiss before he hugs me and tells our baking magician that she should be ashamed for all the future pounds he's going to put on since her bakery will be his new addiction.

Us ladies spend another half hour chatting, laughing, and filling out the order form before Morgan and I take three boxes to go.

When we pour out onto the street, I'm blissfully full.

"Are you ready to aim and fire that registry scanner gun?" I let out an invigorating squeal. My sugar rush has kicked in. "Anything you want, and boom! Ooh, you won't believe how powerful you'll feel with that thing."

"Mm-hmm," Morgan hums.

Except, she doesn't sound nearly as thrilled about this as I feel.

The second I glance over at her, I know she's holding back. *But why?*

"What's up?"

Her eyebrows dip. "No, that cake was… I think we made the right choice."

Uh-huh.

"So, nothing's bothering you?" I ask, knowing good and well we never take the first objection with each other. "There's nothing you want to talk about?"

Stubbornly, she insists she's "fine," which, by her avoidant gaze and unusual silence, it's a bold-faced lie if ever I've heard one.

But I play along during our short drive to Target.

I sing along with John Legend's "Stay with You" and Tony Terry's "With You," hoping if it's wedding-related nerves, love music will get her to talk to me.

By the time Avant and Keke Wyatt start crooning about first love, she shoots me a strong side-eye.

I'm like this.

Whatever it takes—sappy music, nagging, an extra bite of cake—I'll get her talking. *Even if it does feel like it's working more on me than her.*

The entire drive, my stomach muscles are clenched, and

moisture gathers in my mouth thinking about these past few weeks with Stefano—and the ones without him since.

Every sensation in my body is heightened around this man. The electric pulse shooting through me, the delicious curve of his lips as he sank his teeth into his lower lip and quirked his brows. The way he teased me with his tongue...

With each love song, Stefano is all I can think about.

Except, the second Morgan and I pass under the giant red and white bullseye and the clerk at the counter hands us our scanner guns, my best friend swivels around to face me.

A ghost of a smile plays on her lips.

"You're seriously going to go on pretending nothing is happening with you and Stefano?" Her eyebrow shoots up.

By the sheer contours of her voice, I know she knows, which means my entire Sister Circle is still discussing, ad nauseam, the details about me and Stefano getting busy on the side of the building then slinking out early back to my place. *How many times do I have to shut this conversation down?*

"Listen, I really wish you'd stop with the whole crush thing. There's nothing happening between me and Stefano."

Morgan's lips screw to the side.

I'm fooling no one.

"So, y'all were outside Il Sapore for almost thirty minutes, talking?"

With our bodies. "Yes."

She aims her scanner gun and me. "Avery Ellis, how long have we known each other?"

"Too long." I snort.

"Correction. Too long to lie to each other and think we

can get away with it."

I flick my gaze skyward.

I'm not budging on this. Whether it's pointless, given the way Stefano couldn't get away from my house fast enough—*almost three weeks ago now*—we made a promise.

Three weeks.

Morgan pulls the trigger. "Your face is giving it all away for free ninety-nine, ma'am. Try again because I'm not buying your lies."

An exhausted sigh blusters out of me as she turns on her heel into the book aisle.

"What do you want me to say that Monica hasn't already?" I ask. "Stefano Fortemani is fine as hell, single, and I sure would've let him spank me and tell me what a bad, *bad* girl I've been."

She snickers. "All of that?"

"Yes, I *would've*. But it's not going to happen. We're two different people who want different things and it's not going to work."

Pursing her lips, she glances over at a shelf full of fiction romance books before she scans one with a woman draped in the arms of a blue alien.

I scan it, too, removing it from her registry.

"You don't need this book."

She shrugs and studies the cover again, then the one beside it, and the next.

"You're telling me you and Stefano are so different, but these women are falling for aliens, barbarians, and wolves. The man doesn't have freaking tentacles."

Laughter rumbles over my shoulders.

"No, he doesn't. But he does still have feelings for his ex-wife, who's coming to your wedding, at Victoria's request. There's still ties there. Otherwise, why else would he have been with me right after he saw her pregnancy post?"

"Um because it's shocking."

I tilt my head. "Exactly. What a surprise, the woman who you married, loved, and wanted children with is having a baby. What better way not to think about it than banging it out with someone else?"

She snaps a you-just-told-on-yourself' finger at me, and I don't bother denying it.

"Again, *ex,* as in divorced and it's over for many reasons we couldn't possibly know about."

I suck my teeth.

"And anyway, from where I'm standing…" She breaks off, and I sense that "I'm" includes Dante plus the Sister Circle, and whichever groomsmen care enough to comment about us. "The chemistry between you two is off the charts. We saw the sappy glances and lip-licking. And just now, in the car, you looked about five seconds from self-satisfying. So, tell me again, why you're *pretending"*—she emphasizes the word—"nothing is happening between you?"

This time, I know there's no chance she's letting this go.

Stubbornly, I scan Kennedy Ryan's sweeping romance, *Before I Let You Go,* on principle, then *Marriage Be Hard* by Kevin and Melissa Fredericks as I dip out the aisle toward candles and flatware.

"I can't talk about it."

Naturally, she treats this like a challenge, which she gladly accepts. "Theoretically then…"

Coming to a hard stop at the aisle cap, I shoot a Prosecco-scented candle before I meet her unwavering gaze.

"*If* he'd left the private room at Il Sapore, and went out to the alley, then *maybe* I would've followed him to ask why he couldn't spend two minutes with me before he had to run out. And that Monica was right about paying attention to the details because I should be the one running."

"And *if* you did, what would he have said?"

I shrug. "*Maybe* he'd have said he wasn't frustrated with me, but at the fact that his ex-wife was pregnant with another man."

"And then?"

"And *maybe* at the time I wouldn't've known it was a glaring red flag." Morgan winds her finger in circles, signaling for me to stay on track. "*Maybe* he might've said he didn't want me to run before buttering me up with sweet talk, and I suggested we have fun until it isn't anymore. Then we'd hook up against the wall in the alley before we went back inside, wishing there was time to do it again. So, we'd leave ten minutes early, and drive to my house to continue all night before Ace got home the next morning, and he saw no further reason to continue this charade."

A gasp pushes past her lips.

"Yeah, so like I said…" I wince as I adjust my bra. The underwire has been killing my boobs today. "*Theoretically*, we're different people who want different things. Particularly, not to be someone's fun fallback plan, if you get my drift…"

Morgan nods, her brown eyes darting to my pained expression before they widen with consideration, and we start walking again.

She meticulously scans a pale purple flatware set, rattan placemats and napkin rings, and aubergine napkins.

I duck into the restroom.

When I get back, Morgan picks up right where we left off.

"So, when would be the last time y'all saw each other?" she tosses back.

He asked to meet last weekend, but I just couldn't.

"This coming Saturday."

Her stride falters. "You haven't seen each other since—"

"Two Sundays ago." *In three days, it'll be three Sundays, but who's counting.* I blink too many times to be natural, wishing we could skip the conversation altogether. "Now we're meeting on Saturday at the winery to finalize the catering and wine menu."

She presses her free hand to her mouth, ignoring everything I've just said.

"Not even for the ChatVideo meetings?" she asks.

"I've been slammed with other events." I scan a stand mixer, knowing neither Morgan nor Dante can bake to save their lives. "Anyway, it's fine. A month and a week left. August is going to fly by, the wedding will be here before we know it. Then we'll see each other every now and then for you all."

"And that's it?"

"Yup."

Forty-five minutes pass. We've scanned everything under the sun. From a Dyson to super-plush bathrobes to cookbooks, luggage, bookends, picture frames, and million-thread-count sheets, we've got a ridiculous list going. And I've made another bathroom stop. Even my bladder has been irritable today. *Probably, stress from talking about a man who got what he needed and moved on.*

Before long, we get sidetracked in the snack aisle.

Morgan's arms are loaded with chocolate bars, chips, and pink Starburst.

"What?" she asks when she registers that I'm staring at her. "Aunt Flo is in town."

"Oh." *Oh no…*

And that's when it hits me, why I've been putting off seeing him. Why I've been an empath on steroids, acting like "having fun" wasn't my idea. Why I ate more cake than the bride and groom, and I'm contemplating a tub of ice cream with extra chocolate sauce.

I'm off track.

It's been weeks since Aunt Flo visited me.

CHAPTER FIFTEEN

Stefano

NATURALLY, INSTEAD OF answering any of my dozen or so calls or leaving a voicemail, Mother chooses an impromptu visit to the winery, half an hour before Avery's scheduled to arrive. She's dressed in a pale pink, made-to-measure skirt suit with burgundy suede pumps and simple diamond studs. Her hair is laid smoothly against her warm brown skin.

I've sat at her right for every quarterly meeting for the past seven years. I know when Victoria Fortemani is biding her time before she broaches business at hand.

"I'm sure you've received my messages," I grumble.

Mother lingers near the barrel-lined wall of the cellar, her raincoat draped over her arm, her back to me. She's quietly inspecting a barrel that was quality-tested, approved, and filled months ago.

"Darling, you know how I hate it when you mutter. Now, speak up," she demands.

I think about the podcasts Avery recommended. *Reclaim your own identity. Be firm. State what you want clearly.*

Straightening, I clear my throat.

"As I stated in the texts, voicemails, and emails, I'm asking you to rescind Carina's invitation," I say sharply. "We're both moving on with our lives."

Her slender fingers steady on the wood.

When she turns to face me, a placating smile evens her expression.

"Darling, it wouldn't be right. She's already RSVP'd. She's our family, and we don't throw people away simply because the dynamics of your relationship have changed."

I hate the patronizing edge to her tone.

Her hand hovers tellingly over her chest the way she always does when she's uneasy. "Besides, would it really be so unbearable for one afternoon?"

An exhausted laugh blusters from my chest.

I drop my head in my hands, scrubbing them over my face before I meet her unreceptive stare again.

"Yes!" I scoff.

My mouth tenses.

The edge to my tone echoing in the cool, enclosed space seems to take her by surprise. I never raise my voice with her. I've never had to. But I can't budge on this.

Her face contorts.

"Who's more important, here, hmm? Me or my ex-wife, who's parading around her new boyfriend?"

Mother's posture shifts.

I feel her attention fixated on me, studying me, reading my energy, looking at me with assessing eyes. Almost like it didn't warrant her focus before, Mother's gaze catalogues my unkempt curls, casual, loose-fitting khaki chinos and heather grey quarter-zip sweater. As she works her way down to my white leather sneakers, I'm grateful I decided against the DREAM TEAM shirt, lest she question whether I'm her son at all.

Self-consciously, I rub my hands along my pants.

"Obviously, I choose you," Mother says, but her searching brown eyes beg: *Tell me what all this stems from.*

I hate that I'm letting this conversation get under my skin, when it's not Mother's nor Carina's feelings I'm concerned about in this situation.

Avery deserves more than I gave her.

If I'm really going to try with her—and make no mistake about it, I want to—I can't do it with my mother clinging to the past.

Especially, not if I'm going to ask Avery to be my wedding date.

Briefly checking my watch, I suck in a deep breath, then steady my gaze on her again.

"Listen, Mother, if your tea party gave us any insight at all, I'd hoped you'd have seen that it's hard enough with everyone commenting about our divorce. Inserting themselves in Carina's efforts to start anew." I'm still struggling to keep my head but the question I'm working toward is steady on my tongue. "What if I found someone new, too?"

Mother perks up.

She arches a curious eyebrow.

But then the corners of her mouth pull down, and I sense she's suppressing a smile. She's putting two and two together. My attire, checking the time, now uninviting Carina, it's all a riddle she's intent on solving. Mother's highly sensitive intuition is firing on all cylinders.

There's no denying to Victoria Fortemani that this is about a woman.

But she doesn't know who.

It's the only card up my sleeve. I've got her full attention now.

"What if I wanted to bring someone to Dante's wedding? Don't you think it'd be hard enough for this woman to imagine herself in our family, especially when her spot is still occupied by my ex-wife in her delicate condition?"

If I'd have blinked I might've missed her sharp intake of air.

I've surprised her.

Only, I'm not sure about which part—that I'm mentioning bringing a wedding date, that I'm at the point I'm considering this woman's inclusion in our family, that Carina is pregnant, or all of the above.

I've given her a lot to chew on.

As I watch her incessantly blinking, grappling to digest it all, I refuse to lead her.

"It seems I've missed a great deal in these past few weeks."

"Indeed."

She worries her lips, nodding like she's still turning over everything in her head.

"Delicate condition?"

Of course, she starts with the gravest news. Reduce worry, and end on the best note, she always says.

I shrug, ambivalently. "Yes, it would seem so, if her social media is any indication."

She shoots me a pointed stare, scrutinizing my seemingly

cavalier response.

"I see." A small sigh seeps from her lips. "I wasn't aware."

"At the end of the day, I've made my peace with it. We gave our marriage one hundred and ten percent, and now, we've grown apart. Together, we made a choice to consciously uncouple so we can both live happily *even* after divorce. She's finding hers, and I'm…working on mine."

Mother releases a hysterical laugh like she's exhausted by all the neologic language people use to sever ties. To her, whether by death or divorce, losing a spouse isn't something she takes lightly.

It's why she hasn't remarried since we lost Dad. I suspect, why she's maintained a relationship with Carina, and even entertained sending an invitation.

She loves to the roots.

"Very well then." Her downcast gaze settles on the door where light rain is coming down. Then a faint smile curves her rosy lips. "I will do as you've asked and call her today."

"Thank you."

Again, she considers me, and I'm guessing I know what else is nagging at her.

"Is there anyone else you'd like to tell me about? Someone special, perhaps…" *Anyone else I'd like to tell her about.*

My cheeks burn under her teetering smile.

"No."

I wonder if I should reconsider, tell her that, somehow, without my consent, Avery's snuck into my life and possibly my heart. In a matter of weeks, she's become important to me, and there's a *slight* chance I might be falling for her in a way I'd never fallen, not even in my marriage.

With us, although I suspect I wouldn't mind, it's not about building an approved nuclear life together. It's about passion and purpose and feeling good with a person who knows my entire mess, and still makes me laugh. She finds silver linings, plays twenty questions on video chat, makes up ridiculous dances, and genuinely, wholeheartedly loves with everything she has.

I'd be a fool to let something as small as fear get in the way.

I want to earn her love if that's where this takes us.

But I don't say any of that to Mother.

Nor do I sense she buys my answer. Still, she graciously lets me off the hook for now.

The rain picks up, falling in fat drops.

Not wanting to get caught in it, she hurries to slip her arms into the sleeves of her raincoat, retrieve her umbrella from her purse, and dash out into the fray.

What seems like a minute later, Avery rushes insides with her coat shielded over her head, her feet squelching with every footstep.

She's drenched.

Her usual bright sundress, kelly-green this time, clings to her swollen breasts and round thighs. Her hair is stuck to her face, and her shoes are covered in mud.

"Oof, it is coming down out there, but I made it." She chances a quick look at me before her attention snaps to the tasting table heaped with the menu options from our restaurant, Bramoso, and a flight of glasses filled with a selection of white and red wines.

"Glad you made it safely," I say.

"Thanks." Avery inches toward the table, plucking at her soaked dress. She's clearly uncomfortable but she seems resolved to get straight to the business. "This looks amazing. It'll be early afternoon, so a starter salad, a few protein options with pastas and vegetables, and we're good."

I nod. "Should we maybe have a specialty item like truffles or dulse-wrapped grapes."

"Oh my *God* that would be great with the vineyard setting and Morgan's lavender and gold theme. Maybe we can skip the spring salad and go for a Waldorf with Concord grapes..."

Snapping my fingers, I grab my pen and jot down notes. "Paired with a light-bodied red, or even a Riesling, a nice Pinot Grigio—"

"I love it." Avery's voice buoys with excitement before she seems to realize she's falling into our easy, comfortable ways, and tamps down her enthusiasm.

A shiver vibrates her shoulders.

Again, Avery plucks at her dress, and I know I shouldn't overstep. I should do nothing. I should put in the action. Double down on my prayers.

But try as I may, I can't stand here and watch her suffer.

"Can I get you a blanket or offer you my sweater?" I'm already pulling it over my head when she leans in and steadies my hand.

My skin feels electric.

My heart flutters as our eyes connect.

"It's okay, I'm fine."

I toss her a challenging stare. "You're shivering, and I may have noticed your teeth chattering."

Despite herself, her attention falls briefly to my lips.

"Let's just focus on the menu and wine list," she says sharply.

But her gaze falters, and I can't let the moment pass. Not without opening to her.

"Avery?"

"*Please*, let's focus on the menu and wine list," she repeats.

Her chest rises and falls punctuating her nerves.

My desperation heightens as I study her beautiful features. Her dark, sweeping eyelashes over warm brown eyes. Her smooth golden-brown skin, and those lips.

Inching closer, I reach out and glide the pad of my thumb over her lower lip, drawing her eyes.

I want to kiss her so bad.

"I'm sorry." My heart rams against my ribs. "I can't tell you how sorry I am for letting even a moment go by without reaching out to you. I should've called. You should be sick of me texting and emailing, and doing everything in my power to let you know I miss you."

She shakes her head. "Just stop. You really don't have to say anything, Stefano. We never said this was serious. Remember, *fun until it isn't anymore*?" She shrugs. "I get it. It stopped being fun for you."

"What are you talking about?"

"I didn't mean to eavesdrop, but I overheard you with Victoria…"

I bark out a laugh.

"You think I'm going to tell my mother how I feel about you, right now? Fresh off my divorce? As eager as she is to grow her family?" I snicker. "Avery, you do remember she was the mastermind behind the whole selling-the-vineyard hoax, right? The woman knows no boundaries when it comes to her kids. Of course, I said there was no one special."

She grins, and her shoulders relax.

"You know as well as I do, Victoria Fortemani would be so quick to orchestrate a shotgun wedding. Another son down the aisle, plus a grandson as great as Ace..."

We both laugh.

Although, I can't deny how much I love the idea, myself. "So..."

"At the risk of sounding like a broken record, I'm sorry. I miss you. My fear got the best of me, and I let too many days go by, but I still want to try. If you're willing." I blow out a soft breath. "We can take our time because *you* are special to me."

Avery blinks slowly, like she's still turning over everything I've said. Then she asks, "What are your fears?"

I drape my sweater over Avery's trembling shoulders, training my focus on her eyes. *And* not *the way my abdomen aches at the sight of her dress riding up her slick, smooth thighs.*

One by one, I tell her every concern I shared with Dante at the tux fitting—her, losing her husband; me, unaware how to move on while my ex seems to be an expert; whether I'm father material; my uncertainty around doing the work to get to know her, and it turns out to be all for naught; the risk of building a connection with Ace, and hurting him if it doesn't work out. *Whether I deserve the woman I'm falling for...*

Before I can get the rest out, I bend down, pulling a cardboard box from underneath the table.

"I know you come as a package deal, so I'd love to spend some real time with Ace, if that's okay with you," I say. "This is for him."

Avery's gaze flutters disbelievingly at me before she glances at the name on the box.

"Is this?"

"Junior is my son's name. He would've been Stefano Elias Fortemani, Jr."

She swallows, her expression softening with unspoken empathy. "I can't take this."

"It would mean so much to see Ace play with them. There are trucks, robots, balls, and a tiny baseball mitt." Emotion lodges in my throat. "I may have stocked up on a bunch of Hot Wheels and *Cars*-themed merch, too. Lightning McQueen is cool."

A laugh sputters from Avery.

"I can't believe you did all this. Are you kidding me? I'd love for you to hang out with us. He's going to go out of his mind when he sees this box full of toys."

"You know…" I let my eyes sweep over her body. "I also got you a toy."

Avery's mouth falls open.

But then her eyes darken.

"Is something wrong?" I ask, knowing full well I've just turned her on in public. Again.

The air between us smolders.

She sets the box on the table and raises up on her tiptoes. Her lips curve deliciously as she clasps her hands behind my neck and brushes her lips over mine.

The kiss is tender and emotional, communicating without words what we haven't earned the right yet, to say. *I want you. I'm in this with you. If you'll let me, I could be everything you deserve.*

It's real for me.

"You're worth the risk to me, Stefano."

Just like that, in a single sentence, Avery rebuffs my worries and fills my heart.

"Yeah? How about the dangerous task of being my wedding date?"

The way she teases my tongue and fists my shirt in her hands, tugging me closer still…

This firefly of a woman drives me wild.

"Is the winery closed?" she mouths into the kiss.

Immediately, I know the dark, steamy places her mind has descended to.

"Is that a yes to being my date?"

She deepens the kiss. "It's a hell yes."

I wouldn't dare stop to check the time, so I ballpark my estimate based on the time I think she arrived.

"Half hour, twenty minutes, give or take a few minutes." Which, in the throes of passion, feels like an eternity.

It's shameful really, what we're thinking about doing in yet another public place.

This is a business.

One my mother just left, and could return to on a whim. One where my employees' respect and work ethic could be affected.

But I don't care because Avery Ellis wants me.

It feels only right to match my action with this answered prayer.

"Are you thinking what I'm thinking?" She tucks her lower lip between her teeth, and it's nearly my undoing.

I arch an eyebrow.

As she slips her hand under my shirt, I know I'm in the best kind of trouble.

"No one needs to know, right?" she begs.

I nod. "Right. I know a place," I say, scooping her up in my arms, and transplanting us to the far end of the cellar, in the darkest corner between stacked barrels. Lowering myself onto my knees, I hook her knee over my shoulder. "Now, try not to make a sound…" I instruct, knowing good and well my request only makes it ten times harder as I drag my tongue along her most sensitive flesh.

In minutes, Avery's hands are fisted in my hair, her lips are clamped shut as she falls apart in my mouth.

With her wilted against the wall, I straighten.

"Good girl, Pollyanna." I smile.

I've experienced what those words do to her—what that name does.

I see it in her eyes that she's recharged and ready to go again. This is how it is with us.

She's my magnet.

I can't be near her without touching, feeling, clambering to hear my name on her tongue as we bring each other to the edge and fall together.

Soon, my sweater and her wet dress are on the floor, and she's fumbling with my belt and unfastening my pants. We're a mess of lips, tongues, and wanderlust hands roaming freely over each other's aching bodies like we've known each other for years and been apart for months instead of weeks.

And it feels right.

The fit and feel of us, makes me wonder why I wasted so much time trying to force my marriage to work when Avery is every dream I've ever had come to life.

With her panting in my ear and wilting in my arms, I deepen my strokes.

I want it to last.

I want *us* to last.

CHAPTER SIXTEEN

Avery

B Y TUESDAY, I'M paying the price for chasing goose bumps.

My period showed up yesterday, so I'm not pregnant, just regular allergies, I think. Though, not just a few sneezes here and there. Stuffy nose, congestion, the works. To top off my flaming pile of garbage sinuses, the—heavily dairy-based—Alfredo on the pasta I ordered for Turn-Up Tuesday with my Sister Circle curdled in my stomach. Instead of updates about Seneca's now-outdated resignation letter and the forearms on Valerie's Fix-It Felix, I spent most of the night in the restroom, praying to the porcelain gods.

I may have felt like crap the entire time, but I didn't miss our standing weekly appointment.

So, there's that...

Another sneeze tickles my nose.

"Nope. Into the elbow." Monica warns me for the ump-teenth time tonight. She's got too many high-paying Pilates appointments this week to come down with my "random cooties."

Her face twists in disgust as the sneeze lurches out of me

onto the gum-smeared pavement, sending Seneca, Valerie, and Morgan scattering and reaching for their tiny sanitizer bottles.

"And on that note…" Seneca slowly backs away. "Mon, y'all drove together, right?"

Her face lifts with false cheer. "Lucky me."

I swat her playfully, my face still contorted with the threatening sneeze. After fishing out a restroom paper towel from my pocket, I gently dab at my rubbed-raw nose. "But I still didn't get the scoop."

In classic Morgan form, complete with animated facial expressions and wild hand gestures, she gives me the twenty-second recap.

"Felix and his forearms have moved on to Valerie's bedroom where he's been laying pipe. The ceremony dances will be the highlight of the wedding, following the actual vows, of course. I'm SUPER excited about the bachelorette party at Bramoso." She squees. "Then there's Monica. Some influencer took her Sculpting Pilates class, posted about it, and now she's booked for months. And in a full-on plot twist, Seneca has *not* left the bank." She pulls in a long breath and releases it with an exhausted laugh.

Seneca rolls her eyes playfully. "We'll see what's a plot twist when Mike and I dance at your wedding."

A surge of laughter vibrates over the circle like the wave until it gets back to me, culminating in—NOT the stupid sneeze that's been hijacking my nose—but a queasy dry heave.

"Okay, so we've all got work tomorrow." Valerie flips up the collar of her jacket to shield her nose and mouth as she hugs me. "Monica, get her home safe, please."

I try to laugh, but it's just gross, so I give up.

Morgan shoots me a sympathetic stare, though. "I've got late appointments tomorrow. Are you sure you don't want me to take you home? Maybe get you some medicine? Make you some tea?"

"No, I'm fine."

She tilts her head. "It could be food poisoning…"

As nice as that sounds, lying in bed while someone brings me tea and takes my temperature, I'm not a person who likes inconveniencing others. The very idea that she'll have to drive me home, wait on me hand and foot, then make it back to her fiancé exhausted and possibly infected…

No. I can't.

"I'm telling you, it's just a little cold, and the dairy didn't agree with me tonight." I shrug it off. "I'm sure I'll feel better tomorrow after I sleep it off."

She holds my stare for a beat.

Finally, three rapid-release sneezes let loose.

They all bless me in unison.

"Girl, why are you so stubborn?" Monica shakes her head. "It's okay to let someone else take care of you for a change."

"First of all, I live with a six-year-old, which is like rooming with a walking germ," I reason. "I'm used to this."

Standing the recommended six feet away, Valerie snickers. "Ma'am don't blame this on that sweet baby. All night, I've been admiring the cut of your blouse, thinking you might not be sick if you didn't have your boobs all propped up and on display in the open air…"

A gasp spills out of me.

"I've had this bra for years." Instinctually, I peer down at my cleavage wondering if they look bigger. *Are they bigger? Why do they look so voluptuous?*

That question is still ringing in my head after we've hugged, said our see-you-laters, and I'm freezing my butt off in Monica's passenger seat. She refuses to close the windows. Apparently, viruses can't survive in well-ventilated, cool spaces. Nowhere to land (i.e., not on her).

As the light of the city sprawling by outside pierces into the car cabin, I can't stop staring at the full swell of my breasts.

They're just sitting there.

Not that I don't love how they're perched up high, because I do. Honestly, there was a time, pre-Ace, when I would've killed for a perky rack. Who wouldn't want *Playboy*-worthy mounds?

But now, I'm questioning it.

Do they swell when you get a cold? Does an upset stomach push everything *up? More importantly, I'm not pregnant, so WHY do they seem so much bigger?*

When Monica takes a phone call, I tap out a quick Google search about periods and pregnancy. Immediately, the search results flood my screen with statistics, symptoms, and anomalies about women spotting early, or conceiving twins then miscarrying one, before it concludes in bold letters: ***periods usually mean you're not pregnant.***

Immediately, relief courses through me.

Phew, mine was late, but now it's here.

I'm not pregnant. Which, hello? It's way too early in our

relationship to be adding kids, beyond Ace, to our equation.

Except, as I stare aimlessly out the window into my reflection, I can't deny the tiny tinge of disappointment. What if I'm one of those women who spot early? *My flow has been lighter, and it's already looking like it's going to be shorter.* A baby with Stefano? Giving him a junior would make him so happy. Or would it? What if he doesn't want a baby with me?

I look down at my breasts again.

Shit.

"What are you doing?" Monica watches me watching my boobs, before she snaps her gaze back to the road, veering into the left lane.

Another sneeze jolts out of me.

My girl is quick to lower the windows another inch, though. She doesn't even have to tell me to direct my germs into the elbow or slather on sanitizer. I'm on it. Although, the entire time, laughing at her dire expression.

"I'll grab my Lysol when we get to my house," I reassure her before circling back to my eighth and ninth world wonders. "They do look great tonight, don't they?" I shift in my seat, giving her the full display.

"Boobs aside, I think the question we should be addressing is *how* did you get sick?"

Her eyes have been glued to the road. Now, I feel the weight of her assessing gaze, as accusatory as her tone.

That wasn't a question. It was a *you're fooling no one, so you might as well tell me everything* lead into what she's been itching to talk about all night. Rather, *who* she's been itching to talk about.

I release a certified snort-laugh. "Why don't you ask what you're really asking me?"

"Mm-hmm. You're fooling absolutely no one. Out there roaming the wilderness with the silver fox, that's how you got sick."

This time, I don't even bother hiding my laughter.

I'm breathless and gasping for air, holding my stomach. "You are so wrong for that."

"Your secret is safe with me."

As if. The second I tell Monica, the Sister Circle group chat will be blowing up on my phone.

"What is wrong with you?" I giggle.

"Shoot, you already admitted y'all were crushing on each other. *Hypothetically*, I mean." Monica rolls her eyes, grinning like she's the freaking Cheshire cat.

"My lips are sealed."

"Okay, you can pretend you're not dying to tell us, but hear this..." She presses the button to roll up our windows. I'm guessing noise interference won't fare well when we're almost to my house and she wants every word to sink in.

I make a big production, twisting and angling myself to her.

"Girl, you know I live by my Weather app, right?" she reiterates.

"Oh, Lord. I'm dying to hear this."

"A Saturday night. Two attractive, single adults, 'allegedly' curating a wine and catering menu. Chemistry, off the charts," she editorializes. "I'd be willing to bet you carried yourself there, wearing next to nothing, and y'all were alone in that warm, dim, enclosed space of that winery when the rain started coming down. You and I both know you weren't thinking about catching a little seasonal cold."

I drop my face into my hands.

As if underscoring her comment, my phone pings, and I freeze guiltily.

It's a catch-22.

Monica is watching. If I rush to check the message, she'll have visual confirmation of just how hard I am, even for a sound bite of Stefano's voice. From there, it's a matter of minutes before she draws accurate conclusions about everything that's happened since Il Sapore.

Now, I could come up with an elaborate excuse, but then I realize I've got one built in.

Ace is with Mommy. Maybe he's already sleepy, which is totally plausible given she falls for his puppy-dog eyes and allows extra snacks and screen time. *What kind of mother would I be if I missed a chance to tell him goodnight?*

"Oop, close to bedtime!" I say, unnaturally loud. "This is probably Mommy letting me know Ace is off to bed early."

Monica shoots me a sidelong glance.

As my phone illuminates at the bottom of my purse, I zero in on Stefano's name with the tiny cactus emoji I assigned to his contact, and my heart warms.

How's dinner with the circle going?

I'm grinning like a fool.

Quickly, I tap out a response letting him know we've had to cut the night short due to my cold.

"Mm-hmm." Monica smirks. "Because bedtime texts always elicit swoons out of you…"

Sarcasm drips from her tone, and I don't even have the sense to care because his follow-up text is loading.

Except, those annoying little ellipses keep bouncing the rest of the drive to my house. Through Monica's suggestive *Tell him to come take care of you tonight*, and still half an hour after that. So, imagine how embarrassed I feel with my phone glued to my hand, refreshing the message for the umpteenth time, when my doorbell rings, and it's a tall, super sexy and sweet silver fox holding his version of my Fix-it Kit.

"I didn't mean to make you feel like you had to come all the way over here. I'm fine."

I'm wedged in my doorway, torn between wishing I'd picked up Ace's toys and straightened the sofa pillows, and yanking him inside.

Stefano tilts his head, smiling.

"You're not well, so I'm here to take care of you. You never have to ask me, Avery," he says as if that's just an unwritten rule, and not the sweetest thing anyone has ever said to me.

My heart jackhammers against my ribs as I step aside, opening the door wider for him to enter.

He presses a soft kiss to my cheek on his way inside.

As soon as he reaches the kitchen, he gets to work, unloading the reusable grocery tote.

"All right, we've got chicken noodle soup from Bramoso's, ginger ale, and a little vitamin C. We've got to get those immune cells operating on all cylinders again." He tosses me an adorably boyish wink. "For entertainment, I've got my Get Well Soon Movies playlist…"

I climb up on a barstool. "I'm sorry, what?"

He looks at me like he's offended by my surprise.

"Listen, just because I'm a staunch businessman who values nicely cut suits and a great book, doesn't mean I'm not a film connoisseur. I know my movies."

A laugh twitches my lips, but I fan out a hand, giving him the floor.

"Please, enlighten me," I say.

"Since I suspect you're only humoring me because you're under the weather, I'm going to give you five movies to choose from. Then, you'll be relegated to the bedroom." Stefano clamps his mouth shut at my hopeful expression. "To rest and recover," he clarifies.

"Hey, a girl can wish." I shrug.

We could've thrown a pillow over my head to shield him. I've heard of kinkier things.

His expression softens with amusement.

"For the record, as much as I'd love to pick up where we left off over the weekend, I'm here to tend to your health needs." He grins. "We'll take care of the rest once you're feeling better."

Slumping against the counter, I feign disappointment.

"If you say so."

Stefano rounds the island, and plants himself between my knees. Tenderly, he tips my chin up to meet his stare. Every nerve ending on my body stands at attention as he drags his thumb over my lower lip.

"You've got no idea how fucking bad I need you right now," he says.

Lord.

It's the word "need" that makes it so sexy, though.

He doesn't just want me. He *needs* to be with me, inside me, his lips trailing across my aching skin as we chase the feeling...

Ooh, Lord. Save me.

A shiver trembles down my spine.

"Okay, well, at least we know it's mutual suffering."

Stefano presses a petal-soft kiss to my forehead, laughing. "That it is, Pollyanna." He leans forward again, then pauses inches from my lips. "Oh, I almost forgot, I've got one more thing in the bag."

Stretching across the island, Stefano drags the grocery tote toward us.

That's when I notice his goofy grin.

"What?" I ask.

"So, I couldn't spare my prickly cactus. It keeps me warm and safe at night, as one would expect from a plush toy picked out with so much thought, consideration, and care."

I giggle. "I knew you loved him. He's so stinking cute."

Stefano nods. "I'm glad you said that because..." He fishes his hand into the tote, and stalls. "I was able to secure you, an Oopsie Daisy."

A full-body sneeze spills out of me. Into the elbow, thankfully, and not on this beautiful, big-hearted man.

Thanks, Mon.

"Bless you."

"Thank you." I shake away the sneezy haze. "Okay, now an oopsie what?"

Out of the bag, he produces an adorable white daisy flower plush with a friendly, smiling, happy yellow face, and a tiny card affixed to one of her petals.

Now, I'm the one with the goofy grin.

I dart my gaze at him before reading the message. OOP-SIE DAISY, YOU FEEL SICK. HOPE YOU FEEL BETTER SOON. LOVE, STEFANO.

Shoot.

One would think I don't plan elaborate weddings with tear-jerking vows and professions of love for a living.

It's a fun-sized, punny greeting card for goodness' sake.

Yet here I am in all my empathic splendor, tearing up at this beautiful man's sweet gesture and casual use of a four-letter word. Obviously, he doesn't love me. How could he when less than two months ago we loathed each other? Well, that might've been one-sided. At the least, though, we barely tolerated each other.

Now, I'm thinking about him nonstop. I'm finding excuses to call and text. Multiple times daily. The scene of us at the winery reels across my mind at will. He asked me to be his wedding date. That's got to mean something. Yesterday, I was supposed to be finalizing the venue setup timeline for my client Nichelle's wedding, and instead, I lost an hour daydreaming, imagining it was my happily-ever-after with Stefano that I was planning. Dammit, I was low-key excited about stopping at the drugstore for a pregnancy test before my period went and ruined it.

It's ridiculous.

It's too much, too fast, right?

But now, he's here with food and gifts, taking care of me, without me ever having had to ask.

"Thank you." I swallow, focusing on the plush toy. "I

know she'll keep me warm and safe at night, too."

With our ever-present sexual tension acknowledged and my heart still stuttering in my chest, we fill a tray with ginger ale and bowls, spoons, and saltines for the soup. I assume we're locked and loaded to be bed-bound, but Stefano's starts cleaning my house. He's a tidying hurricane, fluffing pillows, folding my throw blankets, and picking up Ace's toys, and I don't know how not to fall harder.

"One thing about kids, it's a constant cleanup." I aim for comic relief. Then immediately vacuum the amusement out of the room when I add, "Sure about that package deal?"

Stefano simply smiles. "I should be so lucky."

Inside I'm swooning, feeling the ache to be more.

When we finally make it to the bed, though, thankfully, we circle back to his soul-healing movie playlist because I'm just a bag of bones and feelings, at this point.

"*Think Like a Man*," Stefano says.

I cringe as I settle onto the right side of the bed, adjusting myself under the covers before I grab my bowl off the nightstand.

My face isn't because the movie is bad.

No, I'm throwing it out, on principle.

"I'm still mad at Taraji for almost letting Morris Chestnut ruin a good thing with Michael Ealy," I explain. "Next."

Stefano chuckles. "Okay, O for one. How about *Two Can Play That Game?*"

"Yes, but I still want to hear the last three options."

He tips his head to either side, considering.

"All right, this next one is a classic. Might give Morris and Vivica a run for their money... *Love Jones*."

I laugh because he says it low and measured like he's on *The $100,000 Pyramid* game show, giving me a clue.

"I would, but—"

"*But?*" The inflection in his voice rises with disbelief. "A but to new love, poetry snaps, and Chicago stepping? Come on!"

"Look, that movie is my *jam*. But you can't tell me you're in the mood for Bill Bellamy 'philosophizing.'" I raise a challenging eyebrow, daring him to tell me otherwise.

"Nope, the next thing you're going to tell me you've didn't love *Just Wright*."

"Actually, that one is a solid yes, for me."

A low chuckle vibrates Stefano's shoulders. "Finally, I knew you couldn't say no to the queen… Okay, we're down to our last option." He pulls in a lungful of air, then dips his chin, gameshow dramatic to say, "*Jumping the Broom*."

I feel my face twist.

"Are you serious?" His eyes widen. "Don't tell me you feel some kind of way about Paula's chicken."

A full-body laugh rumbles out of me.

"Leave that girl alone. That was her momma's recipe. I wouldn't dare judge a movie based off food prep anyways."

He throws his hands up in mock surrender.

My mouth will not close. I'm gasping for air at how surprisingly hilarious he is.

"For your information, funny guy, I would've been fully on board with it. It's perfect for our wedding-themed lives right now. But it's playing at Movie at the Vineyard for Wine-Down Wednesday next week."

"Oh, yeah?"

I chance a quick glance at him. "I was sorta hoping you'd want to take me on a date... Maybe, a little practice before the wedding?"

Realization braids his eyebrows together, and he's suddenly a pile of sappy mush.

"Aww."

He reaches across the bed, intertwining our fingers as he plants a kiss on my lips.

"You're going to get sick, too," I warn, even though I suddenly feel like I'm fifteen again, and I'd love nothing more than to kiss for hours.

"And you think that's going to stop me?" He brushes his mouth over mine again. "Whatever you've got, *we've* got."

We.

He brings our intertwined fingers to his lips.

I bite my lower lip, feeling slightly self-conscious, and strangely nervous about how comfortable it feels sharing laughs, a bed, and now, the cooties with Stefano. "Everyone is going to be at the vineyard movie night, though..."

"You think I'm going to let that stop me from being with you?"

My whole heart on a platter.

"It's the final wedding party get-together."

Honestly, I don't know what response I'm trying to elicit from him by stating this. Part of me realizes we're building this relationship-like thing aside from the wedding and planning. But there's another part that feels like we've only been together because the wedding forced us to be. What if this all ends when my best friend and Stefano's brother say *I do*? What if we're just living in the moment, and nothing real comes from it?

We must both doze off sometime during the second movie because I wake up to the credits rolling in a haze of nausea.

I fumble my way in the bathroom, and barely get my head to the toilet before I'm emptying my stomach, loudly. So, I shouldn't be surprised when Stefano appears behind me, holding my hair and rubbing my back.

"I didn't mean to wake you," I say, so glamorously into the toilet. "I'm okay. You can go back to bed."

"Shhh, I want to be here for you," he says. "Please let me take care of the woman who's taking care of my heart."

For a beat, I consider refusing, insisting I'm okay. It's been so long since I let anyone be here for me. I'm so used to doing everything on my own. Taking care of Ace, solving everyone's problems, holding everyone up. But who's taking care of me?

Now, this thoughtful man with his handsome smile is offering, and I want to let him even though I know I'm falling.

It's too late.

So, I say, "Okay."

CHAPTER SEVENTEEN

Stefano

I'M A HYPOCRITE.

Two months ago, I stood under a tent at this vineyard, warning my brother not to rush into marriage. Good Lord, I was so damn self-righteous. I hounded him about rushing in. I gave him shit about finances, arguments, living arrangements, and freaking decorative hand towels, after being together four months.

I've been liaising with Avery for those same two months, and now I'm at the terrace bar on this fine Wine-Down Wednesday evening, mentally mapping out a life for us.

We don't even have a relationship.

We're, what? The best man and maid of honor? *For a day?* The wedding planner and her vineyard liaison? *That's just logistics. And a sad case, at that.* The Dream Team? Wedding dates? The nice guy who plays with her son, takes care of her when she's sick, and sleeps over from time to time? *Jesus, that could be anyone from a playdate to a nurse to the goddamn milkman.*

It's not that we need some socially acceptable romantic label.

What are we, in high school? Be my girlfriend. Check yes or no? But how's she supposed to know I'm serious?

This is ridiculous. I'm regressing. Just talk to her.

Avery's laugh across the terrace steals my attention.

I swivel around, spotting her at the center of our group. The wedding party. They're all huddled around her, knee-deep in conversation, everyone is sipping from their glasses. Well, she isn't yet. I'm still waiting for our drinks—a Merlot for me and a ginger ale for Avery.

She's still hasn't been feeling one hundred percent this last week, but she's slowly getting back to herself.

"Here, we go, boss!" Tony, our resident event bartender, slides our glasses across the bar. "Popcorn?"

"Not just yet," I say.

"Hey, you're missing out on the cheddar caramel mix…"

"I'll definitely keep that in mind." I chuckle as I slip my billfold from my pocket and lay down a twenty in front of him. But I don't miss the way he lingers, his lips parted and gaze darting curiously between me and the pale-yellow liquid.

"Everything copacetic?" he presses.

"Yeah, uh… What time does the movie start?" I ask. "I was hoping to make a quick trip to the house."

Tony nods, though I suspect he senses my uneasiness.

He flips his wrist. "Another fifteen minutes. D wanted to give the guests time to grab drinks and popcorn, find seats, you know? You've got time."

"Great. Thanks again." I flash him a small smile.

Turning back to our group, I'm not surprised when I immediately connect with Avery's smiling eyes.

For a moment, my shoulders relax.

Since last Tuesday, we've spent nearly every night together. I've been working from the city to be with her. We've gone on dinner dates and downtown strolls. Even tonight, I drove us here. Much to Ace's underage dismay. We're in that hazy phase when the only thing that matters is being together as often and for as long as humanly possible.

She tilts her head, signaling for me to rejoin them.

Instead of walking toward her, though, I match her smile, lifting our glasses. Then I veer off toward the house, holding her stare and hoping she'll follow me.

It's quite possibly the worst timing.

The night is warm, the wine is flowing. Soon, *Jumping the Broom* will be playing on the projector. I should be enjoying a night of outdoor cinema with our family and friends, instead of stealing Avery away.

But there's something I need to get off my chest, and it can't wait.

Ten minutes pass before she finds me in my old bedroom, sitting on the edge of the bed, facing the huge bay window overlooking the terrace.

"Okay, I see what you're going for here. This place really is a mood, but we don't have much time..." She giggles, wrongly assuming my intentions in getting her here are for less than savory reasons.

Which...it's quiet, comfortably warm, and we've got a great view of the screen. If we hurried, we could make it back out before anyone even noticed we were gone.

My heart flutters, heightening my desperation.

I don't want to rush this, though.

If anything, I want to savor ever second of tonight. So, I pat the spot on the bed beside me, and wait as Avery lingers for a beat, raking her eyes over me, reading my energy.

A moment later, she joins me, planting a soft kiss on my lips.

Heat rises in my cheeks.

"Is everything okay?" she asks, slowly pulling back to search my eyes. "You seem distracted."

"Yeah?"

She raises an eyebrow.

I press my lips together, suppressing a smile. I don't deny it, though. My heart is pounding, my pulse racing. Every time we're together, this woman takes my breath away. I physically ache thinking about her when we're apart for even a handful of minutes.

"You're staring," she teases.

"Because you're beautiful." I brush another kiss over her lips, gathering up the nerve.

"Seriously, I can tell something is bothering you. The way you left the terrace, your expression scared me."

Outside, the lights dim. Silence blankets over the muffled din of chatter and mingling. Then the speakers blare to life with the first tinkling notes of the movie studio's intro music, punctuating my heartbeat.

I rub my knees. "We need to talk."

"About?"

Her expression twists with concern.

"Us." I drag in a breath. "Avery, it's nothing bad. I've just been doing a lot of thinking about date nights and wedding dates, and what we're doing in general. We've been spending so much time together, and—"

"You want to stop hooking up?"

I flinch. "No, that's really what you thought I was about to say?"

"Well…" Her expression reveals her worry. "Yeah. You're distracted, your whole demeanor feels solemn, and we're in here instead of out there with your brother and our friends." She shrugs. "So, you don't want to end things?"

I study her beautiful features. The contours of her golden-brown skin, the slight pout to her pink lips. Her bright eyes burrowing past my ribs straight to my heart.

"Avery, I'm working up the nerve to ask you to be my girlfriend." I huff out a small laugh.

"Oh."

"I know this is probably corny or archaic, but I'd never assume with you. Or Ace. I want you to know this isn't some casual thing for me. I'm head over heels for you."

When she doesn't immediately respond, my nerves get the best of me.

"*Damn.*" I drop my head into my hands. "I've read this all wrong. You must think I'm an idiot. We're in my childhood bedroom, and I'm asking you to be my girlfriend like we're some school-aged kids…"

The rest of that sentence dissolves on my tongue as I lift my head again to meet her stare again.

Avery's brown eyes are glassy with unshed tears, and I panic even more.

"I'm so sorry if I…I thought with the wedding around the corner, I should make my intentions known that what we share isn't hinged on their relationship."

"Stefano?"

"I know it's been you and Ace, and I'd never try to replace Justin—"

"Yes." A shaky smile breaks over her face as the tears fall. "I'm such an emotional wreck, even more so, lately, but absolutely I want to be your girlfriend. I want to be your wedding date, your movie date, and your ride partner at the carnival this weekend." She throws her head back laughing. "I want to do it all with you, Stefano Fortemani."

I cover my heart with my hand, releasing a relieved sigh.

"Oh my God, I've been so nervous."

"These are happy tears, by the way." Avery reassures me as she hurls herself into my lap. She covers my mouth with hers and sinks her fingers into my hair like she's done a million times. "I've been so worried because we've only been together because of the wedding. I thought, what if next month, the big day arrives, and we've got no reason to keep seeing each other? What if you only saw this as temporary?"

My heart lurches.

Everything inch of me tenses with the need to assuage her fears.

"I know this makes me the biggest hypocrite for saying this." I suppress a smile. "Avery Ellis, I'm falling for you. And it's not some small crush because you brought me a stuffed cactus and made me an irresistible Magic Mike dancer either."

She laughs a laugh that I feel all over my skin.

"You've definitely got the moves, baby."

"Dante will have my ass for this but…I want to rush in with you. I can see an entire future, whatever that entails, with you and Ace."

"And Lightning McQueen," Avery adds. "You can't forget about him."

"Of course. Who could forget about the car with bold stickers. Or the fact that I've got his girlfriend in my garage."

We both laugh.

"He's going to hold you to that ride in Sally. Promises are in stone with kids."

Suddenly, the air in the room electrifies.

Every sensation in my body heightens as Avery sinks her teeth into her full lower lip. I flex my fingers around the curve of her ass, tugging her forward until she settles over my erection with a soft gasp.

"How are you feeling?" I swallow. "I've got your ginger ale on the dresser if you're still feeling uneasy." I close my eyes. "I just want to feel you."

My body hums with anticipation.

Deep down, I'm praying, at least for now, that she's well.

But then she meets my gaze, there's a smile teetering on her lips like she loves nothing more than knowing I'm turned on and thinking about her.

She leans close to my ear. Her breath is warm on my neck as she whispers, "Right now, your girlfriend needs sexual healing."

Just like that, the tension that's been bundled up inside us for the past week releases all at once.

Avery and I fumble to peel off each other's clothes until it's just us, the weight of my body hovering deliciously above her.

"Don't rush," Avery says, but it comes out low like a plea.

And I don't.

I take my sweet time, kissing her lips, behind her ears, along the curve of her neck until I reach her hardened nipples. I tease my tongue in circles, slowly, taking her into my mouth.

"I need you," she moans, writhing beneath me.

"Tell me what you want."

I dip a finger between her legs, then a second, feeling her warmth as she rotates her hips, her nails biting uncontrollably into my back.

Avery takes fistfuls of my curls in her hands. "I want you, Stefano."

"Good girl."

As I dip my fingers inside her, working her into a frenzy, her stomach muscles bunch, and her breath grows ragged.

"Please, make me feel good."

Only when her back arches and she opens for me, her scent wrapping appetizingly around me, do I lower myself down her body until I'm on my knees and hers are hooked over my shoulders, and I taste her.

"Holy—"

She slaps a hand over her mouth, muffling her cries of pleasure. She is so unbelievably sexy, and I don't how much longer I can hold out, but I'm fueled by the fact that I can make her feel so good. And she's mine.

An orgasm ripples through her.

I push to my feet, settling between her thighs. As I thrust my hips, she clings to me with each stroke of delicious friction, her sex clenching around me, and I know I'm the biggest hypocrite around.

CHAPTER EIGHTEEN
Avery

HERE'S A FUNNY story. My best friend goes and gets engaged, I'm saddled with the—*I thought*—uptight brother of the groom, who I assume will be a wrench in the whole nuptials plan. But lo and behold, he turns out to be sweet, attentive, and kind. *Can't forget smart, he'd quickly remind me.* Oh, and for kicks and giggles, he's amazing in bed, and he makes Get Well Soon movie playlists to help me feel better. Naturally, I fall hard.

I'm seriously rolling around the L-word in the back of my mind.

But that's not the funniest part.

You know how people always say, "If you want to hear God laugh, tell him your plans"?

Yeah, well, I'll bet he's bent over cackling today.

Earlier, I went to the drugstore.

For laughs, of course.

AND to rule out one of my WebMD doom scrolling causes, since Aunt Flo has been here, done her thing, and left me still feeling queasy, and remembering every day of the morning sickness during my first trimester with Ace.

Such is life.

Turns out, I'm one of those early spotters, and my boyfriend of four days is expecting.

No, he doesn't know it yet. I just found out myself. So, now, after giving him a hard time about being distracted at Wine-Down Wednesday, our highly anticipated drive in Sally and our afternoon visit to the county carnival with Ace, it's tainted by my nerves.

I've got to tell him, but I can't just blurt out, "Hey, I know we just made it official, but I'm pregnant. Oh, and by the way, I'm pretty sure I'm in love with you, and I want to jump-start that future you were talking about." Yeah, I'm sure that'd go over well.

Ugh.

A balloon pops at my side. I snap toward the dart game, scanning my surroundings.

All at once, the sounds of the carnival whirl around me—merry-go-round music, rides clinking and hissing, the chatter of the crowd.

The overwhelming scent of popcorn mixed with cotton candy stirs my stomach.

"That one! I want to ride that one." Ace bounces up and down on his small double-knotted red Chucks, pointing to a giant, spinning windmill contraption in the sky that looks like something straight out of a *Final Destination* movie.

Yeah, not today, Satan.

Not my baby.

"Oh, um…" I purse my lips, looking at that thing in sheer horror when I catch Stefano pantomiming height restrictions with his hand sliced over Ace's definitely under four-feet eight-inches requirement. "Maybe in a year or two, big guy. You've got to grow a bit more for that one."

Ace shrugs.

Relief, and perhaps that chili cheese dog I'm currently regretting, surge through me.

My stomach gurgles loudly.

Stefano winces, shielding his hand against the late afternoon sun dappled through the Ferris wheel beams. "Is it your stomach?"

You could say that. "Yeah, there's a lot going on in there."

"Have you thought about going to the doctor? You know, just in case it really is food poisoning."

Shit.

A small laugh bubbles at the back of my throat.

"What's so funny?" he asks.

"It's a frog!" *Not quite.* Ace cheerfully points and announces to everyone in a ten-foot radius. Except, with his missing teeth, it sounds like: *It's a fraud!*

Stefano throws back his head laughing.

Guilt curdles in my stomach.

At the same time, a collective wave of laughter pinballs between us and a handful of sugar-rushed, stuffed-animal-toting passersby with their *omigosh, isn't he adorable* expressions.

Whispering, I tell Ace, "He's in there lounging on a lily pad," before I shake my head at Stefano.

Wordlessly, I'm telling him it's nothing, when I've died a few minor deaths today because of how ironically funny this situation is. It's hilarious, really. You labor, you plot, you make lists, then bam! Now, we're both hypocrites. He's rushing in, and I don't even know if he loves me.

Heck, do I even know for certain if I love him?

My inner voice swiftly chastises me for lying to myself.

Of course, I love him.

I plan weddings. I pay attention to the details from the first consultation. The stolen glances. The constant touching. The sappy way they can't be apart for more than two seconds.

I've got it bad for Stefano Fortemani, and I don't know if the future he mentioned included Ace and me for real. Faced with the reality of us, plus the tadpole in my belly, what then? Will he still want my package deal?

Another bout of giggles spills out of me.

He arches an eyebrow. "Still nothing?" he asks with that handsome smile and easy charm.

This time it's a soft swoon that slips past my lips.

How is he more handsome every time I see him?

"Oh, yeah, it just… The Tilt-A-Whirl plus cotton candy? *No bueno,*" I explain.

"Ah okay."

Stefano gives me a reassuring nod as he tosses me a sidelong glance. I suspect he still isn't wholly buying my story.

Rightly so, on his part.

I imagine I must look like I feel. Nervous and scared to tell him about my positive results and failing horribly at hiding it.

"I'm sleepy, Mommy," Ace says.

Bending down to his level, I meet his big round brown eyes. He blinks slowly and rubs the back of his hand against them.

"Think you can make it a few more minutes until we get through the crowd?"

Ace shakes his head. "My legs are tired," he says, and my whole heart wrenches at his quivering bottom lip.

"It's okay. Don't cry, Mommy will carry you."

But before I can scoop him up, Stefano bends down, too. "Hmm, Mom's tummy isn't very happy right now. Would you mind if I carried you?" he asks Ace.

My son's trembling lip and teary eyes as he nods are one thing.

But it's this moment, exactly, that I know I'm so gone for this man.

Ace adores him. He felt safe with him on rides, shared his funnel cake, and held his hand at the petting zoo. Ace trusts Stefano enough to let Stefano hold him. And on top of their budding relationship, Seneca was undeniably right about women being hard-wired for men who seem responsible enough to take care of their family.

My ovaries are absolutely weeping with joy. I'm sure, so is my occupied womb.

God, if there is something wrong with this man, please tell me now before it's too late because...

I'm standing here like a fool, more than a little hopeful, ogling this man as he sweeps my son up into his arms and rests his tiny body over his shoulder like it's nothing.

As Ace's small hand clings to the fabric of Stefano's sweater, every inch of me aches with love. And a little grief over Justin.

It feels like I'm moving on from the life we shared.

Together, we walk in silence, weaving through the crowd

toward the exit, when Stefano intertwines our fingers.

"I hope this is okay with you?" He darts his gaze to Ace, who's already fast asleep.

"Oh, my goodness, yes. That boy is heavy as all get-out." I giggle nervously. "If anything, you saved me."

Just tell him, Avery.

I take a deep breath, stilling my nerves.

"Actually, I've been meaning to talk to you about, uh…"

I trail off but Stefano doesn't miss a beat.

"I'm not falling for you anymore," Stefano says, stealing my breath. "I'm in love with you, Avery Ellis."

He's breathing so hard. The vibration of his chest passes through to Ace, and I can't stop watching his tiny body rise and fall.

Every plan I had of telling Stefano about our baby news goes straight out the window.

I'm an emotional, empathic mess inside. A bundle of feelings swarming all over me. What I feel, it isn't one-sided, and knowing that makes everything feel within reach.

This is a milestone moment.

The man I love, loves me too. Even though he doesn't know I'm pregnant yet, and while I should tell him now, I don't want to taint this part. I don't want to worry about whether his love will still stand when there's another human involved. I don't want to think about responsibility that won't matter for months.

Plus, shouldn't we come out as a couple to our friends and family before breaking any baby news?

Talk about bullet train bypassing stops.

"Say something, please." His Adam's apple bobs, and he

smiles sweetly. "Because right now I'm freaking out, and I know I should've waited to tell you. I know we said this wasn't supposed to be serious. This was just for fun. But I love you. You and your beautiful son are all I can think about, and you don't wait with something this urgent."

Stefano squeezes my hand and searches my eyes, imploring me to respond.

I peer up at him and smile.

Be bold.

On a deep breath, I say, "I'm pretty sure I've been in love with you for weeks." I shrug.

Stefano stares at me for a few seconds, then he releases my hand and curves his to my cheek. A slow smile bends his lips. "You know we're asking for trouble, rushing in like this…"

"It sounds like fun."

He lowers his mouth to mine and kisses me until my knees are weak. My resolve not to get my hopes up is even weaker. No, I don't want to taint this part.

We've got our last Dream Team meeting on Monday, right?

I'll just tell him then.

CHAPTER NINETEEN
Stefano

MONDAY MORNING IS like déjà vu. Avery and I are back to ChatVideo. I'm in Healdsburg for in-person appointments with two of our wine distributor partners, and she's in the city, working on events, shockingly unrelated to Dante and Morgan's wedding. Just like that first time, the Dream Team is gathering to talk progress and logistics for this final meeting.

"Hey, thanks for logging in early. Sorry I'm late." Avery laughs just as her screen border illuminates a bright blue, and her smiling face appears. "This day has been pure chaos."

"Oh yeah?"

Again, she's effortlessly, undeniably beautiful in a pale purple blouse. Her light pink blush is dusted over her smooth golden skin. Her bright brown gaze hasn't yet fallen on me, but as always, she commands my attention.

I'm so open for this woman.

"My *Lord*, the consult I had with that red-dress bride?" Avery's brown eyes widen. "Total debacle. The bridesmaid dresses are two grand, and she's not footing the bill. Like, what?"

"That's steep."

I minimize the Quarterly Trends and Consumer Health Index reports I'd been reviewing for our next family business meeting, then turn on Gallery view, so my square is centered next to Avery's on the screen.

A smile tugs at the corners of my mouth.

I watch her pull out her giant pink planner and drop it on her desk with a loud thud, and I can't get over how much has changed over so little time. Our first meeting was mid-July. We're just breaking into September, and we're two completely different people.

I'm still learning and climbing, reaching for the next rung. Except, it feels less about career, and more about life. Those decades of management and winemaking experience, marriage even, their collective purpose seems like it was to inform the new life I'm building. *Hoping to build.* I still know the vast, fascinating history of my family's vineyard grounds. I was still that guy who was top of my class in business school. I still read to learn the details of processes and people. And, strangely, those twelve years of marriage, I don't regret them.

They've all shaped me into a man who pays attention, values family, and loves with my entire being.

Most of all, I know I'll never give up on my dream of love and making a family—no matter the blend.

I said I'd never rush in.

But looking at this woman in full-color resolution. Studying her beautiful features, her heart always on display. I feel like she's what it was all for.

I'd never change anything I've been through because

those lived experiences led me to the woman who gets under my skin and reminds me that I'm a man with fire burning in my loins.

She's the best plot twist.

She's my silver lining.

"Long story short, she might not just be down two bridesmaids, throwing off her perfectly balanced wedding party. After this, she's probably down two decades-long friendships."

"That's *no bueno*," I say, using her words from the carnival, and loving that it earns me a low musical laugh.

Under my desk, I stretch out my legs, getting comfortable.

"Exactly." Her smile widens. "Just like Tilt-A-Whirl and cotton candy, asking your friends to fork out cash for expensive dresses that they certainly *will not* shorten and wear again, is *no bueno*."

Silence blankets the virtual room for a beat.

Then Avery squares her body to the camera, a smile teetering on her full pink lips. "What?"

I shake my head like it's no big deal. "Nothing, I just love you so much."

"Awww, don't say that when I can't be with you right now."

A low chuckle rumbles over me. "Sorry, let's just get started. We're finalizing details for the bachelor and bachelorette parties, right? Anything else on your agenda?"

Avery pauses. "Plus, finalizing the guest list. And a few other things…" She breaks off, and I get the sense she's holding back.

I straighten.

"What are these other things you want to discuss?"

Her cheeks flush a faint pink.

"There's something bothering you," I say, stating the obvious. My heart stutters when her face falls. "You know you can tell me anything, right?"

She hazards a look at me.

"Sorry, it's just…I was going to save the personal stuff for last."

My throat constricts.

Fire swarms over my neck and ears, spreading to my cheeks. Briefly, I consider letting it go. Whatever it is, we can talk about it when she's ready.

Then my head swims with worst-case scenarios of her ending this relationship before we've even gotten a chance to get started, and I know I won't be able to concentrate, not knowing.

"Do you think we can talk about it now, then recap the party and guest list details last?"

She clears her throat.

My pulse sprints.

What is it?

Like she did once before, Avery stares at me like I'm a Rorschach inkblot, unsure what she's looking at, and a familiar idea sparks.

Swallowing, I glance at my phone on the desk beside my laptop. "You know, someone brilliant once got to the bottom of our issues with an icebreaker. So, I've reserved ten minutes for us to work through whatever is on your mind."

Avery cracks a smile.

"Great minds, right?" I tilt my head. "Ask anything on our hearts as fast and as honest as possible."

"Right."

Out of objections, and at my mercy, she sucks in a lung-ful of air, letting me take the lead.

On the screen, I tap over to the timer extension, and set it for ten minutes.

"The truth shall set you free," I quip. "I'll go first. Ready?"

She lifts her chin and nods.

Avery's fiery brown eyes flutter wide open as we stare into each other's digital boxes.

Then I start the timer, and fire off the first question. "What's really bothering you?"

Avery's mouth presses into a flat line. She straightens, posture ramrod straight. "Actually, I was thinking we should tell our friends and families about us."

That's what this is about?

She blinks up to meet my stare.

The tension in my chest loosens slightly. "Um, okay. How about after the wedding?" I suggest. "I really don't want to overshadow their big day."

"Do you really think they don't already know?" she counters, her tone taking on an impatient lilt.

Instinctually, I know they do.

Dante and I have been talking in broad strokes and hy-potheticals since the tux appointment. If he's put two and two together, I've got to believe he's talking about us with Morgan, who keeps nothing from the Sister Circle— including my sister as an honorary member. By the rules of the telephone game, Mother knows, therefore, so does her entire Gossip Set.

Only, Avery and I haven't confirmed, which means it won't be public yet.

No one wants false information tracked back to them.

"Of course, I believe they have suspicions." I wait a beat. "Remember when you said you didn't love the way I inserted myself, my opinions, and my personal baggage into Morgan and Dante's relationship? This feels like the same thing, but with us."

"It's not the same."

"Not exactly, but in the same vein. Do we really want to undermine what we've built so far by putting it out there to be judged before we let is grow stronger?" I query.

Avery shakes her head.

"Listen, I love that it's just us," I add.

"Me too." She smiles.

"For that matter, I don't welcome everyone's opinions about us. The mere idea that anyone would think what we have is some reactionary rebound because my ex moved on… I hate even the idea of it. And I know I shouldn't think about the optics, but I want to love you without limits or outside speculation, if that makes sense."

Avery seems to consider this.

But then her shoulders tense and her expression smooths.

"Is that what we are, a rebound?"

"Of course not." I feel like an idiot.

Suddenly, it occurs to me that outing ourselves to everyone is only Avery's surface-level concern, and there's something so much deeper bothering her. Possibly, this question was a test, and I've failed, so I've lost access to the real concern.

"Jesus, no. I hate the fact that word is even on your tongue. I'm in love with you, Avery." I scrub a hand over my face, groaning. "What we have... I've never felt passion and purpose so fierce. Please don't ever doubt that," I bite out.

"Okay," she says softly.

Please believe me.

But as she worries her lips, I know I've put my foot in my mouth with this. Instead of taking her lead, I had to go and bring up Carina, planting doubt in Avery's mind about us.

My God.

"When did you imagine telling everyone?" I ask, circling back. I'm futilely trying to get this runaway train back on the track.

Avery starts to speak again, then she seems to reconsider, and I feel compelled to fill the silence.

"We've got the bachelor and bachelorette parties coming up, then it's the wedding. What's a couple more weeks?" I reason.

She lowers her chin briefly, and says, "No, it's fine. We can wait."

My pulse throbs.

The next five minutes pass in a blur of wedding-related questions about the upcoming parties.

I feel her guards raising, and suddenly, I'm wading through every interaction we've shared trying to determine where I went wrong.

When the timer goes off, her agenda immediately appears on the screen.

"Now, let's get down to details," she says, and I know she's disengaging from the conversation.

I've made her uncertain about us, and there's nothing more I can say.

The muscles at my jaw harden and jut out at the sides as Morgan and Dante join the meeting.

There's no time to catch my bearings.

For the rest of the meeting, I only chime in as needed. I listen to Avery go on about how we've successfully gotten the guest list down to fifty-two people. *Not the goal, but close enough.* Then she goes on to confirm the times and dates for the bachelor's Paintball and Pints.

After she provides Morgan with the pickup time for the party bus to Bramoso, she zips through a few more housekeeping items, including their Mediterranean cruise honeymoon itinerary and flight, confirming vows are finished (or in progress, in Dante's case), my cousin Enzo's arrival for his officiant duties, and marriage license pickup.

All the while, it's on the tip of my tongue to confess my love for Avery to them.

But then she says, "Anything else you want to add, Stefano?"

A humorless laugh hurls out of me.

My head spins, and I'm dying to ask more questions. *What the hell was that whiplash moment back there? How can you sit here talking about parties and marriage licenses like nothing happened? Why do I feel like, with a single question, I've sent us reeling backward? What aren't you telling me?*

Instead, I mumble under my breath, "No, I'm good. No

questions here."

"Okay, great." Avery makes a note in her pink book. Her work done, Avery stops sharing her screen. After informing us she's got an appointment at the top of the hour, she says her see-you-laters, and ends the meeting for us all.

I'm still staring at my computer wallpaper when my phone pings with a text notification. Hoping it's from Avery, my attention snaps to the screen where there's a message from Dante.

What in the hell did you do?

CHAPTER TWENTY

Avery

I DON'T KNOW what I'm doing.

These past two weeks, Stefano and I haven't been alone for more than a few hours at a time.

No, we didn't break up.

It's *not* over. We're not teenagers jumping in and out of relationships because we butted heads over the right time to out ourselves. We text. We still say we love each other. It's a completely mature response for two adults who've yet to find our way to the same page.

You know, except for the whole undercover lovers thing.

I'm in love, pregnant, running on a trip-wire hormone cocktail, and possibly a rebound for a man who might be one-upping his ex. Other than that, I'm on a luxurious bachelorette party bus. The bar is stocked, and I'm surrounded by my friends who've been pregaming for the past hour. What is there to complain about?

A frustrated sigh heaves out of me.

Like a radar alert, Morgan rests her head on my shoulder and peers up at me, sympathetically.

"Are you thinking about him?" she asks.

Why yes, I haven't stopped thinking about him for going on two months now. However did you guess?

I flit a quick glance to Chiara.

That's right, my friend—also, my secret lover's sister—is here to celebrate Morgan's bachelorette party with us. And why wouldn't she be? We've all grown into great friends. She's an honorary circle sister, here to whoop it up tonight over fine Italian at Bramoso's, her family's restaurant, followed by riveting karaoke in a smoky hole-in-the-wall bar.

Heat swarms my neck and cheeks.

I've got no idea if Stefano's told her about us. Or if Morgan, who I'm sure told Dante, has whispered the news into his sister's perked-up ear.

So, not only can I *not* drink myself into a mope, now, I also can't speak hypothetically about Stefano with my girls, either.

The thing is, believing in fairy tales… Solidly my territory.

But Chiara is Stefano's sister. She's Victoria "The All-Knowing" Fortemani's daughter. It's in her genes to sniff out a lie—or a not-so-secret secret—with ruthless elegance and graceful finesse.

Not to mention, she's got me beat in the hopeless romantic territory.

Even if she's been strangely quiet tonight.

"Yes," I finally say to Morgan. I'm hoping against all hopes that she takes the hint that I'm trying to keep talk of Stefano to a minimum. *Or nonexistent.* Just in case, I cautiously add. "It's your bachelorette party. Can we *not* make tonight about me and…" Wide-eyed, I mouth his name, on the off chance the music Seneca's blasting doesn't drown me out.

Morgan nods, not at all discreet.

On the other end of this L-shaped bench seat, Valerie's eyes snap knowingly to us as she sips her bubbly.

She thinks it's pointless to keep talking in code. They still don't know Stefano and I are "officially" together, but I've told them we've been growing on each other. Which, in Sister Circle code, means my heart is involved.

Same thing.

Quiet as kept, maybe Stefano had a point.

The girls and I have been talking about us for the past two weeks. Blatantly telling everyone about our relationship will absolutely overshadow the wedding like it's doing to this gloom-and-doom party bus.

I refuse to let it happen.

"Listen, I love that you all care so much, but I'm telling you, I'm fine," I say, aiming to nip this in the bud before we stop to pick up Monica.

"Mm-hmm. Freaked out, insecure, neurotic, and emotional?" Seneca quips.

I laugh.

In my periphery, Chiara's and my eyes connect.

Smiling at her, I attempt to move the conversation along.

"Yes, all of that, Sen." I giggle and nudge her shoulder with mine then reach over and squeeze Morgan. "But also, I'm so ready to celebrate our girl over delicious Italian food—"

"And sourdough bread," Valerie moans.

"And wine flights," Morgan adds, excitedly.

Notably, nothing over the top like Vegas-style clubbing or a gentlewoman's bar with scantily clad hulks in stuffed Speedos. Nope, not for Morgan Elaine Forster, soon-to-be Fortemani.

She couldn't be further from the dangling penis necklaces, crowns, and neon pink sashes girl.

Her party idea list included the likes of wine-tasting or wine and painting (we agreed, too on the nose), glamping/spa day, karaoke, concerts (British Columbia with Beyoncé), and a Clue-themed murder mystery party down in San Diego at a viral board game store, Love & Games. "Quiet drama." Her words verbatim.

With the jam-packed wedding month, though, out-of-town options quickly got nixed.

So, she settled for wine and dinner at Bramoso's, followed by a pit stop at a karaoke bar in the city.

It's not Queen B killing it like a badass blonde bombshell with fifty outfit changes, but we'll be together.

Win-win.

Valerie's phone rings on speakerphone, piercing the air.

A few seconds later, Monica answers. "ETA?" she asks.

"Two minutes away, so bring yourself outside, and let's start this party!" Valerie shouts and hooks her toned leg around the floor-to-ceiling pole. Flaunting the fruits of the Pilates classes she's been taking at Monica's studio, she whips her body around like a seasoned professional.

"*Ow*! *Ow*!" Morgan and I holler.

Seneca produces a stack of ones from her purse and starts fanning them at Valerie.

"Okay, I see you!" Chiara perks up for maybe the first

time she entered the bus.

I smile solemnly.

Sadly, this is as wild as it's going to get tonight. Dinner and karaoke just don't have that same *I'm almost off the market* feel, I think, when Monica's panicked voice rips through the debauchery.

"Oh, my God. I can't believe this is happening," she scoffs.

The four of us freeze.

"What is it?" I ask.

The line muffles with curses for a beat before Monica says, "Shit, I need you all to come in for a minute."

Then the line clicks off.

"Aw hell," Seneca bites out, which feels wholly accurate.

Monica Mathers is nothing if not the life of every party. She's electric pink stiletto nails, flawless makeup, glossy natural curls, and that banging Pilates body. She's the outspoken alpha of our group, who knows how to let loose. If she isn't ready and waiting on the curb, something is wrong.

The question is, how wrong?

Unbidden, images of a Speedo-wearing Stefano making a surprise appearance rush to mind. That, and either a flooded kitchen or a giant Australian-sized spider on the wall.

I'm already considering where I'm going to get a bucket, a blowtorch, or fainting salts when we pull in front of her house.

"What do you think is happening?" I ask.

Chiara looks as worried as I feel.

"It'll be a few pounds of chocolate and wine delivery she

forgot about," she says, and I feel like someone's zapped me with a lightning rod.

I look at her. *Really,* look at her, down to the sensible heels, muted pink dress, and a single, small section of limp curls that she missed with the leave-in conditioner.

My mouth falls open.

I'm not the only one in a secret mope.

Every atom in my body throbs with the urge to ask her what's going on with her and her boyfriend, Lamar. This is what I do. I fix other people's problems. That is, when I'm not going through personal crises.

But then, in rescue mode, Valerie shoulders to the front of the bus with Seneca and Morgan on her heels.

Chiara heaves a small sigh. "I'm fine."

I smile, letting her exit the bus behind Morgan before I follow suit.

"I know all about fine…"

We march up Monica's walkway, a dressed to impress, bombshell swat team.

Except, the front door is cracked.

Immediately, Morgan volunteers to be the caboose.

None of us argue.

It is her bachelorette party. The least we can do is spare the glittery wedding pumps she's breaking in. From water and charred bug guts—or her soon-to-be brother-in-law's thinly veiled family jewels—we aren't sure yet.

"Mon!" Seneca calls out, tapping the door then fumbling back into us.

We all shriek.

Meanwhile, I've added psychotic murder to the list of

dangers I'm listening for.

Thankfully, a few seconds later, Monica yells back, "I'm in the kitchen."

Since her voice isn't streaked with terror, we stealthily enter the house, and we're immediately baffled about what's going on.

"Um…" Morgan wedges past us into the living room where five chairs are huddled—with a wide berth—around what looks like a raised pedestal of sorts. "What did we miss? And why does it smell like there's a cook-off underway in your kitchen?"

I pull in a long whiff of warm, savory spices.

"It does smell good." I resist the urge to rub my belly, just as Monica, dramatic as ever, enters stage right.

Like a new-age Vanna Black in a sequin blush-colored dress straining to cover her thighs, she fans out her arm toward her kitchen, and announces, "Presenting, your team…"

Under her command, a bare-chested army of stupid-hot men in black slacks and bow ties file into the room holding trays of champagne, hors d'oeuvres, and… *Are those paint supplies?*

What is happening?

As if answering our many questions, finally, the sergeant of this army enters, his arms loaded up with folding trays.

In quick succession, they move assembly-style. Sergeant sets up the trays, and one by one, the rest dole out glasses, an assortment of fruits, meats, and cheeses, pours champagne, and sets up easels and a pre-filled palette with brushes and water cups.

"How did you—" I break off, scanning the room as I watch what's unfolding in front of us.

When a microphone crackles to life in the corner near the television, I take one look at the girl power lyrics cued up on the screen, and it hits me exactly what Monica's up to.

Well, most of it.

"Our sister deserves everything her heart desires. Wouldn't you agree?" she asks.

The rest of the Sister Circle hum our agreement as she proceeds to explain why she had Chiara cancel our Bramoso reservation. As it turns out, while I've been juggling work and a blooming love for Stefano Fortemani—and dropping the ball on an amazeballs bachelorette party—single-handedly, THE Monica Mathers has teamed up with Chiara, pulling out all the stops for Morgan.

The list we whittled down to dinner and karaoke?

They found a way to ramp it back up to everything she dreamed of.

We're performing a Beyoncé-oke (all-Beyoncé karaoke) playlist concert while being treated to a massage and foot soak at the deft hands of a beautiful army. We'll be feasting on fine Italian cuisine courtesy of Chef Rossi on the ones and twos (burners). We're tasting four seasonal wines while we paint.

Our subject?

That's the part I couldn't have foreseen.

He is a true, delectable work of art wearing a truly eye-catching birthday suit that makes us all feel like celebrating. *Truly.*

It's not cheating without touching, right?

But that's not all, folks.

After we've sung our hearts out, sowed our creative oats, and enjoyed a lovely fare, we'll be glamping at chez Monica and playing a Clue-themed murder mystery game supplied by her new Instagram friends, Harper and Nadia from Love & Games.

In other words, Monica saved the day.

And I've been an underwhelming wedding planner and maid of honor.

"Avery?"

At first, I'm confused when my girls rush to my side. Until I register the worry etched on their faces.

I'm crying.

In and of itself, this is not anything new. I cry. I'm a crier. Empath and all.

But not streaming waterworks.

"It's just so amazing that you've done all of this for Morgan." I shift my attention to Monica as she swipes under my eyes. "I'm so sorry I didn't help you with all of this."

"Shhh…" She blows a soft breath over my eyes. "You think I didn't want to do all of this? I realize planning is your job, but we all want to celebrate Morgan."

"And again"—Seneca starts in on me—"you don't have to do everything alone."

Immediately, my mind veers and hooks a hard left into Stefano territory. Without sharing everything about our relationship and the baby with my girls, I feel like history is…not repeating itself, but bordering on it, for sure.

I'm doing it all on my own again.

It's losing Justin. It's me and Ace against the world. It's—

"All right, that's it." Seneca snaps her fingers and slices her hand through the air, cutting my internal spiral short.

Everyone, including our beautiful, half-naked army stands at attention.

She is our completely sensible, logic and straight-shooting line of symmetry, so I'm not surprised when she cuts straight through the mounting emotions in this room.

"Listen, Will got on my last nerve today, so I really, *really* want to fill my eyes with these oily pectorals while doing Beyoncé-oke." Her slicked dark long ponytail whips around as she pivots to me. "Trust me when I say, the Queen is not a good mix with salty tears, so I'm giving you fifteen minutes."

Dang.

I almost laugh out loud, looking at Morgan try, and fail, to stifle hers.

"Like, with a timer?" Morgan sputters as she flits an accusatory glance at me.

I shrug because timers are great order restoration tools. More people should use them.

But Seneca is so serious.

She flips her dainty wrist, all business now. "Let's see, it's six forty-four. In one minute, you start, and we've got until seven o'clock." *Period.*

But the jokester in me can't resist.

"Or else?" I challenge, stupidly.

Ready as ever for my games, she retorts, "I'm sending you home in the party bus with that germy pole, and we're going to have all the fun without you."

Double dang.

My mouth falls open with a sharp intake of air. "You wouldn't!"

"She would," the rest of my Sister Circle says in unison.

I huff out a resigned sigh.

Then, I throw up my hands. "I guess we're doing this."

Satisfied with my answer, Seneca quickly lays out the logistics for me. Which I secretly love. Nothing like order and structure.

"This is how it's going to work," she says. Then she takes the next thirty seconds to efficiently inform me that I'll be temporarily dethroning our model from his pedestal. At which point, my girls will fire off questions, which I'm obligated to answer honestly. If they believe I'm lying, they've got the right to confer with other sources (i.e., all Fortemani family members, winery employees, wedding party members, Stefano's best friend, Dylan, Mommy, and Ace).

Shoot.

"Okay, wow. No pressure," I say, begrudgingly accepting her conditions.

Although, if I'm honest, it's almost a relief. Finally, they'll know. Even if this thing with Stefano doesn't turn out to be my second chance at a fairy tale—for me, and not his ex—I won't be alone.

"Everyone ready?" Seneca settles her attention on me. Then, surprisingly, at Chiara.

What was that?

Morgan bounces on her toes, clapping.

"Based on the entertainment value alone, this night is going to be one for the books. I couldn't be happier."

"Gee, thanks." I laugh. "Glad I can help."

Then, these five women, my mirrors, they get to work, and I'm not even close to prepared.

"Are you in love with my brother?" Chiara asks right out the gate.

My heart beats like there's an entire drumline in my chest about to throw down at an HBCU homecoming.

Swallowing, I eke out, "Yes."

The cackling and cheers nearly pierce my eardrums.

My girls kick off their heels, acting like total fools as they run around in circles celebrating like that's the least of my problems.

Still, I can't help but laugh, too.

"Is that it?" I roll my eyes playfully, knowing it'll reel them back in.

"Not by a long shot, ma'am." Seneca grins from ear to ear. "So, we know y'all did the Oompa Loompa behind Il Sapore, but was there any follow-up sexing?"

Chiara's eyes widen.

Thank you, Seneca, for putting all my business on Front Street.

I pull in a lungful of air, releasing it through my nose as I nod.

It's the snaps and resounding amens that make me love them to my core. We're at a bachelorette party for our girl, and they're still lifting me up. *In their roundabout, prying way, but still.*

"See!" Seneca is positively exuberant. "*Girl*, I told you they've been all up and through her place, his, the winery, the vineyard trails, doing the nasty."

"She's not wrong." I shrug.

Morgan and Valerie high-five.

"Boop, okay now!" Monica blinks a good dozen times with pride.

If we're being honest, might as well get it all out there. Although, there's a part of me waiting for them to ask the inevitable question.

They go off on a timeline tangent, connecting the days Stefano and I've spent time together. Then Seneca asks about him meeting Ace, which leads us down a road of *Cars*, cleanup, and the carnival recap. They end up seated, fully invested, and swooning. Everyone certain "he's so good with kids," which nearly leaves me in tears again, which is strictly against Seneca's rules.

She flips her wrist again, determined to keep tabs on the time.

"It's six fifty-two," she reminds us. "Get to asking if you've still got questions."

In the back of my mind, I'm thinking *my GOD this fifteen minutes is long.*

But also, they've managed to cover our relationship, love, sex, and Stefano's adorable bond with Ace. Beyond the fertilized egg in my uterus, what else could they ask?

I shift on my feet.

Morgan eyes me curiously, and for a split second, it feels like we're at an impasse.

But then she screws her lips to the side and squints. "What about that last Dream Team meeting? You said everything was fine, but was it really?"

I consider her for a beat, reading between her lines.

She knows, but she's beating around the bush.

"No, it wasn't." I meet her intense stare. "Before you and Dante joined the meeting, I'd told him I wanted to tell everyone about us."

"Tell us what about you?" Chiara presses.

Pulling in a deep breath, I blurt out, "That we're dating."

"As in girlfriend, boyfriend." Morgan's smile deepens. She nods like she's connecting the dots. "Y'all are official, aren't you?" When I nod, she speculates for how long. "Since the movie at the vineyard, right?"

Wait.

I scan the room, taking in the elaborate change of plans. We're all here, and no one is in rush to celebrate Morgan. No one was surprised because we're all immersed in my...

Quiet drama.

This isn't a surprise to them, it's an ambush.

"How did you know?" I ask, suspiciously, sneaking a slice of brie and a grape off my assigned tray, popping them into my mouth.

I'm met with five *are you seriously asking that* expressions.

"Ma'am, you and Stefano Fortemani could barely stand to be around each for five minutes at the engagement party." Seneca giggles. "Then he brushed you off after dress shopping, and suddenly every time you're together, you're disappearing for thirty, forty minutes at a time."

Valerie laughs. *"Right?"*

"It's been obvious for a while," Monica says, quietly, but everyone pivots to her. This is her MO. She lets everyone else say their piece, then out of left field, boom! Tough love.

She steps back and folds her arms across her chest, and I

sense the sharp turn ahead.

"Here's what's still confusing me." She pins me with a no-nonsense stare as she commandeers the conversation. "We all knew or suspected as much, but why would he want to keep it on the down-low?"

It's a loaded question.

By the time I bring them up to speed on Stefano's many reasons, including competing with his ex-wife's relationship—I leave out her impending motherhood—they're all on my side.

"At least his intentions seem to be in the right place, though," Morgan reasons.

I fidget with my cuticles.

"So, yeah. I'm a secret until your wedding," I say, nonchalantly, knowing full well Monica isn't done with me.

True to her character, she drops the hammer. "Is that the only secret you've been withholding?"

This is it.

I flit another glance at Chiara, my eyes already threatening tears.

"Can we just sing Beyoncé songs and draw hideous pictures of this beautiful man?" My voice wavers. I'm deflecting and everyone knows it. "Don't you think I've hijacked enough of Morgan's party? We've got Chef Rossi waiting, these gorgeous men are wasting away, the paint is drying—"

"The wine needs tasting..." Monica adds.

One of the soldiers snickers.

"A minute left," Seneca asserts, very timely, kicking Monica into overdrive.

"How've you been feeling?" She raises an eyebrow. "Was

it food poisoning, dairy intolerance, or…" Monica lets the rest of that question hang in the electric air.

As if just catching on, Valerie gasps. "Oh my God."

Morgan and Seneca share a charged glance, and everything feels like it's coming to a head.

My cheeks burn with humiliation.

"Last question…" Monica stands, her entire demeanor softening as she asks, "Does he know, or are you planning to keep the baby a secret from him, too?"

A collective, emotion-ridden gasp rumbles from my friends.

Chills spiral down my spine.

I blink back unshed tears as I chew the inside of my cheek.

"Wow…" Chiara blinks a good dozen times, and I assume she's processing. But then she says, "That explains so much."

The five of us snap to her.

"Wait, like what?" Seneca asks.

Chiara's raises her eyebrows and shakes her head. "After dress shopping last month, I called him out for canceling on Avery…"

"He didn't have plans?" Morgan asks.

My eyes connect with Chiara's as she shakes her head.

"The man built—and immediately deleted—an online dating profile that night, apparently hoping to glean what insight about dating he hadn't yet gained from the ridiculous self-help podcasts he'd been listening to." She laughs, and it feels contagious.

Johnny Timmons's scam of a podcast pops to the top of

my mind, and I almost burst out laughing.

Based on sheer will, I manage to bite my tongue while she continues.

"My brother ended up watching *Door-to-Door Dates*, claiming he wasn't ready to date, but that he wanted to be organized and prepared when the time came. Not long after that I run into him at the store humming that Jagged Edge song, 'Let's Get Married' as he plucked a plush daisy pillow from a shelf."

A giggle spills through my tears. "Oopsie Daisy."

"Yeah, pretty sure we saw her on your couch last Turn-Up Tuesday." Morgan's lips twitch.

"The killer part is, the other day, we were all visiting Mom, and he was in the kitchen making coffee." Seneca pauses. But then she squares her body to mine as she says, "He thought he was alone, but I distinctly heard him say, 'I can't wait for this wedding to be over.' I just remember him being so adamant about Dante and Morgan prolonging their engagement. I guess we all know why the switch-up."

At this point, it's a feat to tamp down my emotions. I don't bother holding back my crying.

No one acknowledges that time's up.

They must know I need to get this out before I can't.

"He doesn't know yet." I swallow to get the rest out. "I was going to tell him during our last ChatVideo before Morgan and Dante joined. When he didn't even want to tell anyone we're together...and after he said the thing about us being a rebound because his ex moved on, I couldn't yet."

"Aww, Avery." Morgan climbs the pedestal to pull me into her arms.

"He tells me that he loves me all the time. I'm complete-ly in love with him, too. It's just...in that moment, though, it felt like he wasn't sure about us," I explain. "I don't want the baby to be a factor when he decides."

I'm almost squeezed death by five pairs of arms banded around me in a group hug.

Then, like they've conspired with Destiny's Child, one by one, my Sister Circle ambles over to the karaoke machine, cues up a song, and collectively hovers over the mic.

As those first tinkling notes of "Girl" spring into the air, I'm ugly-crying.

Monica and Valerie fight it out to sing Beyoncé's part, crooning about how we've come too far for me to feel alone.

Obviously, the song is about some idiotic man who dared cheat on Monica's doppelganger, Kelly Rowland, but the friendship sentiment is strong.

By the time they get to the second chorus, telling me not to be ashamed of crying and needing someone to vent to, I'm singing, too.

Horribly, but with my whole chest.

Soon, the army, the sergeant, the chef, and the visibly cold model—*shrinkage*—join in, singing about us being each other's loving girls.

The entire scene is ridiculous—and so cringy. I'm glad we're not in public, spewing this audible venom onto innocent bystanders.

As we feast on delicious Italian fare with our feet soaking in lavender Epsom salt and strange men's hands groping our shoulders, Chiara leans in close to my ear.

"The bachelor party is tomorrow, right?"

I hesitate, unsure where she's going with this question, then nod.

"What if I told you I've got a plan to blow the cover right off this thing?" she whispers.

It's a sweet sentiment with the slightest bit of edge to her tone. The gleam in her eyes is filled with confidence, readiness. It's a battle cry of solidarity.

In Sister Circle code, it translates to: *We ride at dawn.*

CHAPTER TWENTY-ONE
Stefano

A TALL, BULKY guy in full camo fatigues gear and a red weathered 49ers cap steps out from behind the register.

"Richter party?" he calls out.

The group of guys waiting in front of us excitedly stand, shoving and guffawing as they approach the guy, who introduces himself fittingly, as Riker, who looks like he's been out to the island on a few stints. He begins a safety and personal liability briefing, breaking down the rules as he outfits them with paintball markers, hoppers, air tanks, and battle masks.

I'm straining to hear what he says about the Capture the Flag game they're playing when Jameson elbows me.

The corner of his mouth hitches up. "We're next. Are you ready to come hard?"

"Wow, how long have you been waiting to drop that gem?"

He barks out a laugh.

In a nutshell, this is how life's going. I'm in love with a woman who's slowly distancing herself from me. And now, I've signed a waiver to play a potentially deadly game with an armed man-child who never misses an opportunity to make an ejaculatory joke.

Great.

Over his shoulder, I glare at Marco, who thought beating each other with paint-filled pellets flying at 300 feet per second was a brilliant idea for Dante's last hurrah as a single man.

He looks deliberately at me and fist-bumps Jameson.

In total, there are eight of us. Including Dante and these two Neanderthals, we've got Marcello, Mike, Everett, me, and thankfully, Dylan is here to relieve me of a full day of toxic masculinity.

"Remind me to shoot below the waist," Dylan says low enough so I'm the only one who hears.

I chuckle.

We watch as the other group is escorted out the side door to the fields.

As soon as the door closes behind them, Jameson turns to Dante. I figure he's about to make another adolescent joke, so I'm surprised when he nudges my brother's shoulder and says, "Two weeks until the big day, huh?"

Dante drags in a long breath, grinning. "I wish it was tomorrow."

Jameson nods. "That's real cool man. I'm happy for you."

As Dante thanks him, I'm considering whether I rushed to judgment with this guy. He hurt my sister years ago. Now, they're paired for the ceremony entrance dances, and she hasn't complained, so maybe they've come to a truce. She's dating his best friend, after all.

My shoulders relax.

Like my brother is in tune with my train of thoughts, he weaves Chiara into the conversation. "How's your dance going with my sister?"

Jameson pulls in a breath, smiling with... *is that pride?*

"Let's just say, we're going to give these other fools a run for their money." He chuckles. "Hands down, we've got the best song, and you know, if nothing else, we've got the moves."

"It's that good?" Dante rubs his hands down his jeans, seemingly impressed before he tosses him a sidelong glance. "So, is it safe to say you've let bygones be by—"

"Oh, hell yeah," Jameson says, too quickly to go unnoticed.

Dante's looking at him the same way I am.

We've always wondered if their friendship ever crossed the line. Since Jameson and Chiara were kids, they were tight. Riding-bikes, playing-in-the-winery, building-casks-with-his-dad tight. Until their freshman year in high school when his friend Lamar started dating her. Almost immediately after, Jameson cut ties.

Now, that Dante and I know how unbending love is, it's hard not to wonder, if Jameson did harbor a crush, how difficult it must be—after putting so much distance, and women, between them—now, spending so much time with her.

Dante tilts his head. "So, you all are cool..."

"My dude, we let that shit go a long time ago. Her and Lamar are like this." He crosses middle and index fingers. At Dante's raised eyebrow, he adds, "Just the other day, we were doing our thing, mixing up, dancing, and talking about the other pairs, and I mentioned Avery."

Wait.

Talk about whiplash. Where is he going with this?

My ears perk up like antennae.

"Yeah, she's your biggest competition for sure," Dante says.

At my side, Dylan chuckles, warning me to relax, and I'm prepared to do just that before Jameson scrubs his hand over his mouth and down the scruff of his neck with that self-satisfied smirk on his face.

"I asked if she was single, and Chiara said she'll hook me up with her number." *That smug bastard.* "She's fine as fuck, man. I can't wait to get my hands on—"

"Fortemani party?"

Riker is back with our stack of waivers in hand, ready to give us the same rules, safety, and personal liability spiel. But it's useless at this point.

At least, for Jameson West and his grimy hands, if I have anything to say about it.

My jaw hardens.

Jameson glances back at me. The instant our eyes connect, my body locks up with rage. Fire blazes over my skin.

"Got your game face on, there, huh, big guy?" He huffs out a grating laugh.

He grabs a set of the blue paintball markers and slips a battle mask over his face.

At the patronizing edge to his tone, the tension in my mouth steels under my clenched teeth.

I feel my brow furrow.

I'm going to wipe the floor with him.

Anger and fury surge through my blood to the tips of my limbs, refuting all logic.

Do I have the right to feel anything?

Avery wanted to tell everyone about us. I'm the asshole who thought keeping us in this bubble would somehow shield us from judgment and opinions. I was worried about overshadowing the wedding and undermining what we've built so far. I made us a reactionary rebound because Carina moved on when I should've been following Avery's lead.

She knew better.

"Oh, we'll definitely see you on the field," Dylan says, grabbing two sets of blue paintball markers, and handing me one.

After everyone has been outfitted with paintball markers, hoppers, air tanks, and battle masks, we've got two teams. The red team (Dante, our precious cargo, Marco, Dylan, and me), and the blue team (Marcello, Mike, Everett, and Jameson).

I hate to do my little brother this way, but he chose the wrong team today.

Soon, we're escorted out to a sprawling field that looks like something straight out of a *Modern Warfare* video game. It's set between the trees with rustic hay bales, tire and log stacks, and overturned giant wooden spools and spiral corrugated pipes.

It's legit.

"So, I guess congratulations are in order." Riker slaps Dante on the back.

The rest of us howl encouragingly in solidarity.

"We've got you set up on our Bachelor's Last Stand Run, which should be a good time." Riker takes a sec to recap the simple themed game for us.

Instead of Capture the Flag, Speedball, or a regular Elimination game. We're playing a scenario team-elimination game. Our teams have separate objectives. My team, the red team's, goal is to escort the groom-to-be across the field to the raised platform in the back with single staircase access and a concealed perimeter. The endpoint. However, the blue team's sole goal is to eliminate him.

Basically, it's football with loaded paint guns to fend off the opposition, Dante is the ball, and the platform is the end zone.

Mask on always, and no penalties for unnecessary roughness.

This is going to be fun.

A smile tugs at the corners of my mouth.

"Oh, I see you're hyped about this," Dylan says under his breath.

Indeed.

Immediately, my mind goes to work, zeroing in on the best vantage points.

"Referees will be out there to keep it fun and safe." Riker appropriately settles his focus on Jameson, aptly sussing out my target. "You've got 500 paintballs per person. Typically, reserved events last two-plus hours, but we've got no time limits on our private parties. So, if you've got paintballs, you're free to keep the party going. Any questions?"

With that, the teams scatter around the field.

Marco stays with Dante, and Dylan and I spread out.

I'm flat on my stomach, behind a wooden spool up against a netted wall when the referee blows the whistle, signaling the start.

We're supposed to start slow. No overdoing it until we get comfortable.

Advice that apparently went in one of Everett's ears, and out the other.

Within seconds, this guy, who lobbied for bar hopping over paintball, so he'd have phone access to text with his wife, Sophia, rushes the stacked logs where Dante's being guarded. Rambo-style, he's spraying blue paint everywhere, aiming nowhere, hoping it hits.

But he's out in the open, and it's too easy.

All his obvious hopes of ending this game are dashed quickly when Dylan sprays him in the leg.

Red paint splats all over his pants as he crashes to the ground.

You'd think it was real blood the way he howls, "Holy shit!" as he rolls around in the dirt.

We warned him about the sting, but did he listen?

"What the hell? I'm really hurt, man," he cries out like any of us are going to give up our position to help him.

Around the field, muffled laughs echo into the air.

Dramatically, Everett crawls toward a stack of tires, leveraging himself against it to pull himself up.

One look at him, and it's not hard to see it's a solid hit, which means he's out.

But because we all know Everett couldn't wait to get back to the lobby where his phone is tucked in his locker, Dylan shoots again, in the other leg.

Everett buckles, clinging to a tire.

"Goddammit! That's going to leave a bruise. You got me."

It's a waste of ammo, I suspect as a lesson to the rest of their dwindling team. But until Everett raises his hands and the marker, then calls out loudly for the referee to acknowledge he's been eliminated, he's still fair game.

Showing him mercy, a referee in the middle of the field blows a whistle, the entire time laughing as he fans out a hand, allowing Everett to exit the field.

Except, I follow Everett's line of vision as he tosses a chiding glance toward a tree. Angled behind it is none other than Jameson West.

As soon as the whistle blows to restart the game, I caw to get Dylan's attention. Using hand signals, I point him to ten o'clock near the trees.

On his cue, we both fire.

Red paint splashes into the air as Jameson dives for the ground. "Cover me!" he yells.

Determined as I am, Dylan stands to get him. Like oil and water, the paintballs bounce off him. But not before Dylan is shot by Marcello, who I in turn take down.

"Run!" I yell to Marco, who dashes down halfway way across the field. Shielding Dante, the whole way, he ducks and dodges blue paint, before they take cover behind an overturned spiral corrugated pipe.

The aftermath is an ugly blue and red mess all over the course.

That jealous fury rages through me again as I reassign blame to Jameson, and suddenly, everything around me falls still.

We're down an integral member of our team. Even though they're down two, and this is meant to be a weirdly barbaric display of celebration. What's worse is, it feels undeniably poetic.

I'm doing everything in my power to protect my brother Dante, while dodging the blues.

Breath stifles in my chest.

It's this moment I know I've got to tell them about Avery. Not in hypotheticals or wine lingo. I want them to know I'm completely, irrevocably in love with her.

If I don't want other men asking her on dates or for her number, certainly not Jameson's hands on her, I've got to. How can I expect others to respect our relationship, *her* to feel confident in us, if I haven't claimed what we've built to the people who matter?

"We're out!"

Dylan and Marcello raise their hands and markers for the referees.

Once they exit the field, a renewed energy pulses through me. I can't do nothing and expect to win.

I can't stay still.

With stealthy strides, I whip past hay bales and tire stacks.

Mike is on my tail as I crawl into a spiral pipe, cawing to signal for Marco to keep going. Then I roll out, taking cover in the thick of the trees.

Behind me, a shout ricochets in the blue-spritzed wind.

"They got me, Stef."

At first, I think it's Dante.

But it's Marco who lifts his arms and marker to the referee.

They've evened the score.

It's Dante and me against Mike, who I could've sworn I hit, and Jameson.

In my periphery, red paint catches my eye. It's not until I squint for a closer look that I realize it's smeared on the pants covering Mike's calf.

Smeared.

He's wiped it off.

Though, I'd been only half-listening to Riker amidst my blinding anger for Jameson, I distinctly remember, in between always keeping our masks on and exiting the field with hands and markers raised, he'd mentioned "wiping." Trying to wipe off the paint after being hit, isn't just cheating. It results in a harsh scoring penalty, and an immediate discharge from the game.

Before the whistle sounds, I throw my voice to the referee. "Mike was hit, but he tried to wipe it off."

Guilty as ever, Mike appears behind a wooden spool. "He's lying! I never got hit. I was on the ground. It must've gotten on me as I was diving for cover."

At the referee's request, Mike approaches him to show his otherwise spotless clothing aside from the solid splatter on his calf.

"You're out!" the referee announces.

After Mike argues with him, earning them another penalty, the whistle blows.

Five minutes pass.

It's quiet with only the leaves rustling in the breeze.

Jameson is somewhere in the backend of the field near the platform. Dante is flat on the ground behind a hay bale, twenty feet from the staircase, and I'm waiting in the wing.

Closing my eyes, I aim my marker, waiting.

Then I hear footsteps retreating.

With everything I've got, I unload in that direction until, there's the most satisfying sharp intake of air.

"Damn!"

I got him.

To my left, Dante takes off toward the stairs, mounting the platform with his arms raised in victory.

But I don't run to him.

Instead, I weave through the trees until I locate Jameson lying on his back. There's red paint splattered over his groin, and he's staring up at the muted early evening light dappled through the trees.

As if on cue, the stadium lights turn on, blaring down on me, towering over him.

Like moths to a flame, the rest of the guys pour onto the field to congratulate our last bachelor standing on making it to the end zone, when they find us.

"Oof, the family jewels." Marcello winces at Jameson.

Dante rejoins us to get a glimpse of the carnage.

Now, that we're all here, it feels as good a time as any. I crack my neck on either side before I meet Jameson's stare.

"Stay away from Avery," I warn him.

"Oh, you like her?" he says in his lackadaisical tone. There's amusement in his expression as he licks his lips.

Tugging him to his feet, I dust off his shoulders. Slowly shake my head, feeling a strange sense of calm.

"No, I'm in love with her, actually."

A unified gasp echoes around me. But then it's fused in

with low chuckles and suppressed smiles.

Marcello scratches his head, barely holding it together. "Damn, so it's official then."

Scanning the group, I stretch my shoulders back, sinking into the downward pull of my muscles, and letting my arms hang loose. Lightness blooms in my chest as I scrape my fingers through my hair, taking an easy breath.

"No, but it will be," I say confidently.

Except Jameson is all smiles as he clutches my shoulder in his grip. "That's good to know, old man. Now, thanks to my dance partner, who devised this grade-A jealousy plan, we finally got you to admit it, too, so you can do something about it."

Well damn.

CHAPTER TWENTY-TWO
Avery

ABOUT THREE MONTHS ago, Morgan and I both had client meetings ten minutes away from each other. She picked me up. We drove to a snazzy new restaurant that, of course, only had valet parking. Completely normal in the city. Except, she'd also valeted earlier, and spent the last of her cash. Long not-so-story short, she borrowed ten bucks. Just a simple favor between friends.

No big deal, right?

Wrong.

Morgan reminded me, no less than a dozen times, about the money, until she made it to an ATM. Despite my insistence that it was fine, she paid the highway robbery fee, claiming it was worth to show her appreciation for the favor.

It was that important to her.

Same thing when she first found her city apartment, the Sister Circle helped her move. She returned the favor with all four of us. That's just the cloth she's cut from.

Morgan Elaine Forster, soon-to-be Fortemani, always returns favors with a smile and a touch of dramatic flair.

No matter how long it's been.

So, I'm not surprised on Monday night following the parties, when Stefano and I reach the foot of the vineyard staircase, and Morgan and Dante are standing on the landing, fleeced in matching white and black satin pajamas, respectively, for our double date.

Well, not technically.

As far as the guys know, Morgan planned dinner for us to "finalize last-minute wedding to-do list items." What tonight is about, is returning favors. *Of sorts.*

In the same vein as the Fortemanis' vineyard hoax, which they fabricated to light a fire underneath Dante, Morgan is helping Stefano out of his own way by helping me drop my "oopsie, baby" news.

One way or the other, I'll know just how certain—*or not*—he is about me, once he realizes my package deal recently got bundled.

So yeah, heavy on the flair and dramatics.

The plan is simple.

She's already made dinner, plated it, and set it on the coffee table. *Something about no barriers between us, physical or otherwise.* Once we get inside, we'll settle around the table, and boom! Stefano in the hot seat.

In her words, "show or go."

Trust me, there was a whole slew of "shit or get off the pot" alternatives. Order or get out of line. Fish or cut bait. Puff it or pass it. Daddy up or deadbeat.

We went with the least aggressive, most fitting.

"Oh wow! You all came dressed for the occasion." Dante is all oblivious, charming smile and easy posture as he greets me with a kiss on the cheek. Then he turns to Stefano.

"Matching DREAM TEAM shirts…" He blows out an impressed breath. "This damn sure is one for the books."

"You should talk," Stefano counters. "I feel like I should call you Hef with those pajamas. Did we miss the memo?"

"*Ugh* don't mind those fools." Morgan shakes her head and fixes her wide-eyed, conspiratorial stare on me. "What's more important is I sure hope you brought your *appetite*." She winks.

"*Girlll!*" I let my head and shoulders slump with my exaggerated moan. "Is that even a real question?"

She laughs, pulling me up the last step into a full-body hug, then quickly withdrawing when she notices me wince.

"Relax." A laugh rumbles out of me. The panic etched across her face is proof she's got no clue whether it's my breasts or my belly. Neither of which is she willing to risk squeezing too hard.

Tossing her a *I'm fine, the baby's fine* look, she finally heaves a relieved sigh just as Dante barks out a robust laugh.

"She's got your number, man." Dante spins Stefano around. "Lord knows a good suit is all it takes with you."

With them deep in suits and T-shirt conversation, I quickly hand over the wine bag we brought for Morgan's inspection. Like a seasoned sleuth, she waits for them to be out of earshot before she pries back the sides of the gift bag.

"Well?" I whisper, feeling like I've gone from secret lover to secret agent.

A smile stretches her red lips as she peeks inside at the small stuffed toy crushed discreetly underneath the Cabernet bottle.

"This is perfect!" The inflection in her voice rises unnaturally.

Joy wells up in my heart.

I'm a trail mix of nerves and emotions. "How do you think he's going to react?"

Morgan pulls me, gently, into another hug.

"Do you know how long he's waited for this?"

I nod, clinging to her words for reassurance as we enter the house and weave through the foyer to the living room. Sure enough, the coffee table is set with four steaming plates heaped high with salad, grilled chicken, and halved corn cobs, waiting for us.

"You laugh, but…" Stefano is beaming at Dante "…a tailored suit is life-changing."

"I believe you believe that, too." Dante's shoulders tremble with laughter as he catches sight us rejoining them. Without missing a beat, he hooks his arm over Stefano's shoulder, and congratulates me on freeing his brother from yet another stiff suit. "Look at us. I'm telling you, I could get used to spending this much time with my older brother, laughing, talking, double-dating, making big plans…"

Dante locks his arm, giving Stefano a noogie.

They're like teenagers engaged in brotherly roughhousing and joking about something as insignificant as corny custom T-shirts. Every inch of me loves how much things have changed in two months.

I almost feel bad how unaware they are that I'm about to rock his entire world.

Morgan clears her throats, snagging my attention.

Slyly, she taps her Apple watch, signaling that we need to get this show on the road.

Steadying my nerves for this riveting performance I'm

about to give, I amp up my sigh for maximum effect. "Gosh, I'm *so* thirsty."

The guys have fallen into a mix of laughter and whispers, probably about the bachelor paintball shindig, which, according to Morgan via Dante, no one will speak about. A fact that has clearly gotten under her skin despite our preordained agenda this evening.

Can't fault her for her curiosity, though.

Since they're hush-hush gossip precluded them from witnessing my thespian antics, Morgan shoots me another wide-eyed look, urging me to say my line again. This time, louder, and with more feeling, she pantomimes.

Bracing myself, I readjust my stance.

With a smidge more bass in my tone, I belt out, "Oh, my dear *Lord*, I'm parched. Do you have *anything* to drink?" The last part, I really stretch my voice across the room.

My handsome boyfriend's gaze connects with mine.

"You feeling okay? Need some water?" he asks.

Stefano's already backing toward the butler door between the dining room and the kitchen as I nod.

The plan is working.

Almost.

We need the room to ourselves for a couple minutes to set the stage.

She looks Dante dead in the eyes, watching as his Adam's apple bobs before she lets out two grossly fake coughs.

I've got to bite my tongue to stifle my laugh.

"I guess I'll just go grab you some water, too."

Morgan smiles not-so-innocently.

The second they're gone, she tugs me down onto the

couch, positioning me just so.

"Okay, you sit here on the end," she whispers.

At this point, I'm taking my orders from her.

Grabbing the wine bag, she sets the Cabernet on the table, and fishes out the small daisy plush toy. Gently, she slips it under the throw pillow beside me, careful not to press its button. Then, she breaks out into a silent happy dance.

In the kitchen, the guys' whispers grow loud and intense.

She's mid-bounce when the guys burst through the swinging door, glasses in hand, so she's forced to mask her smile with another uninspired cough.

"Here, drink this." Dante holds the water to her mouth, waiting as she tries to take a small sip.

Except, her lips are twitching from suppressing her laugh, so water sputters everywhere.

"Oh, babe…" Dante dutifully scans the couch for something to mop her spill, nearly grabbing "the" pillow.

"Whoa, there." Stefano comes in clutching the napkin he'd wrapped around my glass, saving the day. He hands me the water. "Both of you all coughing. Could be something going around."

Morgan starts cough-laughing again, her frantic gaze flickering not so subtly to Dante.

It's a surefire *shit or get off the pot* if ever I've seen one.

I blink twice.

We're barely holding it together, so when Stefano squeezes in next to me on the couch, sliding his hand into mine, it feels like my next cue.

My heart is beating a mile a minute.

"Stefano?"

With his thumb, he rubs circles in my palm, and suddenly, I can't tell whether he's the one who's nervous or me.

"I was hoping—" I start to say but he interrupts me.

"Please let me go first." Stefano fixes me with an intense stare.

It's the desperation in his tone that reaches into my chest and squeezes my heart, though. Whatever he's got to say, I can tell it's got a hold on him.

"Okay."

He sucks in a lungful of air.

His voice is low and measured as he says, "Something happened at the bachelor party, yesterday."

"I knew it," Morgan blurts out. Accusation laces her tone. *Guilty of what, though?* "Dante tells me everything, but he wouldn't tell me what happened with y'all."

I force a stilted smile, still unclear where Stefano is going with this conversation.

Short of naked strippers planted around a rustic dirt field, I've got no clue what could be noteworthy for eight guys shooting each other with high-speed paintballs. Stefano hadn't mentioned anything to me.

I figured they went, they played, they got sappy over rounds of drinks. The bachelorette party wore me out, so I needed a recovery day, plus time with Ace. Nothing on the drive here, either.

My shoulders are up to my ears.

"It's not what you're thinking. I asked everyone not to speak about the bachelor party," Stefano explains.

I dart an assessing gaze between Stefano and Dante then back to Morgan who looks like she's still chewing on this version of what's happening, and not the premeditated agenda I'm starting to suspect this is.

"But why?" Morgan asks, genuinely curious.

She reaches up to intertwine her fingers with Dante's.

"I needed time to reach out to Mother and Chiara. Get my ducks in a row for tonight…"

Quietly observing, I take note of the way he keeps rubbing my palms, like he needs somewhere to place his energy. I notice Dante's restlessness and unwavering focus.

"What do you mean, for tonight?" I ask.

"Avery, I don't want to waste any more time. We've already lived and learned through our past marriages. Now, I'm in a relationship with an amazing, beautiful, kind and caring woman, who I want to spend the rest of my life with. I wanted everyone to know."

Stefano slides off the edge of the couch, lowering himself onto his knees in front of me. The desperation on his handsome face heightens as he holds both of my hands.

I chew the inside of my cheek to keep from crying.

"You said all of that?" My voices catches.

Stefano curves his hand to my cheek, and I can't help leaning into his touch.

He smiles sweetly.

"You'd be so proud of me. I told my mother, my sister, plus all the guys at paintball."

"The man was a lethal weapon out there, knocking 'em down and taking names," Dante boasts. "Just ask Jameson."

An emotion-choked laugh spills out of me. "What were you doing, shooting people, then pouring your heart out?"

"That's about the size of it." Dante laughs.

A few seconds pass as the silence thickens and Stefano's expression grows serious.

"Avery, I need you to know that so many things in my life feel uncertain, but you are not one of them." He drags the pad of his thumb over my lower lip before he kisses me softly. "For so long, I'd given up on my dream of love and a family. I figured it wasn't in the cards for me." He shrugs. "Now, I know I was waiting on you and Ace. I want you to be my family."

Stefano's voice wavers.

His piercing brown eyes water as he looks at me, "Avery. Pollyanna, my sunshine…"

Apparently, taking his cue, Dante retrieves a bouquet of daisies from behind the couch, and hands them over.

Morgan stares in open-mouthed shock at her sneaky fiancé as Stefano leans back and holds the flowers between us.

My heart stalls.

At the center of the bouquet is a beautiful solitary diamond ring, glinting off the warm light.

"Marry me." It comes out on a breathless whisper. "Tear down every emotional and physical barrier with me, Avery Ellis. Make me the luckiest man alive by sharing a life and family with me. I'll be the grumpy, silver fox with 'Big Prick Energy' to your Oopsie Daisy—"

"Oopsie baby." I giggle.

He looks confused but he smiles anyway.

"Yes, that too, I guess. Just say yes."

Tears are stream down my face, my throat constricts, and breathing no longer feels voluntary, but I stare at this devastatingly handsome man asking me to spend forever with him, and I've got zero doubts.

"I will." His face lights up. Until I add, "*If...*"

Stefano huffs out a disbelieving laugh like he can't fathom what condition I'd ever put on a second chance at happily-ever-after.

He throws his head back laughing.

"Okay, I'm listening. What more can I give you besides the world?"

Because this double date apparently specializes in secret agendas and world-upending romantic gestures, Morgan dramatically clears her throat. Not even bothering to hide her competitive side, she makes a huge production of fanning out her hands for me to drop the bomb on them.

As I slip my hand under the throw pillow and pull out the small daisy plush, the guys are genuinely baffled. *For only a moment.*

"What more can you give me, you ask..." In my palms, I peel back the white petals until a tiny baby doll wearing a yellow onesie with a daisy affixed to it appears, with a teensy greeting card. "You could give us your heart," I say.

Opening the small card, I watch as he reads the inscription.

Oopsie daisy, here comes baby.

Stefano's eyes snap to mine. "A baby?"

I nod, still holding my breath. I'm waiting for him to reassure me this is indeed celebratory news for him too.

"Holy shit, I love you so much." He tosses the flowers and our plastic baby aside, rushing in to kiss me with his entire body. "You make me so happy."

"Boom!" I hear Morgan clap her hands together, gloating

to Dante, "That's how it's done."

Favor returned.

Soon, though, our kiss grows urgent. In front of our plastic baby, and the bride and groom in over-the-top satiny pajamas, Stefano pulls me into his lap. My hands are in his silvery curls and his are on my face.

We are going to town, two seconds from saying screw it, and going all the way when Dante clears his throat.

We couldn't care less about them seeing us kiss, though. If anything, we're just returning the favor.

But Dante Fortemani is undeterred.

"Okay, but just so we're clear..." Dante says loudly, laughing. "Are you sure you all want to rush in? Surely, you'd want to have a prolonged engagement. You need to take your time and learn each other."

Stefano and I laugh into the kiss.

One way or another, I think we all knew Dante would find a way to throw Stefano's words back at him.

"No? You don't want to learn what's important to you as individuals and as a couple?" Sarcasm floods his tone. "What a shame..."

Morgan is cackling, but Dante isn't finished with us.

"Far be it from me to judge you, but...after only a few measly months?" He blows out a stressed breath. "I don't know. Sounds risky. Maybe you two should consider the benefits of giving yourselves the necessary time to embrace your *union*." He drags out the word.

We finally pull apart. Mostly, because we're laughing so hard we can't breathe, here at brotherly comedy hour.

Stefano is all beaming white smile as he gets a taste of his own medicine. His only option is to join him. "We're in a relationship," he says in a high-pitched, nasally tone, I'm guessing imitating Dante's response in this hilarious quarrel rewind.

Dante shrugs. "Semantics."

This time, I don't mind eating my words.

CHAPTER TWENTY-THREE
Stefano

T HE AFTERNOON OF the wedding, I'm a little on the tipsy side.

Nerves.

Not because of my brother's impending nuptials. No, more than ever, I now understand his rush down the aisle. Heck, I'd be right there with him today if I thought that's what Avery wanted. Funny enough, the past two weeks I've seen some major milestones in my life. I've professed my undying love, proposed marriage, and discovered I'm fathering a child, yet I'm cool as a cucumber about those things.

It's the entrance dance.

I manage a major conglomerate of companies. I run board meetings with billionaires and high-profile clients. How have I developed stage fright over a pairs entrance dance in front of a mere fifty-two people?

To say it's ridiculous is an understatement.

Mother Nature is working her magic. It's the last day of September, and the sun is low in a picturesque, summery, bright aqua blue sky. It's warm and cozy. The main lawn is set up with chairs and a rustic wooden arch draped in lavender and white flowers, and baby's breath. *Freaking baby's breath!*

To boot, the entire scene overlooks the vineyard's panoramic view of Napa Valley's lush landscape and mountainous horizons worth celebrating.

That's not even the half of it.

Business-wise, today is a huge deal for our vineyard and winery. Major bridal magazine correspondents are here to features us. *Lifestyles of the Rich and Wedded* is filming an episode. Our lodging partners are booked, winery subscriptions are up, and our wedding packages are selling out.

Everything is falling into place, and all I can focus on are the four eight-counts I've got to pull off to make it to the end of the aisle.

I don't want to embarrass Avery.

Shit.

Behind us, the deejay whispers to Marcello and Monica, "You're up," amplifying my mounting panic.

Showtime.

A minute later, the upbeat chorus of Beyoncé's "Crazy in Love" spring into the air. Sparkly lavender bridesmaid dress and all, Monica struts to the center of the aisle like it's a catwalk.

The guests jolt to their feet, swaying, clapping, and singing along.

I've got to say, Monica's twerking game is wildly accurate. A fact Marcello clearly appreciates as he licks his lips. He's all shoulders and swerving head movements as he circles her, nodding to the beat.

By the time, he takes her hand, and they split the arch, the music changes.

Mike and Seneca take us back with Donna Summer's "Last Dance," straight Seventies mode. Beyond her long, thick natural hair cascading down her back, their tactic is limited to playing the crowd. No match for Monica's strut-twerk, I think, when Avery nudges me with her shoulder.

"Almost ready to show them how to do this?" Avery smiles up at me. I'm lost in her sparkly brown eyes widening with amusement.

I'm sure she can tell I'm nervous.

She sees me.

Honestly, I think she saw through my walls even before I knew I'd put them up.

"I'm getting there," I say, after a beat.

Like she always seems to know how to calm me, she slips her hand in mine, sending cool relief spiraling down my back. She steadies me. In a world where I'd found myself adrift, she anchors me.

Leaning in, I press my lips to her forehead. For a beat, I linger, letting her sweet floral scent band around me.

At the end of the aisle, Valerie responds to Everett's stellar pining and courting acting skills that ended with him on one knee, with an exuberant yes.

As they bow and curtsy, Chiara appears, arm in arm with Jameson at my side.

"Watch and learn," she says.

Then the music plays.

They take the aisle with Earth, Wind & Fire's nostalgic and apt "September," instantly reviving the crowd. Even though, in my opinion, their montage of hip thrusts and Hustle steps won't likely take the medal, it's a soul classic. Between Frankie Beverly and Maze, and Earth, Wind & Fire, it's almost offensive to our ancestors not to honor this song with dancing and singing.

Jameson twirls and spins Chiara until they're almost to the arch.

"We've got this. Ready?" Avery asks as we take our places.

I suck in a deep breath, letting it fill my lungs. As I slowly release it through my nose, I steel myself for the next thirty seconds.

"Always, when I'm with you."

Avery fists the fabric of her dress.

Then the music starts.

Out the gate, Avery and I are an explosion of bouncing, hard-hitting beats to "Let's Get Married" by Jagged Edge. In sync, we pop, lock, and break, throwing in everything from the Dougie and the Running Man to Krumping, the Jerk, and the Cabbage Patch.

How, in a diamond-encrusted, off-the-shoulder lavender maid of honor gown Avery commands the spotlight, I don't know. But she top rocks. She back rocks. She power moves with the best of them. And the fast footwork in heels?

Amazing.

"Let's get married!" The deejay goads the guests to sing along.

Before the first eight-count ends, it's officially a party.

Dante and Enzo walk out from the right of arch, dancing along with the guests as he makes his way to the arch. The rest of the wedding party is following our moves. Even as

Dylan's four-year-old daughter, Danielle, peppers the aisle with flower petals and Ace holds the satin pillow with the rings tied to it like a champ, the deejay looks like he wants Enzo to hurry up and officiate this ceremony, so we can get to the reception.

"Ayyy…" The deejay hypes us up on the mic. "All right, ladies and gentlemen, let's give a hand to our wedding party. Then stay on your feet. It's the time we've all been waiting for…"

At his cue, a guest seated in the back steps out from the rows of chairs with a violin. It's not a string quartet or an orchestra, just a single instrument. But as she lifts it to her chin and gently glides the bow against it, I don't hear the music.

I feel every word of "I Will Always Love You."

While every pair of eyes is trained on Morgan in her white dress gracefully marching toward Dante, I can't take mine off Avery.

Sometimes, I still don't know how I got so lucky.

Two months ago, my confidence wasn't simply knocked. I wasn't even sure I wanted to explore new sexual, let alone romantic relationships. Then the woman who I thought was Morgan's overprotective, Rubik's cube, mind-boggling best friend burst into my life like a rainbow cannonball. I thought she was too young, too immature, and I wasn't ready to start again. I was listening to ridiculous, problematic podcasts try to learn what this woman taught me in a matter of weeks.

No two loves are the same, so there's no comparing where we've been with where we're going together. There's no best time to fall in love. No prescribed number of days or years because it can't be measured in time, only timing and readiness.

My heart lurches.

I look out at our mothers, friends, and family—and the Gossip Set—aware and watching, and I can't imagine a future without Avery and Ace, and the blessing growing inside her.

Because of them I have purpose and passion. There's no best time to fall in love.

They're my silver lining.

With Ace's tiny hand in hers, we stand on either side of her best friend and my brother, staring at each other as they promise to love and honor one another as long as they both shall live. As they kiss, and the guests erupt in elated cheers, my eyes water.

"We did it!" They raise their connected hands victoriously as they jump the broom then walk toward the two-handed saw.

Tears prick my eyes, and I know I'm ready to share this with Avery.

So, when she glances over at me, I mouth, *I love you.*

Through the celebratory recessional, and both Avery's maid of honor and my best man speeches, I tell her again. After the food and cake have been served, and the best California-grown wine is flowing and the Electric Slide packs the dance floor, I remind her with my kisses. Even once the bouquet is tossed and we lift sparklers into the air, forming a tunnel for Dante and Morgan to pass through on the way to their honeymoon, when the guests taper off and the taillights fade down the vineyard drive, I'm certain.

I'll never tell Avery as many times as she should hear those words to fill the void years of heartache left behind.

But I know I want to try.

With a sleepy Ace on my shoulder, I lead her back to the dance floor for the last song of the night. As she rests her head on my chest and we sway to the tinkling ivories of John Legend's "All of Me," I take a mental snapshot of this moment, committing it to memory.

My heart stutters. "I love you," I say for the millionth time.

Avery lifts on her toes to kiss me.

Except it's cut short when Ace, who I could've sworn was on the edge of snoring, pops his head up. He looks me straight in the eyes, and asks, "You love me, too?"

Avery and I are putty.

We're nothing more than tears and mush.

"Especially you, Lightning," I say, mustering the energy and charisma of his favorite racer Corvette. "Ka-chow! I love you to the moon and back."

Avery laughs through her tears.

As he wraps his tiny arms around Avery and me, and squeezes with all his might, I feel whole.

Everything inside me melts because I'm a fool. I rushed in faster than fast, and I haven't looked back. With a love this fierce, this all-consuming, how could anyone put a time on love? For Avery, Ace, and his brother or sister, I'm willing to be the blissful fool as I learn how to be a father and the best husband I can be. I'm the luckiest man alive to get to spend forever giving all of me—all my heart—for our family.

A love like this is...

Timeless.

The End

Acknowledgments

Thanks so much for reading Avery and Stefano's story. If you got this far, you also know that it's partially Ace's and Lightning McQueen's. *Ka Chow!* Really, it belongs to the entire Fortemani family and our Sister Circle, which is growing, blooming, and beautiful.

In the back of my mind, I knew it would take an ensemble cast this big to help love through unthinkable loss.

The Wedding Crush was nothing short of a labor of love, which I shared with so many important people to get it to your hands, ears, and shelves.

To my husband, who wonders how I manage to sleep at all, thank you for always supporting my dream, and rooting harder for me when the deadlines are staring me down. I love you. To my girls and my fluffy pup, who sneak around Zooms and get excited with me, and always ask "Which book is this one?" and "Go, Mom! Another book!" That's the fuel that keep me writing.

Mommy and Daddy, I love you so much. Here's another one for your entry table.

Denise N. Wheatley, you listen to me unravel my mind until the last page, and I'm forever grateful.

To the Wordmakers. Remember that Plot Party when I wasn't sure where to start this one, and then you helped me torture Stefano with a humiliating podcast meet-cute? This is the one! Your suggestions and ideas set me on the right track. Thank you and see you at the next Plot Party!

To my editor, Roxanne Snopek, you get me. Your sweet comments mixed in with the constructive ones are the best. Ever since *Monopolove*, we've been our own Dream Team. Thank you.

To my gorgeous, growing Sister Circle, Melissa De Grazia, Margo Hendricks, Tia Martin, Alisa Howard, Natalie Berbick, and again, Denise N. Wheatley, we've expanded to a wide, beautiful bookish community, including book clubs like UNLV Rebel Reads, so many amazing romance authors, and the best readers around.

To Alison Johnston, we're still stepping on faith. Ladrea, Ria, Auntie Tami, Auntie CC, Ashley, Regina, Tracy, Rachel, thank you for always supporting my books.

To Randi, Meka, Kris, and D, thanks for welcoming me whenever I resurface.

Tasha and Gab, "logistically" speaking, we've got this!

Thanks to my IG family, Tule sisters, the librarians, Bookstagrammers, bloggers, BookTubers, BookTokkers, reviewers, and my ARC team! Thank you so much for enjoying and sharing my stories.

As always, a huge thanks to Jane Porter, Meghan Farrell, Cyndi Parent, Lee Hyat, and the Tule team for giving the Fortemani family a home on shelves.

To the person who next picks up this book, recommends it, buys it as a gift, and (hopefully) listens to it on audio soon, thank you for the honor of spending your time with my book.

The Wedding Crush Playlist

05:21 MY MY MY | JOHNNY GILL

03:56 CRAZY IN LOVE | BEYONCÉ

03:28 KISS ME MORE | DOJA CAT (FT. SZA)

03:43 DAMAGE | H.E.R.

03:21 SNOOZE | SZA

03:52 SUMMER RAIN | CARL THOMAS

03:59 BOO'D UP | ELLA MAI

03:08 MADE FOR ME | MUNI LONG

03:44 HEY DADDY (DADDY'S HOME) | USHER

03:13 PRESSURE | ARI LENNOX

04:27 LOVE ON TOP | BEYONCÉ

05:05 WHEN I'M WITH YOU | TONY TERRY

03:48 STAY WITH YOU | JOHN LEGEND

03:42 4EVER | LIL' MO (FT. FABOLOUS)

04:21 SO INTO YOU | TAMIA

03:35 SEPTEMBER | EARTH, WIND & FIRE

05:07 BEFORE I LET GO | FRANKIE BEVERLY & MAZE

04:09 LET'S GET MARRIED | JAGGED EDGE (FT. REVEREND RUN)

04:56 LAST DANCE | DONNA SUMMERS

04:18 TWO OCCASIONS | THE DEELE

04:50 (I'VE HAD) THE TIME OF MY LIFE | BILL MEDLEY AND
     JENNIFER WARNES

04:01 ICU | COCO JONES

04:15 LOVE | KEYSHIA COLE
04:30 WHY I LOVE YOU SO MUCH | MONICA
04:46 ALWAYS | ATLANTIC STARR
04:31 I WILL ALWAYS LOVE YOU | WHITNEY HOUSTON

If you enjoyed *The Wedding Crush*,
check out the other books in…

The Fortemani Family series

Book 1: *The Accidental Crush*

Book 2: *The Wedding Crush*

Book 3: *Last Christmas Crush*

Available now at your favorite online retailer!

More Books by Mia Heintzelman

Love & Games series

The Love & Games series follows game store owners Harper Sloane, Rox Sloane, and Nadia Sides—two sisters and their best friend—as they find their happily ever afters and deepen their love for classic board games.

Book 1: *Monopolove*

Book 2: *Trivialized Pursuit*

Book 3: *Clued in Christmas*

Available now at your favorite online retailer!

About the Author

Mia Heintzelman is a polka-dot-wearing, horror movie lover, who always has a book and a to-do list in her purse. When she isn't busy writing fictional happily-ever-afters, she is likely reading, or playing board games and eating sweets with her husband and two children. She writes fun, unforgettable, more than just laughs romcoms about strong women and men with enough heart to fall for them.

Thank you for reading

The Wedding Crush

If you enjoyed this book, you can find more from all our great authors at TulePublishing.com, or from your favorite online retailer.

TULE
PUBLISHING